D0207665

LEADER OF THE BAND

The Citronella Jumpers were to play at eleven thirty beneath the War Memorial; it was difficult to get details of time and place from the Festival Organisers, inasmuch as no one there spoke English. Only the French rivalled the British in their expectation, nay determination, that theirs should be the universal language. I offered to translate but Jack wouldn't hear of it.

'Try and understand,' he says. 'This Band doesn't *want* anything to go smoothly. It's not the way we work. We like to pick things up by osmosis. We do not want to be organised. Efficiency is the enemy of creative energy.'

I'd like to know what the discovery of Athena entailed other than creative energy and efficiency combined. But I was sensible enough not to say so. I called for a bottle of wine, instead.

About the Author

Fay Weldon was born in England, brought up in New Zealand and went to St Andrews University, in Scotland, where she graduated in Economics and Psychology. After a decade of odd jobs and hard times, she started writing and now though primarily a novelist, she also writes short stories, radio and television dramas. Her work is translated into many languages.

By the same author:

THE FAT WOMAN'S JOKE
DOWN AMONG THE WOMEN
FEMALE FRIENDS
REMEMBER ME
LITTLE SISTERS
PRAXIS
PUFFBALL
WATCHING ME, WATCHING YOU
   (short stories)
THE LIFE AND LOVES OF A SHE-DEVIL
THE PRESIDENT'S CHILD
POLARIS AND OTHER STORIES
HEART OF THE COUNTRY
THE RULES OF LIFE
THE SHRAPNEL ACADEMY
THE HEARTS AND LIVES OF MEN

Plays for the stage
MIXED DOUBLES
ACTION REPLAY
I LOVE MY LOVE
WOODWORM
THE HOLE IN THE TOP OF THE WORLD

Leader of the Band

Fay Weldon

CORONET BOOKS
Hodder and Stoughton

The appendices have been published as short stories in the following magazines: 'A Libation of Blood' in *More Magazine* (New Zealand), January 1988; 'Come On, Everyone!' in *Marxism Today*, December 1987; and 'GUP — or Falling in Love in Helsinki' in *Woman* (UK) on 23 May 1987.

The lines from the song 'Why did she Fall for the Leader of the Band?' and the sheet music which appear on the jacket are copyright © 1935 and reproduced by kind permission of Peter Maurice Music Co Ltd, London WC2H 0LD.

Copyright © 1988 by Fay Weldon

First published in Great Britain in 1988 by Hodder and Stoughton Ltd

Open Market edition 1988

Coronet edition 1989

The characters and situations in this book are entirely imaginary and bear no relation to any real person or actual happening.

This book is sold subject to the condition that it shall not, by way of trade or otherwise, be lent, re-sold, hired out or otherwise circulated without the publisher's prior consent in any form of binding or cover other than that in which it is published and without a similar condition including this condition being imposed on the subsequent purchaser.

No part of this publication may be reproduced or transmitted in any form or by any means, electronically or mechanically, including photocopying, recording or any information storage or retrieval system, without either the prior permission in writing from the publisher or a licence, permitting restricted copying. In the United Kingdom such licences are issued by the Copyright Licensing Agency, 33–34 Alfred Place, London WC1E 7DP.

Printed and bound in Great Britain for Hodder and Stoughton Paperbacks, a division of Hodder and Stoughton Ltd., Mill Road, Dunton Green, Sevenoaks, Kent TN13 2YA. (Editorial Office: 47 Bedford Square, London WC1B 3DP) by Cox & Wyman Ltd., Reading.

British Library C.I.P

Weldon, Fay
  Leader of the band
  I, Title
  823'.914[F]

ISBN 0 340 49183 3

Contents

She was a good girl –
And I can never understand
Why did she fall for the
Leader of the Band?

Mrs Jack Hylton's favourite song

1

Travelling South

I, Starlady Sandra, professional searcher after truth, rejector of fantasy, organiser of eternal laws into numerical form, confiner of cosmic events and swirling next-to-nothingness into detail not only comprehensible but communicable to a TV audience, was in flight from my own life, my own past, and the revenge of my friends.

I went south with the Band towards the sun and the gigs and the Folkloriques of summer France, rattling and sweating and leaning into Mad Jack the trumpet-player whenever I could, one leg numb with the effort of keeping myself on my seat while the minibus swerved and jerked and started and stopped; the other leg pressed into his, flesh of his flesh, bone of his bone, and happy beyond wild dreams of happiness, drugged out of my mind with love, zonked out of my wits by sex.

Many are in flight, of course; take to their spiritual heels by way of drink or drugs, and sometimes come back and sometimes don't, but I was off in body as well as mind: run, run, I cried to myself, and run, run I did, leaving home, husband, work behind me, deserting mid-sentence, mid-function, mid-programme, without due notice or warning, leaving others in a terrible fix. I was in love. And those I left behind counted for nothing, nothing: they were ridiculous in their insignificance: even the bruises on my neck where my husband tried to strangle me seemed no more than stigmata, self-generated. But of course, in reality, those I had offended failed to recognise their insignificance, and went on being the centre of their own lives, and came after me, furious, murderous.

Those who pursued me were:
My husband

My lover's wife
The gutter press, the sidewalk papers.
The Producer of *Sandra's Sky*, who was also –
My friend Jude, subject of a story I should not have written,
as was
Alison, my erstwhile friend.
*Harpies
*Furies
*History: personal, political, national.

No escape for any of us, of course, from the three starred items
above; we carry them with us in a cloud around our heads,
products of our guilt, waste-matter of our fate. What we
can't help, what we could have – and how they belabour us,
squawking, with their horrible claws and flapping wings, no
matter how fast we run, how deep we bury our heads into
unmentionable parts of other people's anatomy. But I tried, I
tried. For all our sakes, I tried. And this autobiographical
novel is an account of how I tried, written a year after the
events recorded. Autobiographical, I say, believing I have
invented nothing, but how can I be sure, peer behind my own
conviction? For the further back into the past I go the more
wishful thinking clouds my memory: the more difficult it is to
sort my way through the fog, stumbling against those blocks
of recollection put forward by my ego in the interests of my
self-esteem.

I went south with the Band in a Renault van designed to hold
six in comfort but re-fitted in the interests of profit to hold ten
in discomfort. And these and this is what the van contained:

The Band.
   Rhythm section:
     Pedro (33) guitar
     Sandy (47) double bass
     Hughie (26) drums
   The Front Line:
     Stevie (56) trombone
     Karl (72) clarinet
     Jack (44) trumpet. Oh, Jack, Mad Jack,
     leader of the band!

The Groupies.

Frances (15) Jack's daughter
Jennifer (40) Sandy's wife
Bente (23) Hughie's girlfriend

and myself, Sandra Harris, Sandra Sorenson, Starlady Sandra, Sandra the lady astronomer, all terms apply. The Band knew me as Sandra Harris, secretary, and sometimes one or other would look puzzled and say 'don't I know you from somewhere?' and I'd look vague and say 'oh, I've been around the jazz scene a while'. Starlady Sandra, liar.

Sandy's double bass took up one of the seats, and the van's back door was blocked by Hughie's drums, round which Karl had erected a kind of wooden frame, into which the other instruments, accoutrements, various stands and PA system could slot, but whose stability Hughie doubted, frequently, loudly and at length as we travelled, thus much offending ancient Karl; and there were boxes of wine in the aisle, and the bags and cases of those who did not want to risk getting them wet – for thunderstorms swirled across the wheatfields of France, through which we rocked and slithered, and the roof-rack tarpaulin flapped and fluttered and offered the luggage on top scarcely any protection at all – and Jennifer's iceboxes and dustpans and emergency supplies blocked the side door, and grubby articles of clothing discarded as the storms stopped and the heat began littered what was left of the floor, and Christ knew what would have happened had we been in a collision. As Stevie, a tidy man, kept remarking: making Hughie laugh wildly and take his corners more dangerously. You know what young men are. Nor of course was there any air-conditioning – only a kind of blower, which, when switched on by the driver, blasted out hot air from beneath the stacked drums, and of course overheated and filled the vehicle with smoke and fumes and was so noisy that pleas from the back to switch it off went for a suffocating time unheard: until Hughie realised his drums were suffering and pulled into a layby so abruptly the women squealed and the men shouted. And I was happy, pressed into Jack; and thus love makes fools of us.

3

2

Details

The van was the best the Band could afford. For the Band was no wealthier than the sum of its members. How could it be? Its sound was New Orleans Revival with a touch of folk: it was out of fashion and therefore out of pocket: it was glad enough often enough to play and sing for its supper and no more.

The name of the band was the Citronella Jumpers. Acid green stickers and posters covered the battered sides of the yellow van. 'Revive with the revivers', they begged, a mysterious enough message in its native England: incomprehensible here in France.

The gig was Karl's. That is to say, he it was who had been approached to join the Festival, offered free accommodation and subsistence by Monsieur le Directeur, in return for entertaining the entertainers at the Folklorique of Blasimon-les-Ponts. Karl's sister was Monsieur le Directeur's aunt. Karl had a hearing aid: he was a Marxist, and had been to Eton. But Jack was musical director; Jack was leader of the Band. Jack chose the numbers, beat in the time, kept musical discipline – but it was Karl's gig. That is to say, the moral responsibility for our being in France was Karl's, and Karl's alone. When things went wrong, Jack shrugged; I loved him the more for his insouciance. I, who was in the habit of organising, taking responsibility; who know that to make money you must spend money, who would in a trice have invested in a new van and reprinted the posters and required Monsieur le Directeur to pay for them, who would have written out a schedule daily and had the Festival Office xerox it free, so that all the Band met up at the same time at the same place; who would have consulted maps before we set out, thus saving at least five driving hours of our journey, who would have had

in writing the terms of our contract and presented them to
each of the Band and made sure all understood them before
setting out; who would have ensured that our accommodation
was not in a disused town hall twenty kilometres from the
Festival centre, who would have named as drivers for the
purposes of insurance the two Band members who drank least
and not the two who drank most – I did none of these things.
I shrugged like Jack and twined my limbs with his, and thought
who cares? What has efficiency to do with music? Art and
efficiency are at odds. The worse the Band was organised, the
better the Band would play. Jack said so. Jack knew how to
live. I could feel the life of his body in mine; how could I doubt
it? Besides, I loved him.

Now let my story begin. For three days we journeyed. For four
days we had stayed at the disused town hall, the Hôtel de Ville
of the village of Roc Fumel, twenty kilometres from the town
of Blasimon-les-Ponts, where the Band played by day in the
cafés and in the market square; and by night in the Cabaret
– when it could get itself together that is. And for eight nights
and seven days my mind had been held caught, captive,
stopped like a video with the pause button pressed. On the
ninth night, for some reason, it started up again, busier than
ever.

For some reason, I say, but in my heart I knew why, though
I resisted the knowledge. My disguise had been penetrated.
Jack knew. Sandra the secretary had become Starlady Sandra,
and love was no longer enough: she needed all her wits about
her, yet again.

So Let Us Begin With – A Burst of Radioactivity

I explained my theories on form, style and content to Jack, the mad trumpet-player, but I don't think he was listening. He was asleep. It was three or so in the morning: he'd had a hard day's night; the cabaret audience would rather have had rock than jazz and let the Band know it. The musicians finished early and aggrieved, and for once we came home before two, but instead of making love Jack fell asleep, or pretended to. How was I to tell which? I hadn't known him long. Men are so full of surprises. I ran my forefinger down his hairy thigh but there was no response – in him, at any rate. His flesh was somehow turned away from me. Was it my doing or the world's? There were rich fields for speculation here, but I resolutely turned my mind away from them, quelling as best I could those feelings of resentment and spite which welled up in me. So my grandmother had taught me to do, and her mother her likewise – a lesson which goes back to Victorian times. Too much thought, it was supposed, could overheat and damage the female brain, too much response tip it into hysteria, too much speculation lead it into dangerous erotic areas. Better by far for a woman to train her mind to dwell on pleasant notions and images, to avoid introspection or self-analysis, to sidestep the consciousness of her desires, or else the winds of passion might blow the poor frail thing altogether away. Well, they may have been right. For here I was; I, the lady astronomer, altogether swept away, lying on a truckle bed under a single harsh blanket, a hard bolster beneath my head, in a high square room empty save for four beds – two unused – and a child's desk, the plaster of its walls crumbling, its wooden floors disintegrating, in a disused town hall in a village not far from Bordeaux, France. Swept away, blown away, Sandra the lady astronomer: she who was used to the grace and comfort of Greenwich,

London, from whence the mean time originates It didn't bear thinking about.

I tried Jack's thigh again. Nothing. He had firm, agreeably sinewy flesh – the spirit, forget my body, quite melted with expectation. Never mind. The pangs of unsatisfied desire are easily enough dealt with, as I had learned during my years with Matthew. Treat them like a stomach ache: see them as something disagreeable but temporary and the pangs subside, and no damage done – or not much, not much. In other words, I thought of something else. I had rather hoped not to be obliged so to do with Jack. Indeed, until this moment, when he used his body as an instrument of pain, not pleasure, I had on the whole managed not to.

I heard sniffling from the next room. It was Frances, Jack's daughter; she was crying. If I could hear her crying, what could she not hear (on a good night) of Jack's and my love-making? I did my best to be quiet – and he might or might not have been trying; as I say, I hardly knew him well enough to tell – but I couldn't suppose my best was good enough, as my history teacher Miss Martin would say of my essays, and his was certainly not.
'What do you mean, Sandra, you can only do your best? Your best isn't good enough. The truth is in your marks, and this one is A minus. Not good at all, Sandra. You with a minus!'

I had suggested to Frances that she slept in the room above, not next door – this French town hall, this Hôtel de Ville, could sleep thirty-two with ease – eight rooms with four beds in each, mattressed and blanketed as some civil defence exercise – and the band and entourage occupied only five rooms and ten beds, so Frances could surely have her choice, but she claimed upstairs was haunted and, besides, the stairs were rotten, and supposing her foot went through them in the middle of the night, in the dark – the only light switch which worked was downstairs, by the front door – and so on and so forth, and chose the room next door to Jack and me. So she would have to take the consequences: I had done my best. The girl was fifteen; she was in any case her father's responsibility, not mine.

7

The sniffling stopped. Frances had nothing to cry about that night; nothing but quiet emanated from Jack's and my two pushed-together beds, except that now, half-expected, half-resisted, I began once again to be conscious of, inside my head, silent to the outside world, that awareness somewhere between hearing and feeling, of the wild pitter-patter of thought. Jack's fault. Look at it like this. He had plucked out the needles of my sensuality, raised them like control rods out of a reactor, and now the processes of the mind took off again – electrons and neutrons whizzing here and there where they had no business to be, only barely in control, in their effort to get themselves back in balance.

Form, style, content – in that order of importance. The cosmos is composed of intricate patterns which contain the key to its purpose. That is what I mean by *form*. The cosmos also has a certain *style* which can be recognised and predicted. We can, by observing the particular style of our own galaxy, project ahead our own discoveries: that is to say, know what we are looking for before we find it. (Neighbouring galaxies have different styles, which we do not yet understand, but presently will.) *Content*, mere stars, planets, black holes, and so forth, are the mere stuff of the universe: pawns moved here and there to demonstrate form and style. Content is last and least.

I explained so much and more to Mad Jack the trumpet-player, but, as I say, I don't think he was listening: he was asleep. And just as well, if I wished my disguise unpenetrated. Why should a research assistant be offering this instruction aloud, in the middle of the night: albeit a secretary working at the Greenwich Observatory, for such the Band and Jack supposed me to be. Now everyone knows astronomers are nuts: their clerical staff are supposed to be sane.

Of course, I, Sandra Harris, was in truth no research assistant but – until eight days ago, when I had blown it – was next in line to being Astronomer Royal. I it was, now let me reveal to you, who five years ago discovered the Planet Athena (since taken up by astrologers everywhere as the planet which explained all the things they hadn't so far been able to) and

8

with it, at the age of thirty-seven, discovered the penalties of success, worldly fame and a high income. That is to say, that men don't like you for it. Listen, it's not all that difficult to discover a planet, if you have a mathematical training and my instinctive understanding of form, style and content, and can perceive, by the tingling of your toes, just where the gap in the universe must be. But try telling that to a would-be lover.

Just a tiny little planet, honestly, Jack, and its discovery a small matter in the light of other of my astronomical achievements. To discover a planet is not to invent it, any more than Columbus invented America. But from the fuss, you would have thought so. What a to-do! I would have called it Harris, as the planet Herschel was named after Herr Herschel, that being my prerogative, but what sort of name is that for a planet? The planet Harris? It was before the days I became Sorenson, which just might have been possible. Athena, I thought. Someone childless, as I am, projecting a somewhat pure and disdainful image, as I do. Or try to. Princess Grace-ish.

'Jack,' I said to my sleeping lover, 'Jack, if the audience didn't respond to you tonight it may be that you failed to observe the euphonies of *form*, *style* and *content*. If such things are attended to, even the unconverted will become enthusiasts. Those who love Rock, your anti-god (rivalling only Dixie in your abhorrence) will dance about and enjoy themselves and find in your evening's performance total satisfaction. The Citronella Jumpers don't have to worry about *style*. It's yours and that's that. *Content*, now, I admit, is scarcely under your control – you know only so many numbers between you – but *form* – ah, *form*! If instead of standing on the platform and playing whatever came into your head, in response to your perception of the audience's requirements – quite often a faulty response, if you ask me – you got some kind of rhythm going, a slow number, then two fast, then a blues, then two fast, then a slow – or whatever – the audience would fall into the pattern of your requirements, and you would not have to grope to satisfy theirs. Get the *form* right, grasp the whole before the detail, and then it will surely add up to more than the sum of its parts

9

and that,' I said, 'holds good for an evening's performance by a jazz band touring foreign parts, or a painting on a gallery wall, or, as I have come to discover myself, a short story. *Content* is next to nothing, *style* counts, but *form* is all: just a pity it needs something to work upon. God, the great creator, despises the material universe, his content, as anyone can observe: it is full of errors. Just as you, Jack, playing 'Dr Jazz' in your nonchalant way or 'When the Saints Come Marching In', those numbers which the crowd loves above all, despise the very notes you play, and hardly bother to get them right. Too easy, too straight, too head on, too, God help us, popular! You, who want to be loved, but can't bear to be loved, in music as in life! The notes are tools to an end, the best you can use, not the end in itself. The end is something vague and great you grasp for!'

So I spoke, and spoke, and spoke, and Jack slept on. Just as well, for it's a rare man likes to be told what to do in his own best interests. Even I, Grace Kelly of a lady astronomer, know this. But perhaps he did hear or his unconscious did. For when dawn broke, balm to my unsleeping eyes, Jack raised his narrow head from the hard bolster, and squinted with his brown eyes into the sun which slatted into the dusty room through a broken shutter and said:

'You must get fucking bored, listening to music you don't understand.'

'Never bored,' I said. 'It gives me something upon which I can focus my thoughts.' If nothing else, I am grammatical.

'That's what I mean,' he said. 'Jazz is an experience, not a focus for thought. So don't feel obliged to come along. Stay home if you want.'

Jack wakes up suddenly, into full alertness. Not for him the eye rubbing, moans and groans of other men. Sleep comes to him as an unwelcome interruption in his life's business, descending suddenly, and rising rapidly, like a blind on a too-tight spring, whirr-rr, whizzing. He's very thin, long and thin. Long, blond and thin, with bright darting brown eyes. Women love him. I would see their eyes follow him: and he look back with speculative interest – not so concerned with the state of their bodies – or so he would give the agreeable impression – but their souls. The very thought of it that morning, the very breadth of the arc of his interest, made me feel quite nasty.

'You mean I put you off,' I remarked. 'And that's why you missed notes last night.'

'I don't miss notes,' he said.

'I was joking,' I said, but I wasn't. Even I, a lady astronomer, discoverer of the Planet Athena, planet of the nuclear age (according to *New Astrologer*) can tell a missed note when I hear one, or rather, fail to.

'You don't put me off,' he said. 'You turn me on, that's all. I can't wait for us to get back to bed. If occasionally I do miss a note, that's why. It's letting the Band down. It has to stop.'

You think this speech pleased me? It did not. Judge a lover, judge anyone, by what he does, not what he says. Don't listen to a man: words are treacherous. Watch his body language, how he passes you the salt, or fails to. Is he there by your fire, or calling on the telephone to say he wished he was? These things tell you more, far more, than words. Beware the man, I say, who declares his desire, and fails to demonstrate it. It was not coincidental that these, the first words – rather than deeds – of commitment and passion Jack the mad trumpeter had uttered to me – 'I can't wait for us to get back to bed' – were spoken after the first night of our acquaintance in which we had not spent at least a part struggling and striving each to get nearer the other; to become one, as the lost electron, the stray neutron, cast out by its nucleus, struggles and strives for ever to find a home, whizzing here and there to the great detriment of all around, especially organic matter – butting its head into cells, causing pandemonium, disorganisation, and even death. What Jack meant, but didn't say, was that he had discovered my identity, was discomposed to the point of playing badly, was angry with me, feared impotence, had hardly slept a wink but merely pretended to, and now was thoroughly upset. But would he say so? Like hell he would!

At that inopportune moment, Frances came in. I try to understand and forgive Frances. I explain to myself that no doubt she felt as if she was afflicted by a great burst of radioactivity, as her father and myself heaved away on our side of the wall. She had all the symptoms: she kept complaining of feeling sick, and headaches, and so forth, and her little fingernail was turning black (mind you, she had slammed it in the minibus door) and her father put it all down to foreign food and strange water and the strain of travel, but I knew well enough what it was. It was her father's and my struggle to become one, as the isotope of a metal struggles to lose its oddity, which had poisoned her. I could almost feel sorry for Frances, but how she did tag along! Well, she could tell the story to the papers for all I cared.

'Starlady Sandra in run-away Romance: daughter tells all.' You know the sort of thing. Not that I care about the world's opinion; its inability to distinguish between astrology and astronomy is what really oppresses me. Not the way it behaves but how stupid it is.

'Well,' said Jack, 'time to get up.'

And so ended my hopes of at least some kind of sexual entendre with Jack before the day began. I like being woken in the morning by the thrust of the male member, before the mind is up and working, and the parts are swollen and stiff outside, but responsive and willing within, so orgasm comes suddenly and unexpectedly, taking the body quite by surprise. But words had already been spoken this morning and unwelcome words at that; the mind was working only too well, and the God Eros (or so it is my opinion) doesn't too greatly care for that, so I don't suppose Frances has spoiled much.

Picture the scene, the unedifying scene. Me and Jack sitting up in bed, naked. I small, pale, precise of feature and form, short hair in a blonde unruffled (alas) bob; he tall, olive-skinned, strong, muscly but narrow, fair haired, bright eyed, very white of even tooth: me with two soft round breasts, pink (not brown, thank God) nippled, and those nipples pointing to the ceiling, not (thank God, or my father, as we shall see) towards the door or floor; he with the ribs showing beneath the skin, arching strongly out of the central breast-bone, hair matted; and Frances looking at us, trying not to look at us. She's a big girl; an early developer, beautiful, broad-shouldered, big-breasted, narrow-hipped, long-legged, with a mass of red hair and a white white skin and only a freckle or so and a spot or so to aggravate her, and a wild, untidy look, so at odds with the mien and style of the neat, contained, tough young women of France. Eyes follow her, as they follow Jack, but with curiosity as much as admiration. She feels it. She doesn't much like France, but doesn't know why. (Apart from my presence in that land, of course, where she'd hoped to get her father to herself.) She was wearing white shorts and an acid green Citronella Jumpers T-shirt which swelled firmly and agreeably over her chest. Her long legs were a mass of inflamed and lumpy mosquito bites. Or perhaps, of course, the bites of bed bugs. I wouldn't be surprised. She should have taken the room upstairs. Eros imposes his own punishments, in his own way.

'What's the French for fleas?' Frances asks. 'I've been bitten all night. I didn't sleep a wink.'
'Puces,' I say. 'Les puces. Bitten, were you? Lucky old you.' Fortunately neither Frances nor her father can be bothered working out the last three words, or else are unable to do so, by reason of the slowness of their minds. I do not at first cover my breasts with the sheet. If Frances comes in without knocking she will see what she will see. But Jack frowns: he understands the value of hypocrisy: well, so do I. I respond to his frown. I pretend that I'm only in bed with Jack for medical reasons, or because there's only one bolster available for every two beds, and pull up the covers to make myself respectable. I feel Jack relax.

How odd it is that I should have to take moral responsibility for this affair of ours, as if he, jaunty Jack Stubbs, would be safely and demurely at home with his wife if it were not for Seductive Sandra. Not fair! But then life in its observable patterns is grossly unfair; nor did I, in truth, any more require it to be fair, since the time I discovered Athena and the scales had begun to tip so unjustly in my direction: not just pretty (in a ladylike kind of way) bright (when I cared to show it) newsworthy (if I wanted to be) but a casual picker-up of planets from the sky! Why should I of all people want things to be fair? My legs were twice as long as dumpy Anne Stubbs', my eyes twice as large, my cunt (if you will forgive my bluntness) twice as tight, and I'm fed up with pretending to be what I'm not – that is to say, respectable, reputable and boring. Twice? I exaggerate, but you know what I mean. Why should I want to give up these things? These are the benefits I was born with, the perks I picked up out of mess and muddle, and general bloodiness – why deny them? Those benefits which I have earned – the esteem of my peers, the money due to my status – prove to be no use to me at all, when it comes to dealing with Mad Jack.

If I am this paragon of beauty, intelligence and common sense, I am obliged to ask myself, then what am I doing on a lumpy mattress in deepest France without even a proper sheet to cover my breasts but only some kind of pressed fibre blanket, while this new lover, who only yesterday promised fit to be my knight in shining armour, he who would with his coming explain all things and make me truly happy, indicates to me both moral disapproval, physical non-desire, and professional mistrust? But then I remember the feel of his flesh in mine, and know outrage is irrelevant and that I will follow jolly Jack Stubbs to the end of the earth. Indeed I will even join the adoring throng – and I can see I may have to – who wait for the simple energising joy that the concentration of this man, this particular man, focused through his love-making, can bring. If only I can hold my tongue I might yet be the one he keeps in his bed, for ever. Craven, yes indeed, but there it is. My female lost to his male. I love him. It's hopeless.

'Look!' says Frances, indicating a cheek indeed swollen and sore. 'Just look! This place is swarming with puces. It's disgusting.'

Oh Frances, Frances, what you mean to say is that your father and myself are disgusting. If only you knew! Shall I whip off the blanket and show you what disgusting is, give graphic form to your no doubt vague imagination? What we do, how we do it? His tongue here, mine there? Of course not. How can I even think of such a thing? Ah, if only I could not! Frances reminds me of a girl called Meryl Lee, at school, who would tag along where she wasn't wanted: we kept her in tears most of her school life. I feel inclined to do the same to Frances

14

now, to pay her out for my suffering. But of course her father would never speak to me again if I did anything really disgusting.

At least, I suppose not. It has occurred to me in the last few minutes that Frances plays a larger part in Jack's and my drama than I care to believe: she, no longer a child, not yet an adult, but nubile, fresh and beautiful, with her white cheek and clear, innocent, albeit sulky eye – how can Jack but not look at her speculatively, as a man does a girl, not a father a daughter? Perhaps he fell in love – if that's how I'm to describe it – with me, as a counter irritant to her? Knowing she was coming on tour with him, he made sure I came too. Anyone would have done. The flight from incest – my friend Jude could make a TV programme all about it.
'I know what I'll do,' I say to Frances, as lightly as I can, smiling. I smile a lot – bare my teeth, that is, turn up the corner of my mouth – particularly when working out what to say next, how to defuse anger, turn away resentment, and so forth. 'I won't go into Blasimon today. I'll stay behind. Why don't you stay too? Let your father entertain the entertainers on his own!'

Entertain the entertainers! Can groups as serious as Uruguayan folk dancers, Breton bagpipers and feather-legged Gambian pole climbers be called entertainers? They certainly don't entertain me. How self-consciously, unsmilingly they take their national pride, their ersatz traditions, upon their earnest shoulders. A step and a shuffle here, a head-toss there, a round-and-round we go, male and female facing, passing, touching, breaking, and yawn, and yawn and die from irritation and boredom mixed. La Folklorique! Careful, careful, not to break the languid patterns of the past: cosy and complacent, as if a single nightingale and not the three Horses of the Apocalypse lurked behind yonder tree! (Only the Peruvians, dancing and prancing and piping in an endless circle, like Indian braves around a campfire, make me smile, and that not too kindly. And the Poles at least are less enthusiastic mimickers of long-forgotten, best forgotten rural ways than most, and will even dress up in white muslin and red sashes and dance a drawing room polonaise or so. Otherwise it's tap

15

and tap, and swirl and whirl, and the wild gypsy fiddling vibrating wax out of the ears, and nothing else to do all day but listen.) Sandy has better things to do than drive the Band's women between Blasimon and Roc Fumel, or feels he has, so once you're in Blasimon that's it, until the next morning, when the Jumpers' last gig, down at the Cabaret, comes to an end, and the last local goes home. If Jack wants me to stay behind in the Hôtel de Ville, that's okay by me. But I could do with company; I don't want to be alone, to be at the mercy of my thoughts. I've had eight blissful days spared them, at least in any coherent form.

'I can't stay here,' she says, lip curling. She looks like her father when she sneers. 'What's there to do here?'

'We could look for fleas,' I said. 'Or bedbugs.'

'Bedbugs!' she shrieks, rather nasally. Her voice is not her best point. 'But these are mosquito bites. They've got to be.'

'If you say so,' I say, cool as can be, and leap out of bed, allowing her a glimpse of my figure, neat and contained as hers can never be, and not an insect bite mark on it anywhere (though quite a few of her father's) before pulling on my pants, jeans and Citronella Jumpers T-shirt – the extra-small size. Frances wears the XL.

'Of course they're mosquitoes,' says Jack, who has the male knack of believing what he chooses to believe.

'Of course they are,' repeats Frances, who has the female knack of believing what a man wants her to believe.

'Of course they are,' I agree. If you can't beat them, join them. I'm already relieved that Frances won't keep me company. She finds nothing I say interesting, let alone witty. She doesn't like me and, what's more, I don't want her to like me.

'But you can't expect a lady cosmologist to know anything about insects,' says Jack, and he lies down on the bed and turns on his side; a fairly typical male reaction, in my experience, to bad news. So he knows!

'Ah,' I say, 'my secret is out,' but Jack doesn't reply. Oh Jack, wild Jack, please recover quickly. I am still Sandra, Jack's Sandra, whatever my profession, whatever my income, whatever my fame.

'What's a cosmologist?' asks Frances.

'An astronomer, actually,' I say.

'Are you really?' she asks, interest quite lighting up her blank though glowing eye: it is quickness of thought which makes eyes bright: a surfeit of mere oestrogen will make them glow. And then Frances says, 'What are Leos like as boyfriends?'

'Not an astrologer,' I say, 'an astronomer.' I try to be kind and patient, but why is it so difficult for ordinary people (ordinary people!) to distinguish between those who make a foolish living telling fortunes from the stars, and those who study the nature and destiny of the stars themselves?

'Isn't it the same thing?' she asks.

'No,' I say.

'That's a pity,' she says, 'because my friend Ady has a boy-friend Ken and he's a Leo and someone told her Leos beat their wives so she's going to break it off.'

'Lucky old Ken,' I say. Jack stirs in the bed. I think he's laughing. I hope so. Jack's had some kind of education and has in his time read a book or so, but I despair of Frances, whose mother calls a woman's magazine a book, and comes from an environment where conversation is at best the inter-change of information, at worst a sulky exchange of grunts, tauntings and insults. Children need to be exposed early to abstract notions, or they never get the hang of them, never find the framework which will make themselves interesting to themselves, and so to other people – let alone bother to make the distinction between the vile trade of the astrologer and the noble calling of the astronomer.

'What do astronomers do, then?' she asks.

'Study the stars,' I say.

'How boring,' she replies. 'Our school went to the London Planetarium once. I couldn't see the point. All I got was a crick in the neck.'

'Don't speak to her like that,' says Jack, sitting up in bed. 'She's a famous lady.'

'How did you find out?' I ask.

'Everyone knew but me,' he says, 'as the husband said to the wife.' He smiles too brightly, even for jolly Jack Stubbs, all white even teeth and stubbly chin and the veins and muscles of his thin neck start out, and I don't know that I trust the smile. 'She's on TV once a week,' he says to his daughter, 'and she never even told me.'

'Once a month,' I defend myself. 'Late night.'

'That's not really famous,' says Frances, 'if you don't mind me saying so. All kinds of people are on after midnight.' And she ambles out, victorious.

'Well, that put you in your place,' says Jack, and I know I am right not to trust his smile. 'And you shouldn't walk about with no clothes on in front of her. It may be all the rage in your media circles but not where I come from.'
That said, he jumps out of bed.
'Not media,' I say, 'mathematical and cosmological circles. TV is only the tip of my iceberg.'
'I don't doubt it,' he says, and pulls on his underpants (yesterday's) and I feel like a child deprived of its lollipop or, more accurately, a donkey of its carrot. Jack is, as they put it, well hung. That, I fear, is the carrot I'd followed south. And what with the harpies and the furies wielding their stick, their many-thonged whip, from behind, how could I not? Where it went, I followed.

'I didn't tell you lies,' I said, 'just not the whole truth.'
'Or, as I might say, I didn't get the tune wrong, I just missed a few notes.'
'Sorry,' I said, who am unused to apologising. Craven!
'That's all right,' he says, but I don't think it is. If a man runs off with a bored housewife, that's what he bargains for, not that she should suddenly display herself as a lady astronomer with a hundred ephemerides at her fingertips, and he not a differential equation in mind. All he has then, he must think, to keep her quiet, is his well-hungedness, and what reliance can he place on that? Or should he, if he's a man of dignity and proper self-esteem? Who wants to fuck their way to Paradise? Half the way, perhaps; not all the way: some of it at least must be spent in companionable conversation, minds and hearts in tune.

Oh Jack, wild Jack, leader of the Band! I leaned into him, and put my head against his shoulder − as I loved to do: Jack is six foot two: Matthew the same height as myself; that is to say five foot five, though broad with it − and the arms he puts round me are, I think, dutiful rather than enthusiastic.
'Look,' I say, 'let me explain.'
'Explanations are boring,' he says. And so they are, so I go to

the bathroom and stand outside on bare, splintered boards, waiting for Bente to finish gargling in her musical Scandinavian way. The only water in the Hôtel de Ville comes from the cold tap of the bathroom basin, and that comes in a rusty trickle. Jennifer, Sandy's wife, has put a plastic bucket under the basin so that the WC cistern can be filled when and as necessary, which is often, because fruit, wine, excitement and hot weather keep the Band's bowels active.

And I envisage the bathroom back home at Greenwich, where my erstwhile husband Matthew paces and grunts as is his habit, naked, hot and soft from the bath, his little blunt finger of a willy lost somewhere in the pink, folding flesh of his being. The floor is tiled with flowered ceramic, and the taps are gold and the bathroom suite navy blue, and the bath itself a Jacuzzi.

Bente came out of the bathroom.
'You didn't tell us you were famous,' she says.
'I'm not,' I say.
'Karl says you are.' It would be Karl. Mischief-making at seventy-two! Shaggy white locks shaking; rheumed eyes gleaming.
'Rumours, rumours,' I say.
'Please? I do not understand the word.' She wouldn't.
'Never mind,' I say.
'Jack will mind,' she says, smugly. 'There is a problem with the toilet. It is blocked.' And off she goes, to braid her hair and polish the struts of her boyfriend's drums, or pick the dandruff flake by flake from his pillow, or clean between his toes, or whatever of the many services she provided in return for his love.

And so indeed the toilet is blocked. Disgusting water reaches nearly to the brim. I take the handle of the lavatory brush (provided by Jennifer) and, shutting my eyes, and my nostrils with my spare hand, drive it down into the wodge of newspaper and worse, and am rewarded by the whoosh of water as the mass clears, and is sucked away and clean (well, cleanish) water wells up and steadies at an inch or so below its normal level, indicating that all is well below.

My stepfather would be proud of me. Then I fill the basin and wash, and wash, and wash, but who will wash my sins away? Sins of commission, of lust, lechery and pride. And sins of omission, of failing to leave a forwarding address.

4

Breakfast at the Hôtel de Ville

'Come on, everyone,' Jennifer cried, and her voice echoed in melancholy fashion up and down the dusty corridors of the Hôtel de Ville. Sandy brought Jennifer on the trip because she was, as he explained to everyone, a fool of a woman but useful. She was little and pretty and anxious. Everyone liked her except me, and even I took exception to her on the flimsiest of grounds – that is to say, that she took being called a fool of a woman as a compliment, the best a proper man could do by the way of a wife.
'Come on, lazybones,' she cried out now, into the silence. 'Come on. Let's get the show on the road. The bus leaves at ten and everyone not on it gets left behind.' (Oh she was, she was, a fool of a woman! Perhaps Sandy had it right.)

Now Jennifer was a good kind woman and I could see why her husband had brought her along, in spite of the opinion of her he so continually voiced. She could map-read, and pack swiftly, and thought it necessary (no one else did) to clean out the minibus from time to time, and produce clean, ironed, emerald green shirts for the Band to wear at formal gigs over acid green T-shirts. And also, of course, for the mutual pleasure of their nights together, a pleasure which I did not doubt. He was a deep-voiced, large-nosed (always a good sign) fellow, and I daresay with a deep and powerful stroke or so, of the kind he employed upon his chosen instrument, which could produce an agreeable enough response in Jennifer.

Make no mistake about it, these musicians are randy fellows and the instruments they choose to play, the music they care to make, reflect the manner of their love-making, their compulsion to beget. And if I unfashionably bracket the two, I daresay it is because I was reared by my grandmother more than my mother and am still permeated with the notions of the world before contraceptives were freely available, when the sexual drive was seen as something which suited nature's purposes, not man's; existing to create babies. The associated pleasures and excitements ensured the continuation of the race. Those who liked it fucked, and their genes survived. Those who didn't, failed to reproduce. Thus a race who liked sex was created. Sexual pleasure was both the stimulus and the reward for reproduction: God's way (great-grandmother) Nature's way (grandmother) evolution's way (mother) of making sure we fucked and fucked and fucked again, for the better continuance of the race, the more variant its surviving form. I have a special interest in evolution, in genetics, for reasons I will presently relate. My mind goes to it, whenever it can.

'Breakfast up, everyone,' cried Jennifer. 'Don't let the coffee get cold!' And up and down the corridors floorboards creaked, and the murmur of voices arose, and doors opened, and Jack came bounding along the corridor towards me (a puff of dust rising with every footfall) and whirled me round and kissed me full on the lips.
'Oh, you idiot,' he said, 'you idiot. What do you want with the likes of me?'
'Just you,' I said. 'Only you.'
'It's no kind of life,' he said, 'to be married to a Band. When I think of what you're used to.'
'You mean I'll turn into Jennifer?'
'No such luck,' he said, and vanished into the bathroom.
'This toilet isn't blocked,' he called out, in satisfaction. 'Rumour said it was, that we had to use the lamp-posts like the dogs we are.'
I did not claim credit for the unblocking, for fear of overwhelming my man with my competence.

'Jack, Sandra!' called Jennifer. 'Where are you two lovebirds? Just because Sandra's a star doesn't mean she doesn't need breakfast.'
'Go down and face them,' Jack called to me, from behind the closed door. 'I'll be a minute or so.'

And so I did. I went down to face my audience, my critics, in the high square kitchen, where spiders wove their webs and

22

beetles pattered about the dusty floor, and slugs laid silver patterns on broken tiles, or had done until Jennifer put an end to their fun; she stayed up late the night we arrived, dizzy from exhaustion, to clean up, as she put it. So we could all start fresh in the morning, as she said. And so we did, because it was Jennifer who ran about the house, shifting mattresses, finding bolsters, fairly allocating the grisly grey blankets, while the rest of us just sat on the stairs, and finished off Steve's red plastic flagon of yet grislier red wine, reluctantly shifting over whenever Jennifer pushed by: and so were saved the hours of grumbling negotiations while a consensus was reached on who should do what, and where, and worse, why. Easier, it was silently agreed, for Jennifer just to do the lot.

'So there you are,' said Jennifer brightly, filling in the awkward silence that fell upon the group around the table as I came into the room. They had been talking about me. 'So that's why you looked so familiar! A telly star. Why didn't you tell us to begin with?'

'We would have carried your bags,' said Karl.

'Aren't we honoured,' said Hugh, moving over, brushing not-so-pretend dust from a fruit box that served as a chair. He had a square plump face and was thinning on top, for all he was still in his twenties. He was the best drummer in the country, a distinction he shared with at least a hundred others, similarly described. He was hopelessly dyslexic, and (other than by speech, with which he was economical) could communicate only by drums. Bente thought he was a genius, because he'd told her so; she hovered over him, attending to his every whim. Why not? She had a well drummed upon look. I sat down and smiled vaguely, as I have learned to do when under attack, and Jennifer laid before us fine fresh bread, good Normandy butter, apricot jam with tiny whole (pitted) apricots still observable, hot foamy milk and weak grainy coffee. (I knew she'd slip up somewhere and she did, on the most important item) and some of us (not me) cried 'wonderful! a miracle! how do you do it, Jennifer?' or words to that effect, as expected, and she looked up, modest and triumphant, and looked shyly at Sandy whom she adores, for the pleasure no doubt of his slow base strokes.

And we ate and I thought that would be the end of it. They'd come to accept me, surely. I was the same person I'd been the day before – Jack's doxy, cause of the Reading Embarrassment (Mrs Stubbs had turned up at Reading Station Car Park, the Band's final pick-up point, to discover her husband with me in tow) and if they didn't mind that why mind this? But they did.

'Along with the raggle-taggle gypsies, oh,' observed Pedro. Well, he would: his background being folk. The band put up with him and his vibes, but he wasn't their regular guitarist.

'Slumming along with us ordinary folk,' said Karl (who'd been to Eton and spent his life slumming) and took from his pocket and unfolded (elderly men always *fold* a lot, and tightly, running a firm finger along every available crease: the only firm thing left, I daresay, so they use it whenever they can) a copy of the *Sun* some six months old, not just yellow but brown, and still discernible, that unfortunate photograph of me topless and apparently dancing on a table at a wild party, quite irrelevantly heading a report of a special public meeting of the Royal Astronomical Society. 'New Look at Sandra's Society'. Once they have this kind of photograph on their files they keep using it. I'd begged Matthew (my lawyer husband) to sue, but he said no: better to just let the matter die down.

'That photo,' I said now, tentatively, 'is misleading. I was standing on a table to change a lightbulb, and stretching up, and wearing a tube top, and that's the kind of thing that happens.'

They laughed.

'If you want to dance naked on tabletops,' said Steve, 'that's your business. I suppose the Press is after you now, to see what's next, and we're it.'

'Jack's it,' said Karl, and laughed. Envious old trout.

'All that's behind me,' I said. 'Finished. This is a new life.'

'We must seem very dull and ordinary to you,' said Steve, glinting through his pebble glasses.

'None of you seem the least ordinary to me,' I said. 'If anything, the lot of you are positively extraordinary.'

'What do you mean by that?' asked Sandy, dangerously. It was obvious I was in a no-win situation. And Jennifer, sensing trouble, moved uneasily and said:

'More bread, anyone? Who's for another dollop of jam? I'm

sorry it's not home-made, but it's better than nothing,' but no one took any. They looked at me instead.

'I think the Band's great,' I said. 'And the music's the greatest, and I'm proud to wear the Citronella T-shirt.' And I raised my mug of coffee to them all, and that helped. A simple, sincere act of flattery has got me out of many a tight spot yet! But where was Jack? I needed him. My body, as much as my mind, noted his absence. And then I heard the notes of his trumpet out in the courtyard. Jack was practising scales, pre-breakfast, as was his habit. The notes would drift into a tune and then out again into another key and another scale and another tune. Jack, in fact, was showing off.

'Pity he didn't play like that last night,' said Karl. 'He was all to pieces.'

'He doesn't get enough rest,' said Stevie of the abstemious trombone, leering at me through the pebble glasses, and Jennifer frowned and clucked.

We sat and listened, perforce, and the pure notes shivered the motes of dust from the kitchen shelves and they fell dancing in the streaming sunlight to the floor. But the silence was not easy. My presence inhibited ordinary conversation. Starlady Sandra, discoverer of the Planet Athena, for a short time a media celebrity: still, as they say, just about a household word, a faint flame fanned into brightness every fourth week on TV, whose views were solicited by feature writers as to what they were giving for Christmas, how they cut their toast, what length they wore their skirts, whose naked boobs had appeared in the *Sun*, was not wanted here. They felt as Jack did – cheated, taken for a ride. Silence was their weapon. They fell silent as teachers do when the Head comes into the staffroom, as the Mothers' Union does when the Vicar approaches, as does Claridges' Dining-Room as Princess Margaret enters. No matter how the Head jollies things along, or the Vicar swears the oaths of the common man, or Princess Margaret smokes yet another sinful cigarette, it only makes things worse. We are ordinary folk, they cry in their hearts, and proud of it. Nothing singular about us, no sirree! We're every-day, part of the team; we are the herd whose whole point is our lack of singularity. Bad . . . to you who are singled out, for good reason or bad!

And then Frances said:

'I don't know what all the fuss is about. I've never even *seen* her programme,' and everyone laughed, and felt easier, except Frances herself, who looked at me balefully with her lovely, moist, cowlike eyes. The white showed above the iris, I noticed. No amount of cosmetic surgery could cure that, I imagined.

'Everyone had enough?' said Jennifer, whisking a paper table-cloth away. Did she bring them with her: did she *expect* the disaster of our billeting? Karl assured us before we left that we'd be put up in proper French hotels, two-star. Was it that Jennifer lay awake each night planning how to be everything to someone, to provide something for everyone, preparing for all eventualities? Perhaps as a child she'd read *The Swiss Family Robinson*; perhaps she'd been carried away by its enchantment, grown up always to have at hand the equivalent of one of those convenient shipwreck chests from which necessities could be produced – not a mere rope to tether the wild goat but, better still, a knife to cut the creeper to bind together to make the rope: for here she was with length after length of paper tablecloth that could be cut up into squares for toilet paper (toilet paper, anyone?) or spread on some filthy, wormy old door she could always somehow find and place on fruit boxes to make a table, so that breakfast (which she would also somehow extract from the natives) would not only taste good but look good – ah, this trip, this band outing, this general disaster was Jennifer's moment of triumph, you could tell from the small smile of bliss on her lips. The great hour of the Band's need! Spoiled only by me, bringing with me the flavour of illicit sex, my uneasy mixture of fame and notoriety, diverting the full attention of Jack the mad trumpeter, leader of the Band, he whom every woman fancied (even Jennifer) and I had got.

Jack put his trumpet away, and came to finish the last of the coffee and no one said anything nasty to him at all.

'Time to hit the road, everyone,' said Jennifer, and the Band dutifully rose, and made its preparations for departure, and Jack took me by the hand and led me up the dusty stairs with the broken banisters to the very top of the house, and the small under-the-eaves room, where doves cooed and fluttered (the roof must actually have holed. The French simply don't seem to care about these things) and pushed me up against the wall, or one of them, and unbuttoned my jeans, and tugged them down and inelegantly but powerfully and briskly fucked me, so the ancient plaster behind me frayed and powdered and fell in showers over my heels. I remember I cried out, and the sound echoed. A lesser man would have said 'hush'. Jack didn't bother. He didn't care. Let the Band know. What did they not already know?

'Better?' he said. How did he know? What did my face show? Had I appeared to so much as notice his sexual remissness, let alone care? Surely not! Oh, but I was truly colonised. Jack sent his spies into my head, amongst the crowded passages of my thoughts, taking note, detecting rebellion. He humiliated me as the conqueror does the conquered, making sure that's the way it stays, that no one gets any ideas.

'Better than what?' I asked coolly, instead of saying yes, oh yes, and my defiance seemed to set him off again, and I was glad of it.

'I must be going,' he said. 'They'll be waiting. Mustn't upset Jennifer. She'll have her stopwatch out.' But he kissed me lingeringly, almost romantically, as if in apology for the brusqueness of his behaviour, and I was glad of that too. I did not doubt he loved me – albeit as the conqueror loves the conquered. Let them mutter and murmur and squirm, that's okay, that's expected, that shows they're worth the conquering; but let the spies report back any sign of real unrest, of organisation, and the iron hand descends, and informers turn into secret police, spies turn into torturers, and misery abounds.

'That was to keep you going,' said jolly Jack Stubbs. 'Until I come home tonight.'

'But what will I do all day?' I asked.

'It was you who said you wanted to stay behind,' he stopped at the door and said. He was as tall as the door. He would have to stoop to leave the room, this lengthy man whose lengthiness extended to all other parts. I stayed where I was, my jeans at least modestly replaced, though I seemed to be shirtless – my shirt, I now observed, in a crumpled ball beneath my feet; how had that happened? – still pinned against the wall by the sheer memory of the extent of his presence within me.

'Did I?' I said. 'I must have been mad.'

'It's best if you do,' he said. 'Frances is getting jealous. Give her a day on her own with me, and she'll be fine.'

'Keep an eye on her,' I said, 'or she'll be off.'

'She's too young for that. Fifteen!'

'Growing up fast,' I said.

'We'll have to have a talk some time, you and me.'

'What about?'

'Things,' he said. 'Where we go from here. We can't be on the road for the rest of our lives.'

'Why not?'

'You being who you are,' he said. 'It alters things.'

'How?' I couldn't see it, wouldn't; standing there in disarray. 'A man has his pride,' said Jack, Mad Jack, Leader of the Band. Proud Jack, like any other man. But love conquers all. Doesn't it?

'They'll never have me back,' I said. 'I've burned my boats. You've no idea!'

He looked me up and down, with his bright knowledgeable eyes, and smiled, and moved back towards me.

'Takes a lot of burning to sink a boat. Careful, or they'll tow you back into port.'

'They never will,' I said. 'Never, never, never!'

But Lear said seven 'no's' in a row, and it did him no good at all. And the minibus's horn went, long and loud, and Jack moved away from me, saying, 'I have to go,' and I knew he did, but I took it as a bad omen.

I had better report what happened after Jack left, pounding down the stairs, clatter-clatter, the better to keep Jennifer happy, though I had rather not. I watched the dust of his departure subsiding, gently falling through the beams of August sunlight – already just slightly autumnal – which shone through the cobwebby windows. I was released quite suddenly and irrationally, as when the door of a washing machine after its fast spin finally allows itself to be opened, from my pinning to the wall, and crossed to the window, and saw what I did not want to see. The Renault 12, packed with the day's necessities – bass, banjo, guitar, clarinet, drums, trombone, trumpet, various stands, sound system, microphones, shirts, T-shirts, cassettes, stickers, badges, the Band itself, Sandy already at the wheel and Jack just getting into the back, pulling first Jennifer, then Frances, up behind him, the doors closing, the van driving off, and nothing left, nothing, just the bare French yard, the French morning sun, and a kind of lonely shuttered desolation.

I couldn't bear it. My private parts still buzzed and zinged. What had been replete and satisfied now hungered and thirsted. The doves fluttered and pecked at my feet on the powdered plaster, for spiders and weevils and all the things Jack and I had disturbed. The birds seemed strangely tame and not disconcerted in the least by the odd activity of humans. I looked around for any possible source of satisfaction. It was going to be hard to come by. The door handle seemed about the right height, of cold, shocking metal. I took off my jeans and rubbed myself up against it and, with the aid of my fingers, came and came again, and cried out without shame, so the doves rose and departed through a crack between eaves and ceiling into somewhere less desperate and agitating. Then I felt better, as if I had involved just not the organic world but the inorganic in the patterns of the changing universe. Drawn them in, united them. My flesh and cold metal had had business together and very right it seemed. Thank you, long Jack. Thank you, brass door handle. May the electrons fly, may the cells of the flesh learn how to welcome them, and not resist them.

Perhaps I am mad.

5

Mother's Got a Headache

My mother was mad. I don't mean mad in the way of wearing unexpected hats, wearing bright tights when everyone else wore dull, or talking too brightly and too long, or spending too much money at the shops, all of which can classify a woman as mad, that is to say disconcerting – Tamara? Oh, Tamara's mad! Such fun, on a good day; really trying on a bad – but clinically, definably, schizo-phrenically mad. An inhabitor, on and off, of lunatic asylums, a plodder in wrinkled stockings down shiny pale green smelly corridors, a hearer of voices in the head which urged her to burn and murder, a perceiver of visions before the eyes which made her see devils in corners performing hideous obscenities, which she would, en crise, attempt to nullify by imitation.

Or thus a kind psychiatrist once tried to explain the voices and the visions to me, sorting out a little of my confusion and despair. I belong to the school of thought which sees mental derangement as a matter of chemical imbalance in the brain – if the balance is out of kilter, however minutely, the mind picks up information from itself and processes this alongside what comes in properly and in an orderly fashion from the senses. If you're sane, a dog is a dog, yellow is yellow, bread smells like bread. If you're mad the dog is more than a doG, possibly God in reverse, yellow is something sinister, bread smells like shit so perhaps is shit. Everything is more than it should be. The mad are not happy: they are overloaded. They hate.

Now there are many driven by circumstances to dwell in lunatic asylums or let their stockings wrinkle and their jackets stain in what is known as 'community care': their eyes may dull and glaze, their face muscles stiffen in imitation of the real thing, but they are merely refugees from life, the ones who can't stand it a minute longer. These are mere pretenders, they are not the genuinely, tragically, frighteningly mad.

Do you know, if good people, and many such there be and I do not include myself amongst them, opened a hostel for the mentally unbalanced next door to me, I'd move out. I wouldn't be one of those who joined a protest meeting – 'We Don't Want The Mad Here' – that kind of primitive hysteria which always bubbles up in the general populace to prevent social improvement, prevent the arrival of Utopia – I wouldn't have the face; I'd lose street credibility. 'Starlady Sandra in Madhouse Feud'! I'd just keep my mouth shut and move out, saying the place was too damp.

At times in my life I'd tell myself that my mother was merely one of the pretenders, one of the 'driven mad' not 'born mad'. Driven mad by my father. (There's another story, and certainly one my grandmother liked to believe.) But I never quite convinced myself: the desire to murder was there in her brain, the devil's glare in her eye, as she stared at me, her daughter. And the frequent approach of the madhouse staff, syringes and strait-jackets at the ready, made it difficult to maintain the illusion. No, here was no pretender to the mad state: this was the real thing. Mad Tamara was born, mad she remained. In my veins runs the blood of the past. My mother's insanity, my father's sanity. Now there was a man who was sane: whole committees of sensible men (not a woman amongst those jurors) and some of them most cultured, agreed that he was sane. That was in 1949, at the Nuremberg Trial. Then they took him out and shot him dead. Sane, sane. But all that's another story. I notice I have said 'they' shot him, those cultured, censorious, shocked folk, but of course they didn't do it themselves: they appointed a firing squad of rough soldiery to do it for them. Officers seldom actually kill. The judge doesn't switch on the electric chair, let alone slam prison doors. Lesser men do that, who don't have the same sensitivities. Well, we all know this. In the meantime, my father doesn't have a grave, so we can't lay flowers: we, his many, many children.

Of course I'm in flight from the past. Who isn't? There is a good deal to escape from. None of us are born to ordinary parents, but to the one way or another insane, the one way or the other cruel. I am just an extreme example of the human race, scratching away with my pen, thinking this, writing that, working out a story about Jennifer, on a door on two boxes which makes a satisfactory table if I don't lean on it too hard (if I do, it tilts) from time to time moving my chair, with its one almost-broken leg, out of the sun, as that splendid orb creeps up and round the courtyard rooftops; and as and when the white paper throws up too much reflected glare for comfort, conscious of the pleasure still lingering between my legs, and confident of its eventual renewal; with a couple of doves – perhaps the same two? but who could tell? (Doves? They all look alike to me! Seen one, seen 'em all) to peck and coo about for company. Even I can be happy: mothered as I am, fathered as I was.

So happy I was, in fact, that I put down my pen and skipped around the courtyard a little – the sun was not yet so high and hot as to make such an act unthinkable – and saw my new life stretch ahead of me, my life with Jack as Sandra Stubbs, no longer Sandra Harris, Sorensen or Starlady. When Jack understood I was now Sandra Born Again, that he was my saviour, that I had been reborn the night I met him, the hour his body entered mine, why then he would be easy in his mind, as would the Citronella Jumpers. All would be well. True, the body of past that pursued me was powerful and heavy, more than most had to put up with, but I'd do it, yes I would! Who wanted a proper writing desk when a door on two boxes would do? Who needed gold taps and a navy bath and the dinner-time conversation of astronomers and barristers; water came as well from a rusty tap: a truer, more honest converse from musicians. For I could see, even in my elation, that if I lived with Jack I would also live with the Band. Musicians today live as they always have; as actors have: nothing changes. The troupe is all, the Band is one; like footballers, back-biting and sniping off the field, divided by temperament, but on the field united by common experience, exhilarated by a common joy, totally loyal, each one nothing without the group, everything within it. And women have always up and followed, off with the raggle-taggle gypsies oh, as Pedro would have it, away from the warmth and safety of their familiar lives: in flight from boredom.

It isn't wise to be too happy: to dance around empty courtyards in a state of elation. Something will happen to bring you back to a sober state, a proper mode of anxiety. Something happened.

Something happened in the shade of the fig tree which leaned its branches over the courtyard wall. I've never liked fig trees. The branches are too bare, the leaves too oddly shaped, their green too muted: the flesh of the fruit too delicately, corruptly scented. A man was standing there: or not standing there. Perhaps not a man – hardly more than a boy. I saw the thin wrists and the red and yellow knitted cap he liked to wear, and knew it was my half-brother Robin. I couldn't see his face clearly and I was glad of that.

'Is that you, Robin?' I asked.

'That's me,' he said, or didn't say.

'What is it now?'

'It's all very well,' he said, 'but what about my grave?'

'Oh my God,' I said, 'I knew there was something!' Every August it was my habit to go to the cemetery and clear my brother's grave, picking up the litter the year's winds had swept in: his grave was in a walled corner – rather like the corner where he now stood, I realised – where rubbish was apt to accumulate. This annual clearing of Robin's grave was the only gesture of sentiment I allowed myself – and see how it confounded me!

'I just thought I'd remind you,' he said. 'It doesn't really matter!'

Was he in my head, a memory taken flesh? I scarcely knew. What difference did it make?

And he smiled, my dead brother Robin smiled, and shrugged, and left it to me, in death as he had in life. Up to you, sister Sandra, do what you want!

'I won't,' I said to this non-existent lad. 'I'll work something out. I will not go back. I'm with Jack.' What woman doesn't do it – use her duty to a man to get out of an obligation. Can't see Mum today because she has to cook her husband's dinner: can't bake the PTA cake because she has to meet him at work. Can't lay your ghost, Robin. Sorry. Jack needs me!

'Tell you what,' I say. 'We'll compromise, Robin. I'll get your grave seen to, somehow. I may not do it, but it will be done.'

And he goes, though whether or not he's satisfied by this, I can't tell. Or I dismissed him. At any rate he wasn't there any more, though for a time there lingered on the wall a slight Hiroshima-type shadow, and it did seem a little chilly. A lizard on the wall even scuttled back home. I wasn't frightened. The ghosts of the past are always there – I just hadn't reckoned on their tenacity, their capacity to travel.

I went into the village in search of a telephone box. I would have to ring my friend Alison. I had sworn not to, of course, but to make a clean break: give in but once to the longing for continuation, for familiar voices, places, and you'd be doing it all the time. Alison today was fine, but what about Central TV tomorrow, and Matthew the day after next, and the *Sun* peering through windows trying to get my boobs in the bath next week – and oh Jack, dear Jack, goodbye Jack, common sense triumphs over love, or lust.

Since Robin's death I have become both tough and frivolous. It was not my will: it has just happened.

My brother Robin was mad. Either he inherited insanity from my mother, or acquired it from her, or else his brain, from close proximity to hers, learnt the same painful but no doubt interesting tricks, of wandering in and out of those areas of consciousness barred to decent folk, for their own protection. My mother, though mad, was beautiful, and married when I was five, a pleasant Englishman called Simon, a breeder of horses, frequently bankrupt, in one of her more apparently sane periods, when she didn't stare at me, or him, with her mad glare, her devil's brow, plotting how best and horribly to murder us, but softly and sweetly, though always sadly knowing, only too well I fear, the temporary nature of her kindness. Robin was born when I was six and I loved him greatly and not enviously at all: he was witness not just to my mother's ordinariness, but to my kind stepfather's promise of permanence. And a bright, handsome, beaming child Robin was. Only sometimes, even when he was very small, would his face fall into a kind of stillness, a remoteness: and sometimes if I disturbed him in this state, offered him a sweet or a ride on my bicycle to stir him out of it, he would look at me with a hostility which I could not bear to see, and which reminded me of my mother. I did what I could to please him, to protect him from her fate.

'Mum's got a headache,' I'd say, 'that's all,' when he seemed upset at one of Tamara's bursts of violence, or when she washed the same knife ten times over, complaining of germs, dashing with every jerky movement our hopes of ordinariness. Simon resisted to the end the notion of his wife's, my mother's, insanity. But I knew it even before they were married: when I was four, five. I was a wary child, given to smiling and turning away wrath, in case it was murderous. Robin, a fraction more obtuse than I, just a little more self-defending, wilful in his insistence on being happy, became merely confused. Tamara showed him once how to pull the wings off flies. 'You're a boy, so you're bound to do it,' she said, demonstrating. 'There! Now you know how.' It was as if, doing her best, she'd learned the maternal role by heart, but got it wrong. She taught me how to do it too –
'It isn't right for a girl to know less than a boy, in order to get to the same place.' So I pulled the wings off flies when she was looking, and didn't when she was not, and instructed Robin to do the same. I daresay I merely added to his confusion. He had her Knight's move in thought to come to terms with, and I, zooming my pieces Bishop-like here and there, must have made his poor head dizzy. My stepfather was the King, a slow mover from square to square, always under financial attack, always moving out of trouble just in time. The Queen, the all-powerful, she who should be obeyed because she could be trusted, had long since left the board. We were on our own, Simon, Robin and I, playing a dismal end game we were bound to lose while wingless flies lay in heaps around. I knew my value, though: knew my way out: survival at home, steeling my heart against the pain of fearing my own mother, and progress at school. I would educate myself out of home, into

freedom. When I was nine, and Robin was three, I taught him to read. I saw the same solution for him.

By the time he was twelve I could no longer hide from myself his resemblance to my mother: by the time he was fifteen he was expelled from his school; he took odd jobs and was fired from them: he was abusive and hostile at home and stared day after day at the television, trying to work out some connection between the images on the screen and the real world, and then, when he felt he had succeeded, had learned the patterns of behaviour and response which other people seemed somehow just to know, would go out and do likewise. Batter, bash and snarl. Better, I daresay, if only just, than copying the behaviour of invisible masturbating demons, as my mother did, and for which when Robin was nine, and myself fifteen, she was first put away. If anyone looked at Robin wrongly, in a bus, or on the street, and it was difficult so not to do, for his eyes looked so bright and odd and he wore a battered straw hat with the crown punched out, and a wing collar and tie, he would follow John Wayne's example and knock them down with a cry of 'A man's got to do what a man's got to do', which would have been funny – and I think he meant it to be funny; there was always an underlying quality of double-take in his peculiar behaviour, which from time to time gave me false hope: he was just a pretender, then, after all, taking refuge from trauma, not just flesh of her flesh, brain of her brain, mad of her madness – but which in the event meant prison sentences, probation officers, social workers, and definitions of insanity, but no treatment, no hope, no cure.

Enough of all this. Robin is dead: he jumped under a train, a brave kind final act of kindness to me (if not the train driver) and his father and his grandmother, with whom we presently all lived, who could then put his existence behind us, consoling ourselves with the thought that he, our brother, our son, our grandson, had been merely one of evolution's mistakes, and had to go: the sooner snuffed out the better. This was certainly Robin's own view of his life. And better he went before the genes had a chance to carry on into the next generation, and prove themselves viable: for the mad, albeit distressing to themselves and others, can survive and propagate very well

36

thank you. He was punch drunk in the end, of course, confused, whether by the drugs or electric shock therapy they gave him before throwing him out and saying 'there's nothing we can do' – or else, more likely, by the sheer battering of the thoughts within his head, panicking like the birds in a chimney, soot flying, black everywhere, apparently exitless. Our existence, if you pay it any attention, is unbearably distressing.

6

A Telephone Call

I called my friend Alison collect, at the Royal Society for the Prevention of Handicap, where she worked. The French operator did not really wish to connect us, and let me know it, but my will prevailed upon hers.

'Alison!' I say, expecting warmth, pleasure, 'where have you beens, what's been going ons, oh you wild mad impetuous thing; are you okays' and so forth. But no: her voice is cold. 'Oh, it's you, Sandra. I'm just off to a meeting.' Now I live in fear of offending my friends. I don't have so many I can afford to lose them. If I don't hear from them for a time I get nervous: I think what have I done, what have I said: if they're curt or quick or off to meetings I'm sure it's my fault.

'I'm phoning from France.'

'Oh, that's where you are. What do you want?'

'I want you to do something for me.'

'That figures.'

I consider this. The phone gives three sharp peeps to remind me that time is money. So much the French do for each other. An old man with a gnarled face and wearing a dusty black beret peers through the glass at me. Perhaps he is the ghost of Tourist France. He dribbles a little and goes away, leaving a wet patch on the glass, but that may still be an effect, rather than a fact, like Robin's Hiroshima shadow earlier.

'Alison, what's the matter?'

'Nothing's the matter, just some things are more important than others, and the hydrocephaly rate is up 2.8 per cent over last year, and another eight children without brains were born in the London Regional Authority in the last quarter.'

'A statistical anomaly.'

'I certainly hope so. I heard you'd run off to France; I thought you'd be back by now.'

'This is for keeps.'

'So you keep saying. Actually, I am rather cross with you, Sandra.'

'Why?' My heart beats faster. The dribble has evaporated, leaving a milky patch on the glass. I think he was real.

'I've settled down: it's time you did. You're – how old – forty-five?'

'Forty-two.'

'And I don't like being taken advantage of. I don't like being your raw material. And poor Matthew! You've led him such a dance, Sandra.' And this is my friend. He's been getting at her. Ringing her up, putting his side of the story. It isn't a story, of course, only an event: but he's trained to make consecutive sense out of random happenings, and get people put away for years as a result. He's a hot-shot for the prosecution: a no-hoper for the defence.

'Raw material, Alison?'

'A story you wrote, Sandra. At least, I suppose you did. It's my life story and in this week's *Nursing Times* for all the world to see.'

So there it was. They'd actually published my 'A Libation of Blood' and Alison, the spoilsport, was kicking up a fuss.

'You just flail about,' she says, 'making trouble for everyone. Why don't you have a baby and settle down?'

'Because it might be in fashion and not have a brain,' I say, and she has the grace to laugh – she's not hopeless, Alison, and I'm curling and uncurling inside with joy, and can't show it. A story published! Only in the *Nursing Times*, it's true, and who's going to read that, except by bad luck Alison herself. It must be something to do with her job, I suppose. 'Nursing of the paediatric problem case' or some such article, drawn to her attention. But it's a beginning. Will Jack mind me being a writer? Will he encourage my talent, or stifle it? I reckon he'll be all right, so long as I write about my friends, not him.

'The story's not about you, Alison, not really,' I say, more craven because she is my friend, than I would be with a colleague, an acquaintance, a stranger.

'Oh yes,' she says coolly, 'separated from her husband, pregnant with twins and in genetic counselling, and nothing at all to do with me! I really must get to this meeting. I can't sit gossiping all day.'

'This is not gossiping,' I say. 'Robin's birthday's coming up. Will you visit his grave for me and tidy up?'
There is a long silence.
'No,' says Alison. 'Do it yourself.'

Alison's end

Alison put the phone down, and then picked it up and called her boyfriend. What was his name? I had to remember back to my story in the *Nursing Times* – I could hardly give the poor man a face, let alone his name – though I'd met him a dozen times or so. (Truly. acceptable good kind men seem to me somehow anonymous: or perhaps it is that I don't truly believe in them.) Yes of course – Bobby – a steady enough name, in fiction as in life. Lucky old Alison, mother of more than enough, now with Bobby.

Alison put the phone down and then picked it up and called Bobby. (What I am writing now is, of course, wishful thinking. This is how I imagined it, walking down the dusty, bungalow-and-geranium lined French road, towards the market square, the heat of the pavement seeping through the thin soles of my canvas shoes, upset, trying not to cry. And perhaps, who's to say, I get it right.)

Alison put the phone down and then picked it up and called Bobby at the BBC.
'Bobby,' she said, 'Sandra just rang from France.'
'That's nice,' said Bobby. 'What's she doing in France?'
'Don't you remember,' said Alison. 'She left Matthew a couple of weeks back and ran off somewhere with someone and the *Sun* was in our front garden trying to find out all about it.'
'Darling,' said Bobby, 'I can't keep up with your friends. My friends are not like yours, thank God.'
'And I was upset and put the phone down on her.'
'Then call her back and say you're sorry. Do you mind, darling. I'm in the middle of a recording. The spina bifida scandal.'
'Well, I'm supposed to be at a meeting about hydrocephalus funding.'
'They can't start without you.'
'Nor can your lot start without you. And I can't call her back

because she was in some village in France in a phone box. Poor Sandra. I'm afraid I upset her.'
'What did she want?'
'She wanted me to tidy up her brother's grave. You know, the mad one who died. And I said no.'
'But why?'
'She can't go on using her family as an excuse for ever.'

That's enough of that conversation. You get to the painful point and it's time to move on.

I'll take up Bobby and Alison's conversation later on that evening, as they sit in front of the fire, or more likely, lean side by side against the rail of the oil-fired Aga, warming their bums. (Forget it's mid-summer. This is author's licence. It's my first novel.)

'Of course I'll go and do the grave,' said Alison.
'Do you know where it is?'
'I was at the funeral. Poor Sandra. Her mother was there with her keepers: they'd let her out for the occasion. She didn't even recognise Sandra. Her own daughter!'
'What about her father?'
'Men never played a large part in her early life.'
'She's making up for it now.'
'Yes,' said Alison. 'And biting the hands that feed her.'

Ouch. I'll take them on to in bed, after love.
'What really gets me,' said Alison, 'is that story about me and you. She's using us.'
'What story?'

Let her get out of her nice warm bed and go all the way downstairs in her nightie, stubbing her toe on a child's toy, to find a copy of the *Nursing Times*. Then let Bobby have to sit up in bed and read it, first finding his glasses. They'll be tired in the morning.
'What's wrong with that?' said Bobby. 'It's a good story. It's based on you and me, but perfectly affectionate, and very nice about your mother. I like the title. You're being much too sensitive.'

'Now I feel dreadful,' said Alison. 'Supposing she needs me? I think I'll brave Matthew in the morning and try to find out where she is and go over to France and bring her home.'

'That's better. That's what friends are for. What about our work?' asked Bobby, suddenly cautious, like his author.

'It's a Bank Holiday weekend,' said Alison, and though her author is aware that there isn't such a weekend so early in August, she chooses to overlook this inconvenient fact. Thus plot makes liars of us all. I shall put Alison and Bobby's story 'A Libation of Blood' in the appendices. Turn to it now, if you so wish. Otherwise continue with the main narrative.

Jennifer's story 'Come On, Everyone' – the one I stopped writing when faced by Robin's ghost, as a consequence of which I made the painful phone call to Alison, is the second story in the appendices. I have even changed Sandy's profession in the interest of his anonymity, and because I am becoming more prudent. I really like Jennifer (on the whole) and don't want to upset her.

7

Trying to Get Through

After Alison had replaced the receiver so abruptly and un-kindly I walked further into the village in the hope of diversion – laughter, conversation, conviviality, but of course these are not the hallmarks of a French village in the middle of August. Anyone who cared for them must be off to Blasimon, listening to the Citronella Jumpers, living it up at the Folklorique. The streets were deserted, the windows shuttered. I looked for the dribbling Ghost of Tourist France, but even he was gone, back to the postcard from whence he came. Red and orange flowers grew in tidy patterns in bungalow gardens, and a few hens pecked about in the road. A dog barked and danced about at the end of a chain as I passed, but it was a puny thing and I barked sharply back and it stopped. (I identified the creature with Alison, rather sharply. Somehow, consciously or uncon-sciously, she had sent her spirit out to invest the animal.)

The village square was equally deserted and lined with short stubby tidy trees, which afforded no shade in the midday sun. On one side was a closed boulangerie, a closed charcuterie, and a shuttered, all-purpose store. The only cars were four parked Citroëns, none of them new. One tilted to its side, was covered by a plastic awning and had a very flat tyre. The metal rim of the wheel rested on the road. I was sure the owner, who took the trouble to shade his car, would be distressed to know that this was so. Perhaps he had gone away, on holiday? But did he have no friends, who must see, and would replace the tyre in his absence? I wondered if, when it came to it, I had friends who would do such a thing for me. Alison would not: not at the moment. If she would not visit my brother's grave, selfish bitch, why should she change my tyre? Jack would, of course he would, but then he was my lover. Matthew, my lawyer husband, would not: firstly because he'd think it was a mechanic's task, and then because it might have some legal significance in the matter of our divorce, suggesting that he still saw me as an extension of himself and therefore entitled to maintenance, which would not do. He'd let my car rot, and me if he could. Jude, my friend and colleague, producer of *Sandra's Sky*, and a practical person, would do it at once, of course – or see that it was done, wishing to preserve her white fingers and polished nails. Unless, unless of course, some obscure magazine chose to publish 'Falling in Love in Helsinki' in my absence, and she happened to come across it, and recognised herself. I felt like crying. I, who so seldom cry.

During the past year, and because I do not believe in wasting time, I had looked for a way of productively filling in the evenings at Green Gables, Greenwich, while Matthew was out with the Masons, or the League of Lawyers against the Common Law, or whatever. I had hit upon the idea of writing short stories. I would manage one a week, print it out by the score, and during the following week feed it through the Royal Society's postal franking system to all appropriate magazines, whether literary, house, trade, or hobby, from the *London Review* to the BBC's *Ariel* to the *Nursing Times* by way of *Fisherman's Weekly*, *Aerospace* and *Autocar*. By thus flooding the short story market, it seemed to me, and indeed opening up new ones, and with very little capital outlay, I could almost guarantee eventual publication. And so indeed it had proved. But there were, as so often, consequences of my actions I had not properly considered. I had not taken sufficient steps to render my characters convincingly fictional – and now being separated from the word processor had no means to recall the particular magazines which had received 'Falling in Love in Helsinki' and so could not calculate the likelihood of Jude coming across it by accident.

I stood outside the telephone box in the square and wondered whether or not to call Jude, and find out if she were still my friend. There was no wind: it was very hot. I enjoy heat, but not in a place like this, not when it's a conspiracy between desolation and discomfort. My T-shirt stuck to my skin and my jeans chafed, and I was hungry and thirsty and alone, and I thought eyes might be peering at me from the cracks of shutters. How could I know? There was a kind of shrieking in my head: the harpies beat about me with their wings, and clawed me with their talons, saying, no, no, run, run, you can't look back, look what happened to Orpheus when he looked back – lost Eurydice and got torn to pieces by the mob, and he was a man, what hope is there for you, a woman? And the furies buffeted me too, saying this is your punishment, this desolation, put up with it. Pride goes before a fall. So I could hardly hear at all the calm reasonable voice which said look, she's your friend, your colleague: you owe her something, indeed a lot. Get in touch, let her know what's happening: she'll want to know. But ah, was she my friend?

I stepped into the shade of the booth and found all my loose change and rang Central TV in Norfolk (where, where, asked the operator) and was put through to Jude.
'Hello,' she said, and I put the phone down. How, where, could I begin?

I like to think that after I put the phone down the conversation between Jude and her assistant Marcia went like this.

Jude: That sounded like Sandra. I hope she's all right. We got cut off! Perhaps she's been kidnapped.
Marcia: I do hope not! I couldn't bear it if anything happened to Sandra!
Jude: She's been under a good deal of strain lately. It's a nuisance about the programme but we'll manage somehow. Keep her place open while she decides whether or not to return. She's so popular with the public, in any case, we really have no option but to put up with anything she chooses to do.
Marcia: On full pay while she makes up her mind.
Jude: Of course. She must have been very unhappy with Matthew to run off like that. What a tedious bore that man is! She had every justification.
Marcia: Or very much in love with someone we don't know about!

Unfortunately this conversation is making the harpies and furies shriek with laughter. I sit on a stone bench in the little

45

patch of shade afforded by the lopped and pollarded tree above and try it again. This time Jude is speaking to Alison, over lunch. They sometimes meet up.

Jude: I just so happened to come across this story by Sandra in a FinnAir magazine.
Alison: I suppose it was all about you.
Jude: Let's say it was written round me, rather than about me. Well, that's the writer's prerogative, isn't it. All life is his, her raw material.
Alison: You don't feel, as I do, that she's parasitic on our lives, has betrayed our confidences?
Jude: Oh no, not at all! And nor should you.
Alison: I did, but I've recovered. I'm off to France with Bobby at the weekend to see if we can trace her, make sure she's okay. Perhaps you should come too?
Jude: I'll think about it. Because, I must say, I do get rather tired of being treated like her mother. I'm so much younger than she is. So why is she always so desperate for my approval?

Ouch! Let's bring that one to an end. Now the question is posed I can get on with my life. I blank my mind out and roll up the bottoms of my jeans – with difficulty because they're as narrow as can be – to let the sun get at least to my shins. I wish I had gone into town with the Band: I would be spared the pressures of my own company. 'GUP – or Falling in Love in Helsinki', my story about Jude, forms Appendix III of this book. It deals with GUP, or the Great Universal Paradox; the one which states that what you want you can't have; what you do have, you don't want. If it seems appropriate, read it now. Otherwise, let it wait a little, until such time as I suggest.

8

Bringing to Life

I did not wish to be defeated by this town. I wanted to bring it to life. It seemed to me that money might be the magic required so to do. Money, I had often been told, opened many doors. I had money in my pocket – six ten-franc coins and four hundred-franc notes. I sat on my stone bench under its deformed tree and jingled it. My experience is that if you do this, sooner or later, and usually sooner, someone will come and, taking you for a fool, do their best to extract it from you. This at least is activity, energy in action. I longed to see some.

Sometimes of course you have to wait quite a while. I remember going on an outing with my mother, when I was nine and Robin was three, and she was in, if not sane, at least competent mode. We went to the beach for the day. We sat by a rock pool, clear, deep and happily and prettily fringed with seaweeds and salty flora: and my mother Tamara prised open mussels and dropped little portions of pinky yellowy flesh onto the clean pale sand of the rockpool floor, and said 'Wait! Now wait!' And Robin and I waited, and presently a small crab appeared out of nowhere, and then half a dozen prawns, and feasted, and such was their joy, such the commotion, that the very rocks around began to move and a giant claw shot out, and grabbed the best for itself. 'See!' said my mother. 'First the small fry, then the large. A sprat to catch a mackerel.' And we puzzled over this, Robin and I. It made sense, but no sense. Nevertheless, I have always observed – jingle money and wait, and something happens, whether you like it or not.

I sat jingling in the square for ten minutes or so: a shutter in the house next to the boulangerie was thrown back with a clatter that made cats hop and pigeons rise and a young woman appeared in the window. She had a baby on her arm. What did she find to *do* all day, I wondered, behind the blank façade of the house? She seemed cross. I was not surprised. Then the blind of the boulangerie rattled up: fermé became ouvert. I went in and bought a long thin loaf with a ten-franc piece. The bearded woman in the faded navy dress who served me counted out change unwillingly, as if knowing it would just give me more to jingle in my pocket. It did. The doors of the charcuterie and the supermarché were now open. I bought sausage from the first and wine from the second. On both occasions I was served by women. As I left, the doors closed behind me in a kind of exhaling breath which I felt to be part relief, part disappointment. The relief was that peace had been restored: the disappointment that no one's fortune had been made by its disturbance. But there, nothing is as bad as one fears or as good as one hopes. I was disappointed in them, too. What is the point of a town without men? Or inhabited only by the ghosts of men?

For I must report that as I walked back with my provisions to the empty Hôtel de Ville, I heard footsteps behind me, echoing my own. I stopped. They stopped. I looked back. No one. An echo, perhaps? But I could see no wall to make such a reverberation of sound; just the dull, empty, hot street, and ugly wrought-iron gates with their tubs of practical red flowers. Dogs which should have barked didn't. And when I resumed walking, the steps came after me again – and not with the shuffle of the dribbling ghost, or the light tentative movements of Robin, but with a strong, young, forceful pace, so I kept thinking whoever or whatever it was would catch up with me, that someone would appear at my elbow, but of course no one did. The unseen follower did not pursue me into the courtyard of the Hôtel de Ville: the footsteps stopped as I came up to the little grassed slope to the gate – and I looked behind again and saw nothing unusual except that the sturdy-if-rusty child's swing, which for some reason stood on the slope, was creaking to and fro, to and fro. And that of course could have been the wind. Winds do get up quickly in these parts – not that I felt any when I licked my finger and held it up. But of course, my not feeling it did not mean it was not there. These things are so subjective.

I nodded towards the swing and went inside the gate. It never does to show fear, even to ghosts: which is another way of saying we must face the past and our own guilts unafraid. And even if this one was, as it were, nothing to do with me, I doubted the capacity of any ghost to do the here and now any harm. I was not afraid. Was I not Sandra Harris the great and famous, next in line to Astronomer Royal (if so I chose), mistress of Mad Jack Stubbs the trumpet-player, dweller in the here and now, and invincible? All the same, the hairs on my arms stood up, the back of my neck tingled, my body betrayed me. I showed the physical manifestations of simple fright.

Now it is important, when presented with the unknown or unexpected, not to panic; not to flail about with limbs and mind, but to switch smoothly into emergency gait, and deal swiftly and calmly with the symptoms of the untoward at once, and ponder underlying causes later. So no doubt my father would have done.

So, a ghost stood at the gate, waiting and listening: summoned up by myself, raised by some accord between myself and it? His ghost, perhaps? My father's?

My half-brother had already been to visit: bringing his disordered soul to bear on mine. Why not my father now, a visitation of malicious order, to bring me back to heel? But the universe would hardly be so concerned with me, and besides there seemed no threat or danger here: nothing even very personal: just some kind of statement that needed to be made, in the strong, steady, unseen step. I breathed deeply: the tickling feeling of impending fear receded. Let him stand and wait, whoever he was. I would just get on with my book, and he, or it, would drift away and become one with the hot smell of mint and lavender mixed, on the other side of the wall.

We all have ghosts to haunt us. Mine seem particularly near. Sometimes as I stare up at the stars, when the heavens arch above me, before I begin the defining and focusing business that brings this section or that of the galaxy into precise and narrow attention, I seem to catch sight of a face, formed no doubt by the vagueness of the starry clouds, as do the hills and valleys of the full moon – why, there's the man in the

49

moon, romantics amongst us say to a race of children who know well enough there's no man there, only that bleak and rocky emptiness. He's taken a step or two back, I daresay, into the constellations of the Milky Way, and that's who I see. 'You're always seeing things,' my friends complain. I saw Jehovah himself once; I was on a tour of Israel, with a group of astronomers. We went round in a minibus, escorted by a handsome army captain, armed with a machine gun. We took the narrow dusty road to the Dead Sea, through a land bleak and rocky as the moon, but as hot as the moon is cold, baked rather than frozen, and up and up the hill to the cleft in the rocks which would let us down again into the valley of that salty, mechanical sea, which is nothing more than heavy metals in suspension and good for neither man nor beast – though I believe they have spas there nowadays; and use the black and sinister mud to cure psoriasis – and I saw Jehovah's face loom down through the clouds: he was the God of Vengeance all right; a surprisingly personal Patriarch; he would have spoken to anyone in his bearded old man ire, his eruptions of outrage, and made them tremble. Both paranoic and obsessive, I thought, with his vengeance wreaking and his detailed rules for his terrible laws, and his insistence that everyone kept them, and, seeing him, I was more than ever glad my brother had died young. I bowed my head and closed my eyes, and when I ventured to open them the vision was gone; all there was by the side of the road, viewed briefly as we passed, was a burning bush: flames flickering, flaring, quickly dying: a wisp of smoke; gone. 'Was that a burning bush?' I asked the captain. We were lovers, as it happened. I hadn't slept properly or long enough for four nights: it makes one visionary. He laughed. 'It happens,' he said, 'people throw cigarettes out of cars.'

Well, I see these things, or think I do. Sometimes I am pursued by the pattering of little feet, and know they are the ghosts of my dead children. All women have these, pitter-pattering round them like leaves rustling from a tree in autumn: the spirits of children conceived and destroyed, or merely unborn by virtue of her disinclination to allow them life. Every month she keeps her legs crossed, takes a pill or whatever, another one rustles and falls, reproachful, wasted. It's the aborted ones who are vociferous, bold in their game of Grandmother's Footsteps, tugging at the coat of their ferocious mother. 'I got so far,' they say, 'so very far. Why did you stop me?' And the answer 'why, for the sake of those already living' is as little satisfactory as my Israeli captain's answer to me, when I beheld a burning bush – 'People throw cigarettes out of cars.'

But I won't have them brought into being, I won't. I make myself deaf to the pleas of the unborn. As many as my father brought into existence, I will keep out of it. I will make things even, as the whole universe craves to do: to balance its books, as the isotope struggles for ever, to the detriment of all around, to bring itself to heel, to get electron and neutron in proper proportion.

Let him stand outside the wall and breathe his ghostly breath, and wait; I won't have his children, no I won't. Though the hot scent of mint and lavender rises – perhaps as he moves, and the herbs crush beneath his feet. For that's what he is, I bet. He is the universal father.

He is Godfrey the bearded goatherd, with whom I lived for five years, who at first begged and pleaded with me to have his child: but I wouldn't. I knew how they'd be. Little country-cottage children, muddy, shaggy-haired; with slow minds and droopy eyelids. Their noses would run in the icy winds, which the cottage walls would fail to exclude. And how would I get on with my work?

For I knew what pregnancy did to the mind, the animal stupor which descended upon the will: the horrible apathy: the seductive voice in the head which said 'what is the point of striving, of endeavour? Just be, be; split, procreate; forget yourself, be the vessel through which the future can express itself' – a feeling so strong it made the journey to the abortionist almost impossible. The footsteps lagged: the will only just triumphed, I can tell you.

But that was when I was eighteen: look, the father was sixteen. It was impossible. Everyone said so, even the family doctor.

Around thirty, I was broody. I would look into prams, coo at babies. I hated myself for it. For still I would be me, me: I would not split myself, define myself; I was flesh and spirit: I would not let the flesh win. I would take what pleasures I could from it and not pay the awful female price. My place was somewhere else: my business pulling the stars down to earth, not motherhood.

Matthew wanted children: I did not. It was our chief quarrel – or at any rate his. But I knew what they'd be like. Little city children, of the wealthy, well-groomed kind: smooth and orderly, with the clear complexions and sensitive mouths of those who go to private schools. Matthew's children! One would trot them between dancing class and the orthodontist, and produce another race of Matthews. It was not to be borne. Neither were they.

Jack's child – ah, now there was another matter. But too late now, thank God.

My friend Clare, mother of so many, would reproach me for my determination not to have children. 'It's unnatural,' she'd say. Only through motherhood, her thesis was, could you embark upon that journey of self-discovery which was the purpose of our existence upon this earth. Poppycock, I'd say. Romantic twaddle. What is this talk of 'purpose'? Nature sets traps to lure us into motherhood, that I'd agree: but once the trap is sprung she offers precious few rewards for her Nature's purpose. I could as well declare victory, to finally produce a generation which wouldn't *want* to reproduce itself. Enough would be enough. And I'd make Clare shut up about her virtue in thus producing her noisy, tormenting children: I liked her, almost loved her, in spite of her children, not because of them. I remained lean, lithe, small-breasted, flat-stomached, barren, a defiance and a lure to men, and that's how I liked it.

Forget the breather at the wall, the watcher by the gate: the steady footsteps after mine. Perhaps the first child, unborn, claiming life through me? He'd be in his mid-twenties now: of military age. It didn't bear too much thinking about. I was sorry to have deprived him of his sexual pleasures, the joy of

52

young strong limbs – but then think what I'd saved him, all the humiliations and despondency flesh is heir to. He should thank me, not haunt me.

Just then the scent of mint and lavender mixed, and the hot sun beat down, and the doves cooed and pecked, and I wished that Jack would hurry home, and all of a sudden I was scared out of my wits.

9

Scene in a Car Park

We will put the matter of my haunting to one side, stop
nagging and picking away at this ghostly knot – for no doubt
it has many strands, composed of my own guilt and the world's
past – and consider the scene at Reading Car Park. It was a
scene made quite unnecessarily by Jack's appalling wife Anne,
and if I were the kind to be embarrassed, I would have been
devastated.

Now Jack and Anne had been living under the same roof but
apart for some years. They had separate bedrooms. They kept
together for Frances's sake: the girl had her schooling to get
through. Any formal separation, they felt, would upset her too
much. Jack was away a great deal, playing with the Citronellas
and other bands in various parts of the country, or on tour
abroad. And Anne had a good job which was her main
preoccupation.

When I told Clare all these things, she fell about with mirth,
saying it ought to be on the back pages of *Cosmopolitan*, it was
how all married men described their marriages, and I was a
little offended. She'd missed the point.

Jack was a musician. Musicians make bad husbands: women
who want good husbands should know better than to marry
them. They are frequently drunk, or high on drugs or both
and are seldom available for ordinary social events; dinner-
dances on Saturday nights for example, or Friday meals with
friends. How can they be? Those are the very nights they're
doing a gig. How can they take the children to Saturday
afternoon football when they're playing from three to six at
the town Fête, the local Agricultural Show? They leave home
anxious and nervy and come home over-excited and abrim
with either self-pity or self-congratulation. They conspire with

other members of the Band to denigrate the role of wife, girlfriend, mother – women and their claims and desires being the common enemy of all musicians. For it is WOMAN who wants them to stay home – a terrifying adult extension of the original mother who keeps their boy in when he longs to go out.

A musician is a bad husband but a fine man, he inspires love. But woe betide the woman who believes she'll change him, confine him, alter him, as Anne did Jack. (I would never do such a thing. I wouldn't be such a fool!)

But alas, alas, the musician needs a wife, and a smiling, cheerful one too: someone to wait up for him at night with interested questions and hot soup: someone to pay attention to the bills and answer the phone and keep his diary: to keep the roof mended and the children educated. How else but by having a wife is he to live, once he's past the first flush of impetuous, noisy youth? In a bedsitting room: in a converted van parked over a city sewer? Some do: they have to: their wives get fed up with them and throw them out.

Unless of course the wretched woman manages to turn herself from wife to mother. But that's of short-term benefit: in the end a thankless task. The man cries out for his mother, and gets her, but it wasn't really what he wanted – no, not at all. Women who play mother – who nurture, cosset, bite back harsh words – get left, as if they were the real thing. The wide erotic world beckons: why should he stay at home? It isn't natural. Such wives are left not just because they're boring – which they are – but because every beautifully laundered towel, every well balanced, timely meal, every caring constructive word, is seen as an octopus coil which will tighten, confine and strangle unless severed. And the man is right to go. For the woman who lives her life through a man is truly manipulative and dangerous: she has him retired and in slippers, or pottering round the garden in no time at all. Or worse –

The telephone rings. The musician's wife answers. 'Can Bill, Tom, Harry, do a gig this Saturday night?' 'No, sorry, hadn't

55

you heard? He's had a stroke.' At last, at last – the wife sings in her heart. Bill, Tom, Harry will be home on Saturday night, not out with the boys. Or what's left of him. And the horror stories fly round the musical world – another good man, a true fighter, bit the dust, destroyed by womankind! Those who give life, also bring death.

When the minibus arrived at Reading Car Park, to pick up Jack and myself and take us on to Newhaven, it was followed by a nine-year-old rusty Ford Escort, the kind that only the depressed and poor consent to drive.
'Oh, Good God,' said Jack, 'what a bitch!' (I think he was referring to fate, rather than to his wife.) 'It's Anne.'

And this dumpy little lady got out and came towards us and I didn't like her one bit, nor the expression on her face.
'You bastard!' (him) 'You cow!' (me) 'How can you do this to me? In front of everyone! In front of Frances!' For there was Frances, pale face pressed against the glass of the minibus window. It was the first time I'd seen her. I didn't deign to reply to her screeching mother.
'I'm not doing anything,' said Jack, mildly. 'Just standing here in a car park.'
'Do you want me to kill myself?' she shrieks. 'Is that it?'
'Well,' says Jack, 'that has to be your decision. You certainly make my life scarcely worth living.'

Sandy gets off the bus.
'I did my best,' he apologises to Jack. 'But she followed us all the way from Maidenhead. I offered to take a message but she wouldn't have it.'
Karl gets off as well.
'Look,' he says, 'can't you two settle your differences some-where else? It's bad for the girl.' And if you look, you can see tears roll down Frances's cheek, smudging into the glass.

Anne collapses from the heights of rage into the depths of self-pity.
'I thought I'd see you at Maidenhead,' she whines. 'You said you'd be there. Me and Frances thought you'd be there.'
Ungrammatical, too; to add to her failings.

'I was going to be there,' says Jack, patiently. 'But I had to do a fill-in job for the Pilots' Association at Heathrow. So Sandra and me picked up the minibus here. Was that wrong?' She is too chokey and teary to speak. She looks terrible. She has wide feet in collapsed brown flat-heeled shoes. I tap my neat little boots impatiently. I take a size 4 and am light enough to wear high heels with ease. Jeans tight over slim tilted calves, a gap of flesh and then the curling top of leather boots – and what old cardigan was that that she was wearing? One longs for a decent rival.

'I asked if you wanted to come along,' says Jack, 'and you said you didn't.'

'I didn't know you were taking *her*: that flashy bitch.' She meant me, Sandra, she of the clear profile, neat hairdo and high buttoned boots, who monthly presented the Marvels of the Night to the waiting millions. She, who discovered the Planet Athena, a flashy bitch! Imprecise and inaccurate, as well as ungrammatical. There was nothing to recommend her.

She'd followed the minibus from Maidenhead. Karl had picked up Pedro, Steve, Hughie and Bente outside Camden Town Marks and Spencer, Jennifer and Sandy at Slough, and Frances at Maidenhead. (Bands go in for these elaborate arrangements: that they ever get to gigs at all always amazes me.)

Everyone knew Jack was bringing me along; his mistress, not his wife. Everyone knew he'd been seeing this woman for at least two months, since he met her at the Royal Astrological Society in the grounds of the Greenwich Observatory, and they'd gone off together into the shrubbery. These things do not go unnoticed. It had therefore been the more embarrassing for the gang to have Anne following in the Escort.

'Try and lose her,' Pedro had muttered to Sandy, and Sandy did try, but Anne had been too clever. The spirit of vengeance sharpened her eye, made her foot nifty on the accelerator, her hand on the steering wheel.

'Anne,' says Jack, reasonably, 'Sandra's just a friend. She loves jazz. You hate it. She'll be company for Frances. It's not as if we were still married.'

This confuses her.

'But we are,' she stutters, looking round for help, which is not available. Even Frances isn't listening. Frances is mulling over her own problems. She doesn't see her father all that often, and had hoped to have him to herself. I reckon her tears are self-pity, rather than distress. Just as her mother's are manipulative, and not grounded in any real emotion.

'Only in the eyes of the law,' says Jack, 'and I wish you wouldn't make these scenes in public.'

'We've got to get on,' says Sandy. 'We've got this ferry to catch.'

'You'd hate it where we're going,' says Jack. 'Hardly a souvenir shop in sight. So don't spoil it for the rest of us, okay?'

It's not okay. She hasn't finished with us yet. She boards the minibus and tries to yank Frances out, shrieking that Jack's not going to take her abroad, but Frances resists.

'Oh, Mum,' she says. 'Do give over. I *want* to go with Dad. Why don't you just go home and make yourself a cup of tea.'

At which Anne just gives up and gets back, sobbing gently, into her mouldy little car, and drives off into the night, and Jack and me unload our things from the back of my snappy little Citroën (six months old) and find our seats and we're off.

Not that we had much luggage. Jack had his two trumpets, the briefcase with his music, and a battered old suitcase. I had a swiftly packed nylon bag. I was running away from home, not to mention my life. I needed to travel light, though stylish. I had taken no books; I was bored with my mind, and the feeling of non-encumbrance was delightful.

Just a pity Frances existed: was there sitting on the bus, her eyes swollen with reproach and self-pity. Her mother's daughter – except the daughter had youth and looks, even I would admit that. Most things are forgiven the young, so long as they're not drugs, when they join their elders in the invisibility stakes – the ones we do not see but like to blame.

'If we ever get back,' I said to Jack, as the minibus took the M3, and Sandy misjudged the speed of the oncoming traffic and there was much swerving and honking and catastrophe was narrowly diverted, 'you ought to do what you keep talking about, and sell the matrimonial home and split the profits. As it is, she obviously feels she has some claim on you.'

'Oh,' he said vaguely, 'there's Frances to think about. And if I had money in the bank I'd only spend it.'

That's how it is, between musicians and musicians' wives. Nothing ever quite settled or definite: sentences no sooner said than forgotten, arrangements no sooner made than changed.

Jennifer said 'Oh, Sandy! Do be careful! There are some terrible drivers on the road!' and everyone laughed except Sandy, who muttered under his breath, and Jack took my hand and held it to his chest, as if I were a precious possession.

But just a little, just a little, I think my passion for Jack diminished that night at Reading Car Park: his connection with Anne, she of the bloated face and wide flat feet, rubbed off a little of the sheen of love. I wanted a better rival.

10

A Summons from Afar

The ghost had gone: that is to say I no longer – how can I put it? – felt waited for, as if some moral bailiff stood by the gate. I went out into the road, and a dog – a mangy, yellowy animal with a pointed snout and little sharp eyes – trotted by about its business, loose skin wobbling beneath its belly, elongated teats dangling. Bitches after childbirth are not a pretty sight. See, I thought. There! If there were some presence standing there even this ribby thin creature would have the energy to react. And no sooner had I thought this than the animal cast a sideways glance at me, and stopped, teats quivering, and stared, and its hackles rose, and it looked at me with terror and hate, and turned tail and fled, howling. I promise you this happened.

And I thought whatever it was is no longer outside me but *in* me: now what was I to do? Or had it always been there, and I had somehow left it behind, in my mean-minded, snarly shopping trip to the village? And now it was back in again, and I had succeeded in stirring up some awful sediment to such an extent that even a passing bitch, running back no doubt to her pups, had noticed and reacted?

I used as a talisman against my inner demons the memory of Jack and myself, out to sea, in our berth on the ferry, fucking and fucking while the ship (one of those roll-on, roll-off, roll-over types) banged up and down into the waves as if in sympathy with our cause. Let the stars drift unobserved in the heavens, unannotated and recorded, let Matthew rant, let Anne weep, only this country, in and out and up and down, and the swooning blackness pierced by light as we remade the universe, Mad Jack and me.

A butterfly alighted on my hand, and fanned its wings a little, and then flew off: a gesture of reconciliation, perhaps: or else the thing was just too drunk and simple to understand its danger.

Then the telephone rang inside the Hôtel de Ville. Now this was not surprising: a town hall, even in France, even one not used for its bureaucratic purpose for a year or so, may have a line still connected; a wrong number may have been dialled: or indeed for all I knew Monsieur le Directeur du Festival was trying to contact the Band – an extra gig, perhaps tomorrow morning, early: or – and this I did not want to contemplate – perhaps I had stirred up sufficient sediment, in my calls to Alison and Jude, to allow my whereabouts to be traced.

I thought at first I would let it ring unanswered, and then something struck me as odd. The ring was not the long-burr-silence-long-burr-silence of the French system, but the burr-burr, burr-burr of the English. Now how could that be? I stood in the kitchen and the ringing disturbed the motes in the air, where the low sun shone through the window above the shallow stone sink; otherwise I would have thought the sound was imaginary. I went looking for the instrument – into the big empty front room whence, once, the business of the town had been conducted. The ringing stopped – nor was there a telephone there that I could see, or anywhere in any of the other big square ground floor rooms. A thin torn cotton cloth hung before a doorless cupboard beneath the staircase and on one of the shelves, indeed, rested one of those old black wall telephones, but it was broken; more than simply disconnected – discarded. All the same I felt nervous of touching it. When I moved the cloth it threw up a cloud of dust, and I sneezed, and sneezed again and startled myself.

Now from much study of the heavens, since I was a child, I know how difficult it is to find anything one does not have the confidence of finding and how easy to find anything one means to find. I looked again for the instrument, willing myself to see it. But still to no avail.

I was, I admit it, frightened. Of course the sound might have been produced in my own head: the dancing motes of dust caused by the burr-burr, burr-burr could have been visionary.

It was unusual for two senses to be involved in these phenomena, but not, I suppose, impossible.

I went back to sit in the kitchen and heard footsteps outside in the courtyard, and looked out into the dusk, relieved, glad of human company, but there was no one there. The pang of disappointment which seized me was very great: it made my throat tighten: and I thought, how strange, this is altogether the wrong emotion: fear would be more reasonable. And then indeed panic set in and I ran from the Hôtel de Ville – taking up my pad and the rest of the bread (I'm not daft and was certainly hungry) – and set myself up beneath the yellow arc light which stood where the N89 crosses the little D9, just to the right of the Hôtel de Ville, where the companionable and sensible traffic passes, and where notions of life and death are practical things. Stop and wait for the lights, or you're dead! At least these small matters appear to be within our control; do not contain the menace of evil rampant and malicious – the lights, for example, staying green of their own volition when they should have turned to red, causing some head-on smash by accident on purpose of malice. Or does the driver just see green, when others see red, so great is his/her underlying wish for death, if only to ease the burden of guilt? Perhaps only the guilty see and hear ghosts, are afflicted by demons? And only a few of the guilty at that, not all of them, or we could scarcely move about for paranormal phenomena, pick up an egg without it leaping from our hand, breaking on the ground, and just sitting there, frying. Or whatever. And the death rate on the road would be vastly, vastly higher.

11

Return of the Citronellas

So what if the Hôtel de Ville was haunted? It was pleasant enough sitting outside on the wall with the crumbling majesty of the grey façade behind me, dangling my legs, watching the heavy lorries pass, and the bold little Deux Chevaux; as the hot day relaxed into its pleasant evening, and the sky tinged from a red haze to orange streaks and then dimmed into misty boredom, and the yellow French headlights came on, and I could only tell from the thunder and rumble what was a lorry and what was not.

I kicked my heels against the wall and considered the nature of possession, and whether it was my own eyes, or a demon's, which regarded the world. Would I, to any passing observer, have the kind of cunning, sideways look I saw on my mother's face, from time to time, and on Robin's? Or my father's cold eyes? I assumed he had cold eyes. Nazis always do. Though how exactly a cold eye is defined I can't be sure. How is it recognised? My mother's eyes were brown and people described them as warm and kind, but to me, when not animated by their demons, they looked simply blank. I once saw an optician bring down a tray of glass eyes of all possible shapes and sizes and colours from a top shelf. He blew the dust off them, and there they were, blues, greens, browns and in between: some red veined, some rheumy, some young and clear; eyes for all possible matches. He sold them to an antique dealer who said they were in demand for ear-rings. And I tell you, the expression, the mood, the warmth, the chilliness, was there in these eyes, just waiting to be brought to life. They were invested by sleeping demons. I wouldn't have worn them to parties, not on your nelly, not ever.

The Citronella Jumpers returned. I could tell them from afar. Their headlights were white, in the English style: a source of annoyance to French drivers. The van was painted acid yellow, but the street lights switched the colour to green. It pulled up behind me. Jack embraced me. Everyone was in fine good humour. A good night's playing, a receptive audience.

'I met this feller,' Frances confided in me. 'His name's Jock. He's one of the Scots Guards. He's the one who heel-and-toes it round the swords when they cross them on the ground.'

I did not regret not going. I did regret my phone calls to Alison and Jude. Cowardice. Hand in hand with Jack I went into the Hôtel de Ville, and his love, or at any rate, lust folded itself round me like a protective cloak.

Jennifer had contrived sausage, bread, carrot salad and bottles of wine. We sat round the table and ate and if the telephone rang I couldn't hear it, nor if somewhere Anne wept, and the babies stirred in Clare's womb, and the fax machines chattered in Jude's office with their messages from distant Time Zones: 'Where is she? Where is she?'

12

So, Starlady Sandra

That night after love Jack said, 'So, Starlady Sandra.' And I said well why not, somebody has to be. It is, I suppose, my habit to diminish myself: we'll have no vainglory here. I am a guilty person: I have to punish myself. My mother is mad because I am sane: my brother is dead because my suppressed rage killed him: my father was shot because my birth was used as evidence against him. My anger is all powerful; could blot out the world. So it is never expressed. I am cool, rational, and for ever guilty. I punish myself by ignoring my worldly success. Even the adjective 'worldly' diminishes its noun, don't you see – as if there were some other realer kind of success somewhere else, more worth having. So a therapist – a Jungian, I think – told me before I left her after four sessions, murmuring that I was far too busy to continue seeing someone who merely stated the obvious.

'Why do you murmur?' she asked, at the door. (I don't write these difficult things to people: I don't hide behind letter and stamp: I have it out face to face.) 'Why don't you shout, stamp and scream these things to me?'

'Good heavens,' I said mildly. 'You're far too nice for that!' And so she was. But she had cold eyes, which reminded me of my father. I didn't quite trust her. I felt I could have blown her away with a breath, for all she was nearly six foot and I a mere five foot five. She had bought a couch more fit for her than for me, and I felt its length reaching far beyond my feet, far beneath my head: as if I was on a rack and in danger of being stretched for ever.

'The reason I felt I'd known you all my life,' Jack complained, 'is that I'd seen you on TV.'

'You might have felt it anyway,' I said. 'How will we ever know?'

'Men are more comfortable with women who are lesser than they,' he said, 'but personally, I can put up with a little discomfort.'

'A degree in astronomy,' I said, 'is nothing. A master's in mathematics paltry. I can't make an audience feel a common cause, lift its spirits, get its blood singing, hormones pumping. You raise your trumpet to the stars and sing to them. I just catalogue and annotate. I am mere secretary to the heavens, if not, as I let you believe, research assistant to the vice chairman of the Royal Astrological Association.' Or words to that effect, whenever I could, for want of breath, his mouth on mine.

'Jack,' I said, in other words. 'You are greater than me. I look up to you and admire you.'

'And look,' I said, 'it's not a high-profile programme: not all that many people watch it, and those who do are mostly senior citizens, half asleep in their chairs, too tired to put out the cat and switch off the telly: trapped by their own inaction.'

Jack, Jack, I said, in other words: don't worry about the spectacle of me, ogled by millions, by too many – for all I could do with high collars and genteel voice, it made me more the stuff of fantasy than ever. Take 'em off, rip 'em off! How can the woman who is everyone's be for one alone? Of course I hadn't wanted Jack to know: ever to say 'So, Starlady Sandra.' Fame in a man is for a woman a great aphrodisiac: fame in a woman appeals to the man who likes public fucking. Pity.

'Look,' I pleaded, in the name of love, which would now have to conquer many hazards, 'it's only half an hour or so once a month, and most of the time on screen it's charts, diagrams and special effects, not even me. I'm just a passing presenter.'

He laughed and said not to worry, it didn't matter one way or another how I earned my living; I was to stop overpresenting my case, I was protesting too much, but wasn't it me who discovered the Planet Athena?

'Only by mistake,' I said. Well, almost by mistake. A couple of orbits askew needed some kind of explanation. I invented an explanation, focused the lenses, clicked the cameras, and lo, there it was! 'The Press latched on to it,' I said. 'That's all that happened.'

'No one cares any more,' I said. 'Five years ago is for ever ago. I'm a whatever-happened-to person. Honestly, you have nothing to worry about.'
He appeared to sleep.

'Look,' I said, before he could wake, or appear to, and forestalling a discussion initiated by him on the alleged difference in our incomes, 'I don't get paid a great deal; not in terms of, say, what the makers of TV commercials make. Peanuts. A pittance. And what I make I spend on clothes. I did have a little house in London before I married Matthew but he wanted me to sell it, as a token of my love for him: he wanted me, as it were, to demonstrate a wholehearted approval of our togetherness. No bolt holes for either of us! So I did, and Matthew invested the money for me in high-risk investments and lost most of it in last year's stockmarket crash. So I was more dependent on him than ever. Or so he thought. He didn't know I didn't mind being penniless. He would have minded very much, and didn't understand that not everyone was like him: or rather, believed that everyone not like him was eccentric, or in some way untrustworthy. He had his own money invested in the money market, and did well enough, as many with friends in high places did at that time.

'Jack,' I said, or words to this effect, 'I can't tell you how good it is to be lying on a lumpy mattress with you, with nothing but a nylon bag of possessions to worry about: travelling light, travelling free.'

Jack asked into the dark, and I knew then he only appeared to sleep, to listen to my monologues the better, 'Weren't you angry about the money?' and I replied no, I didn't have the time, and he said 'Yes, you were angry or you wouldn't have run off with me. I am your revenge.'
'No, no,' I said, childlike, 'it isn't like that.'
'I don't mind being your revenge,' he consoled me. 'If I have to put up with your being the centre of attention I will: and if I have to put up with your earning more than me, how about

buying me a new trumpet case in Bordeaux, so I don't have to mind so much?'

'I will, I will,' I promised. Love, honour, obey and support, as long as we both shall live. Been to India, lately: seen the men *sitting*, while the women building workers heave and shovel: been to Africa, where the men smoke ganja and the women hoe the brick-hard soil: been out to dinner and counted the number of times your hostess *gets up*? No wonder the men feel bad about it.

This is no complaint, only a comment. The women like doing it, so where's the harm? Any man, cries the woman – unless she's pretty, educated, a good earner and under thirty, when she reckons she can pick and choose – is better than none. Half a man, if she's a Muslim and has to share him with another – better than indignity and No Sex. My friend Jude made a TV series about it. *Women Who Serve*. She sees *Sandra's Sky* as a rather boring sideline: a kind of tarted-up late night science programme of minority interest. The ratings we get seem to astonish her.

'It's the high-necked blouse,' I say. 'It attracts the porno audience.' That's the kind of thing Jude's able to understand. That mankind is also interested in its origin and its destination and sees in the heavens, quite rightly, the pattern that will solve the problems of its existence, quite escapes my media friends. The gorilla idly masturbates behind bars in London Zoo, and the audience gawps, but it's the gorilla eyes that really get to them: that sad black wisdom.

Alison said to me when I told her Matthew had proposed marriage –

'Well, well! Aren't you lucky. Not many men will marry a star.'

'Firstly,' I replied haughtily, 'I am not sure that marriage is the end all women must automatically desire: secondly, what do you mean by lucky; it is no more than I deserve: and thirdly, far from Matthew loving me in spite of my fame, it was my fame that led him to seek me out.' That was at the very height of my starladydom: I had recently discovered Athena, and named the blasted rock in a public ceremony, and was wanted on game shows, chat shows, as token woman

68

in shows discussing anything from the decline of socialism to the nature of the arts/science divide. I was blonde, as well as bright. Former boyfriends crawled out of the woodwork then: old one-night stands; faces I had forgotten (and parts as well, thank God) to remind me of a past I had assumed I had put behind me for ever. Only Matthew, carrying assurance and the world's approval on his stocky shoulders, came to me out of the present, offering me a life worthy of my sudden new status. Little me.

'You're wrong,' I told Alison. 'Somebody wants me.'

'You are your sample of one,' she said, disappointed. Whoever likes to hold a faulty theory, so easily disproved. I preened; she fidgeted her unbelief.

I like to have these conversations with other women about the nature of our sexual selves. They deal in generalisations, they come to no conclusions, but they pass the time agreeably: the problem for a childless, unmarried woman lay in providing sufficient fuel for the conversational fire. I was glad to have this new episode with Jack, this new experience, to pile onto the general conflagration. Presently no doubt I would also have a divorce to discuss and compare. Pity my poor grand-mama! Her family life was such a pattern of shameful secrets – illegitimacy, insanity, cancer, divorce, bankruptcy; all un-thinkable, unsayable, weaving in and out: each by itself the cause of doom, gloom and anxiety, family secrets and night-mare, of pacing up and down behind closed doors – let alone piled on top of one another as they were for her. And no telephone helplines at her fingertips, just think of it! Else she might not have wished me and Robin unborn so often, and Robin might not thus have rendered himself. He knew he brought shame on others, and that's what in the end he couldn't bear. Oh, the shame of it, Robin! The disgrace. Well, well. And all my fault, for sopping up such sanity as there was in my mother's nurturing blood, leaving nothing but madness for him. But the devil's work, not mine, surely, thus to reduce my glory, my despair, to this kind of grim, bleak banality. If Robin had kept going until, say, a year ago, and had then jumped beneath his train, all of us involved would have reacted less grievously. The train driver could have looked at the statistics and learned that he had a one in four chance of such a thing happening to him in his working life, and gone to British Rail Medical for counselling: my grandmother and myself would have joined a Mind support group and learned how-to-cope, comparing ourselves to others in the same situation. Robin's torn and bloody corpse and his tormented mind would be thoroughly devalued, but we would have been saved. But it was a full twenty years ago he killed himself, and the world was still young in the ways of emotional self-preservation. There is of course no support group for children of such fathers as I had, nor will there ever be. We are too few, our fate . . .

Only the State of Israel, boring the world with talk of the holocaust (that old thing! Forty odd years ago. Forget it!) nags on, and has become, of course, a dab hand at a passing massacre itself. But that, they say, is not the same. That was unpremeditated. Dead's dead, say I, and may the living never again envy the dead. The nations of the world limp on, denatured, as are their citizens, unable as ever to face their own past. Well, I can say no better for myself, can I?

13

Breakfast Time

'Eggs, anyone?' asked Jennifer. She'd acquired a dozen, from somewhere. The scrawny hens, then, must be capable of laying. There were no egg cups, so we ate scrambled eggs on fresh bread. I offered her money, but she said no – Jack paid into the Band kitty for himself, Frances and Anne, and since Anne hadn't come along but I had – We're doing the washing up. That is to say, she does it, and I politely hover.

'Do you know Anne well?' I asked.

'No,' she said. 'She used to come to gigs sometimes to keep an eye on Jack, but she wasn't really interested.'

Ah. That almost sounded like a gesture of friendship.

'You didn't come yesterday,' she pointed out. Not so good.

'I wasn't feeling very well,' I said. Better than that Jack preferred me not to go, which she would misconstrue.

'Oh you poor thing! Would you like an aspirin?'

'I'm better today.'

'So you'll be coming with us? Good. That's company for Frances. I'm sure it's all perfectly okay, but there are all those soldiers and she is only fifteen, and I'm not her mother –' Her voice dies away.

'Neither am I,' I say, and her hands move busily in the dish water, where they seem very much at home. Good Lord, how has this woman achieved a *dishcloth*?

'Did you ever read *The Swiss Family Robinson*?' I ask.

'No,' she says, surprised. And then, 'Should I have?' as if I were the one able to judge 'shoulds' and 'shouldn'ts'.

She polished up a saucepan really nicely, and quite unnecessarily. Presently she said –

'Poor Anne, she doesn't stand a chance, does she?'

Rejected wives have few friends. They die for the unmarried women who were once their friends. They must make new

71

alliances amongst their own kind – the abandoned and deso-
late; the un-coupled.
'Not much,' I said.

I tried to explain that Anne was out of the running before I
turned up and that notoriety is a contradiction to sexual bliss,
but she wasn't listening. Sandy came in, with his big double
bass and she dived for her all-purpose bag and brought out
Brasso and a cloth folded into a neat plastic packet. Sandy
smiled kindly at her, but his eyes flickered to me, Starlady
Sandra, Jack's sex kitten (a kitten rather past its first youth,
admittedly): if she'll have Jack she'll have not anybody, no,
not Pedro the guitar-player or Stevie the trombonist – but
surely she'd have king of the back row, the bass player, and if
she would, he would: and Jennifer caught the look. Too bad.
Now what would I do for a friend? Sandy took polish and cloth
and saw to the brass keys which wound the strings. I watched
amazed.
'I'd do it but he doesn't trust me,' said Jennifer. 'You know
what these men are like with their instruments.'
'Just wonderful,' I said with feeling, and she looked at me with
her mouth puckered, wondering if I meant what she thought
I might have meant. Sandy knew I did, and raised his eyebrows
ever so slightly at me. Why do these men, I asked myself,
always choose women less quick in the mind than they? (To
say 'more stupid' would be unkind.) The answer, I daresay,
is that only such women are prepared to rush after them
proffering Brasso and cloth. Or perhaps it's the very preoccupation with dishrags and polishing cloths which renders a
woman puzzled and slow. Poor men, I think, poor men, always
in such a fix.

The washing up finished, Jennifer called through the echoey
building. The ghosts didn't stand a chance in the face of such
good-hearted practicality.
'All right, everyone! Time to hit the road!'
'Don't *say* that,' muttered Sandy beneath his breath, but if I
could hear it so could she. She was meant to. She took no
notice, just wrinkled her nose at him, flirtatiously, and he
wished she wouldn't do that either.
'So it's okay for me to come today?' I said to Jack. He had no

made it plain whether or not I would be welcome on the bus, for reasons of his own but very much to do with whether he or I would henceforth have the upper hand. I'm not daft. These things must be worked out.

'Of course,' he said, apparently surprised. 'Karl wants to talk to you. He has an idea for a TV series about a travelling jazzband and wants to know if you'd help him get it on.'

'Ah.'

'Will you?'

'No.'

'Good.'

So in I went with the Citronella Jumpers to Blasimon-les-Ponts, where the street flags fluttered up and down the streets, and stalls selling ethnic niceties from every corner of the globe lined the square; you could buy freshly made prawn crackers – smelling of real fish and quite disgusting – tortillas (from a microwave), African beads and bangles so high in the asking price, so cheap in the selling you'd think it's some kind of plot and wouldn't be seen dead in them. How do these street traders survive so far from home? Can they even tell one coin from another in a foreign land? I fear not, despite their reputation as shrewd and mean: it is they who get ripped off, not do the ripping – and not a thing on sale which couldn't be bought in Camden Town Market, London, any day of the week, so universal have become the gewgaws of the world. Little groups of folk dancers, in the intricate, uncomfortable costumes of the past, danced and skipped and sang their way along the streets, to the music of pipe, violin and drum, while watching crowds grouped and applauded and dispersed, glad of at least something happening in what could only be the infinite boredom of their lives. What goes on behind the fastened shutters of the small French town? Nothing, I fear. The young and the old stare into space, and brood, and wait, sweltering in summer, freezing in winter. I said as much to Jack, who reproved me for my attitude. There was obviously something about gypsy fiddling he knew, and I did not.

Frances, after last night's softening, will have nothing to do with me. She went off arm in arm with Jennifer. I sat with Jack and drank café au lait from agreeably large green cups, gold-rimmed. My wrist looked thinner and browner than usual. My hair had bleached in the sun. Nothing much mattered. I could live like this for ever. Close the shutters: be content, like anyone else round here, just to be. The Citronella Jumpers were to play at eleven thirty beneath the War Memorial; it was difficult to get details of time and place from the Festival Organisers, inasmuch as no one there spoke English. Only the French rivalled the British in their expectation, nay, determination, that theirs should be the universal language. I offered to translate but Jack wouldn't hear of it.

'Try and understand,' he says. 'This Band doesn't *want* anything to go smoothly. It's not the way we work. We like to pick things up by osmosis. We do not want to be organised. Efficiency is the enemy of creative energy.'

I'd like to know what the discovery of Athena entailed other than creative energy and efficiency combined. But I was sensible enough not to say so. I called for a bottle of wine, instead.

14

Under the War Memorial

By some magic not worked by me the Band had assembled under the War Memorial by eleven twenty-nine and, what is more, all had their instruments in working order. In the time between the parking of the minibus in the Festival Car Park – an acid yellow David between rows of Goliaths, for the other groups came in massive coaches with national flags flying, on-board loos, catering facilities, and some kind of embroidered garment hanging from all available windows – there had been the repeated customary panics – broken strings, snapped keys, valves stuck, music missing, the sound system without its master plug, the van locked and the keys lost, one or the other of the Band refusing ever again to play with another, but all these difficulties were, as ever, resolved in time. A little organisation, a little system, a little tact, and none of these problems would have arisen – but then where would have been the fun? Most of the ills turned out to be imaginary, of course, as I began to realise. They were no more than little spasms of paranoia or despair – the stolen notebooks were under the seat; or Hughie had been trying to unlock an already unlocked door: the damage to instruments almost non-existent, obvious only to an obsessive owner, and of course Jennifer was there to sort things out – mother to this group of wilful, talented naughty elderly boys – who needed me, bossy little sister that I was? And look, eleven thirty came, and there they were in their green shirts, and a kind of gleam passed from one to another, of exhilaration and complicity, and Jack's foot was beginning – one, two, three, four – and they were off, and the pigeons fluttered and soared as the first notes struck, fit to raise the dead. He had listened to me. I was part of the Citronella Jumpers. My heart soared: form, style, content, in that order! I had made an impression! A gust of wind blew through the square; trees tossed about above: what did the morts-pour-la-patrie think, the roll-call of their names the backdrop to this strange band of unlikely men? Did they too want to get up and dance? The living certainly did. French crowds, acclimatised to the genteel rituals of the folkdancers, usually took time to respond to these half-New Orleans, half-idiosyncratic sounds: hard to make sense of it if you were not accustomed to it, a kind of overlapping of random sounds, of oddly assorted instruments. But today a sense of excitement gripped them almost at once: feet stamped, faces beamed, they were delighted: the sense of complicity, of being naughty children, themselves presented to themselves and far, far nicer, more at one, than they had ever realised, the threads of individual exultation pulled together to make one universal, joyful sound – the wind blew, the trees tossed, even the dead came to life: the people danced. Well, it wasn't often like this. Just sometimes. It was the moment the Band worked for, hoped for, put their wives through hell for, annoyed their employers for, ran off with women for, drowned their sorrows in drink for, savagely bantered with each other for, practised hour after hour for, in garages, lofts and fields: just to bring these few minutes into existence, when the music took off, and took the crowd with it, and everything added up to more than the sum of its parts, and they could do no wrong. Form, style, content! Told him so! Whispered the secret into his sleeping ear: not like poison into Hamlet's father's ear, but the elixir of the universe into Mad Jack the trumpeter's ear – my knowledge the same as his: what works for the stars will work for you. I was dancing: so was Jennifer, so was Frances, so was Bente; in and out we wove, the bad women and the good, the undecided and the stolid; the stern French faces relaxed in smiles, peasant feet stamping, old hands clapping – and then it was over, and the wind dropped and the hot, hot sun won – but some benign presence had been there and we all knew it. Well, where there are demons there are angels too. Perhaps I brought them with me. I think I carry them. But what was this? The Band was leaving; the Citronella Jumpers had been taken on board the Cuban coach (no one wanted to be seen with the battered British minibus); everyone except wives, children and hangers on had gone off to some mayoral reception in the next town: they wouldn't be back till evening: the groupies were left behind: no room even on the half empty Polish coach – a bad case of food poisoning had kept many of

76

this vast-ankled, sharp-nosed group confined to their quarters – what a vehicle, we see it leave, darkened windows, coffee bar, loo – we have no passes they say, sticklers for order – and of course Sandy's taken the keys of the minibus with him – and that's us put in our place, me, Frances, Bente and Jennifer. Not part of the real business.

So there we stood, the four of us, in the suddenly deserted market square, with the stallholders putting up their boards, because it was midday, in our uneasy relationship: women deserted by men, pretending it didn't matter.

'I'm going for a walk,' said Bente, and strode off in the direction of the castle, her sturdy lace-up shoes clomping. She had a big bust and a big bottom and wore a pale blue track suit not quite large enough. She ate a great deal, I noticed. She and Hughie exchanged chocolate bars a lot; and she would butter French bread for him, and he for her; and tempt him to delicacies: a nice way to go on, but fattening. And of course musicians drink a lot on gigs: especially beer, to quench their thirst: and in France, perpetual wine in between, because it's everywhere, and his woman drinks to keep him company, or he suspects reproach in her gaze.

'She'd do better jogging than walking,' said Jennifer. 'Get some of that weight down.' It was the kind of thing she said. She wore a blue and white striped cotton dress, belted; it looked as if it came out of the fifties, but not the fifties returned to, but the fifties never left. A pity. She had a pretty face and a nice figure and an acid tongue. But then Sandy had left her without a word or gesture, still on his jazz-man's high. Jack had at least smiled and glimmered at me.

'I think they're disgusting,' said Frances, 'leaving us standing here like fools. And Dad hasn't even left me my lunch ticket.'

Festival folk ate self-help canteen fashion, up at the college at the foot of the castle, queuing up in the shade along the wooden banks of the moat, each national with his/her own group. Tickets were handed out to group leaders, who distributed them amongst his troupe or, if he employed power, used them as a means of discipline. No ticket meant no food, which was a pity, because it was good in the French fashion, well cooked and sauced and served by enthusiasts – carrot salad, egg mayonnaise, chicken legs, pork steaks, beans in quantity, melon in profusion, chunks of bread and tin jugs of crude red wine on every table. Also in the French fashion, cooks made no concessions to the dietary fancies of ethnic minorities, so there were constant 'pork strikes', as Jack called them, amongst the Muslims, and 'beef strikes', amongst the Hindus, and the Israelis wouldn't eat a thing, and the Poles contrived food poisoning, and of course the Citronella Jumpers had the British suspicion of foreign foods, but were too small a group, and too diffident, to make the fuss that other nations made, shrieking and banging along the counters, chorusing their national pride, walking in huffs, with Monsieur le Directeur called up every meal time to deal with one crisis or another, through inadequate interpreters. I could see why Frances would be piqued to miss her lunch.

I offered her my ticket. She was wearing a white T-shirt and white shorts, and had very long translucent, apparently sun-resistant white legs and her red hair was untidy and frizzy and be-ribboned in the English fashion, and bunched on top of her head, and very different from the glossy cropped business like chic of the French teenager. The alleged flea bites on her legs and cheeks stood out in an oddly exotic and personal way. Her large blue eyes were liquid with angry grief: they filmed over with moisture, I noticed, when she was in the grip of passion. I thought she looked terrific.
'I don't want your stupid ticket,' she said. 'It's all your fault. I'm worn out with all that fucking dancing.'
'Language!' said Jennifer.
'Fucking dancing,' repeated Frances. 'I only did it for Dad's sake, to get everyone going. Not that he cares. He doesn't even notice.' (to me) 'He doesn't care about anyone or anything except his fucking music. I hope you realise that. My mum's well rid of him if you ask me. He's been a rotten husband and a rotten father.'
She stared down at me, waiting for my response. She was twice my size.
'Well,' I said, 'he's not a rotten lover.'
That shrivelled her. She snivelled.

'Sandra!' reproached Jennifer. And then. 'I know, everyone!
Let's go and have a lovely lunch, all by ourselves. Who cares
about the men!'

'I do,' said Frances, 'and I'm going off to find Douglas.'

'Douglas?' said Jennifer. 'I thought it was Jock.'

Change seemed to frighten her.

'I've gone off Jock. He's just a boy, no more use than a sick
cat. Douglas is the one who clashes his swords above his head.
He comes from Ilvercuddy. He's something else. A real man.'

'But he'll be at the Reception,' said Jennifer, 'along with all
the others. So come to lunch with Sandra and me.'

'No, he isn't,' said Frances. 'They won't let the Scots Guards
in, in case they get drunk. Only the officers can go. They're
really pissed off. They're going to break up the town tonight.'

Rumour travels fast through the lands of the young.

'I know you want to stop me,' said Frances, terrified. 'But I'm
old enough to know what I'm doing. And everyone else does –'
(glares at me, her father's doxy, bad girl of the Band) – 'so
why not me.' And off she went, one could only presume, to
lose her virginity to Douglas, or Jock, or whoever. (Difficult
to tell one from another beneath a busby.) No doubt about it,
those sturdy, strapped, socked and be-ribboned calves below
the swirling kilt would be hard enough to resist. And why
bother, as she herself had pointed out.

'She'll get AIDS,' said Jennifer, all but weeping. 'And it's all
your fault.' She stood in the French market square and shook
her English finger at me. The nail varnish was chipping. I
mentioned it. She took no notice. It was the bright red kind I
most dislike. I favour beigy pink crystalline. It was bound to
chip, I suppose, considering the amount of housework she did.
'What sort of example have you set her?' she demanded. 'Don't
you realise your responsibilities? If you take on a married man
you have to behave decently towards his children.'

'Why?' I asked.

'Because it's only decent.' She was frothing and spitting.

'But they're a nuisance.'

'You take them on when you take him on.'

'No, I don't.'

'He didn't start life the day he met you. A married man brings

79

his past with him.' She was quoting a hundred women's magazines. I told her so. She frothed more.

'You are a monster!' she cried, and I thought that was that, she'd come to her conclusion, and now perhaps we could have lunch. French restaurants fill up quickly after twelve. But she thought of another tack.

'As a public figure,' she said, 'you ought to set an example.'

'Why?' I asked. 'Napoleon was a public figure and he didn't. The less well public figures behave, the more public they become.' I am argumentative, it is true.

'Oh you and your stupid media world,' was all she would say. She did quite like me, in spite of her disapproval of me, as I quite liked her. We went and had lunch. Crudités, steak and frites, fruit and cheese, but she began to cry over the cheese. She missed Sandy. And now the really hot part of the day had begun, and her hat was locked in the van, and whatever was happening to Frances – even as we ate, the dreaded virus might be passing from the Scots Guards into her young body. I was going to have to pay for Jennifer's lunch, because Sandy had gone off without leaving her any money.

'Sandy this and Sandy that,' I said. 'Can't you organise your own life?'

'No,' she said. 'I like Sandy to organise it.'

'Then you'll cry for ever,' I said, and then I cheered her up by saying that Jack and I couldn't help it, love was its own imperative, a greater good overwhelming all the little wrongs, and of course Frances wouldn't get AIDS, and she'd have a far better time with Douglas from Ilvercuddy than she would with some local boy back home who'd betray her and disappoint her and be around for ever to remind her of it – as it was Frances could write Douglas love letters and tell herself it was circumstances kept them apart, and she could hug her love to her bosom and save her face and be the envy of her friends, and if I was instrumental in Frances losing her virginity to a soldier in a French provincial town, then good for me. That was what soldiery were *for*. Think of all those younger sisters in the Austen novels – the minute the Regiment was in town they would be off; there was no controlling them: nor should there have been. Kilts and busbies and sweaty brows and dancing feet and puffing cheeks – wow! Lucky old Frances, said I.

She actually smiled, and discovered she was eating goat's cheese – crumbly and white and not tough and rancid as imported goat's cheese is. Poor old Britain, fobbed off with the world's culinary cast-offs.

15

Lying in the Shade

Look, one thought leads to another. After lunch I parted gracefully from Jennifer and went to lie in the shade of an oak tree on the grassy slopes that led down to the moat at the foot of the castle. On the far side of the moat a thousand senior French citizens milled around the big marquee where the afternoon concerts were held. They had come in by bus from the villages around. For four hours they would sit in a confined and unventilated space, on uncomfortable chairs, watching endless heel-and-toeing, swirling skirts, gracious bowing and ferocious thigh-slapping (Turkish) and listening to gypsy fiddling, Creole mourning, and thirty-piece orchestras playing melancholy, energetic but always folksy pieces. This they would do with an intensity and appreciation which made me, a mere lady astronomer, feel ashamed. The women wore dark cheap cotton dresses on their bolster bodies; their arms were fat and flabby, or thin and fleshy. The men had little sharp elderly eyes, tough burned skins and wore greasy Sunday suits. To such an end must all peasants come: nothing left in life but to be bussed in to Folk Festivals to witness the artificial celebration of a daft and dreary life.

I catch myself thinking like my father, the Nazi beast. That is what happens when the work machine gets turned off: you find out who you are, how nasty you can be. In the sudden silence of non-attempt, non-effort, you hear the furies flapping round your ears. If there are no papers to write, no graphs to decipher, no lectures to give, no dinner guests to entertain, you see ghosts. You drive dogs shrieking in terror from the mere sniff of you. You are yourself. To what end had I come, forget my elderly peasant brethren. I leapt upon Mad Jack the Knight Errant's horse as he galloped by and he landed me in the fire, not the frying pan. The truth of the matter is, no amount of fucking can stop you thinking and the time had come to think.

I felt obliged to give some thought to the matter of my father. My father, the supplier of the genes that gave me the Aryan cast of my countenance, the precise lines of jaw, cheekbones, nose – the rather thin mouth, the small perfect teeth, the long legs – all so different from my gypsy-girl mother Tamara, plump, dark and somehow diffuse, and she herself, in her turn, so inappropriate a child for her mother, my grandmother Susan, who had the kind of English horse-face seen at its best in an English vicarage garden, pruning hands protected by thick cotton gloves. Susan ran off with a gypsy: she was, I like to think, the original for the girl in the D. H. Lawrence story, *The Virgin and the Gypsy*. I am one of a race of misfits, that's for certain: the result of a surfeit of miscegenation, and would have come to nothing had it not been for some chance mutation in the genes, which gave me the kind of brain which is useful in worldly affairs – one that can do sums, pass exams, consider the heavens, discover a new planet, and has a gift for teaching, for making the improbable facts of the universe seem probable to a television audience. This I do by throwing myself around a studio, pretending to be the sun, or a black hole, or a red dwarf, or whatever, demonstrating the Doppler Shift by putting a brass band on a railway carriage and zooming it past the mike – in imitation of what Christian Doppler himself did, long ago – and so forth. I am good at it. Look, I'm really something, me. And also I am nothing. I am the debris of the world, product of a series of unconsidered and unnatural matings, between the proud, the mad and the murderous. Once things start going wrong in a family they certainly go wrong. (The brass band I chose for the Doppler Effect show were a staid and boring lot, by name the River Kwai Beat. If I'd known then what I know now, I would have employed the Citronella Jumpers. They'd have got, for once, Musician Union rates – a rare event in any musician's life. (Then I would have really impressed them.) Though, now I come to think of it, it was the sousaphone player of the River Kwai Beat who gave me the card of the Citronella Jumpers, which I in turn gave to the Centenary Organisers, which was how I encountered Jack, meaning of my life. Love at first sight!)

83

I wonder if my father, donator of the genes, ever fell in love? Or did I get my capacity to do so from my mother's side of the family? This business of genes really intrigues me. I devoted two whole programmes to evolution – I find myself a stern Darwinian when going into the possibility of, for example, there being life on Athena, that miserable, chilly little planet. (Unlikely: improbable to the factor of a trillion or so, in fact.) And my ratings, never vast, dropped 5 per cent while I told the audience so. This was news no one wanted to know. What, no life out there! And we're all waiting for the starship to arrive and explain all! Someone has to.

I wonder if my father was tall or short? I had only ever seen his face in an old newspaper cutting, and, back in the last century, Mendel had explained to anyone interested that genes don't *blend*. It's not my father's tallness and my mother's shortness that makes me of middle height. (My head at Jack's chin: what a pleasure it is to look up to a man – I had to lower my eyes to meet Matthew's.) No. We inherit attributes from a male and female parent, but we don't end up hermaphrodite, do we? So I can't work back from me to discover my father's appearance or temperament. What we have are particles of inheritance: maleness being made up of a million million inheritable particles, femaleness likewise. Depending on where the preponderance lies, we turn out to be one or the other. Majority decision, as it were. We inherit, randomly, all kinds of things unnecessary to our survival, simply not contra-indicative of it. We can survive (as a species) pretty well with our remnant appendix: it's merely an irrelevance, as are the stripes on a zebra. (The schizophrenic gene will presently, no doubt, breed itself out, particle of inheritance by particle. Presently. It's just tough in the meantime.) As human beings we have a vast surplus of intelligence over what is required for our survival as a species – it may even be contra-indicative to that survival. Down's Syndrome people, with their extra chromosome, seem more appropriately equipped than the rest of us; they have just enough sense to feed and provide for themselves, an active desire to reproduce, and are far less given to suicidal/martial behaviour than we others, who are in actual danger of wiping ourselves out, something no other species, as far as we know, has so far done. I didn't put that bit in the programme – Central would have censored it. Talk of Down's Syndrome in anything other than tones of hushed sympathy they simply won't have – talk of nuclear death-wish smacks of CND, and ill manners. As for me, Starlady Sandra, I mean to help the evolutionary process along by failing to reproduce. I guess I may have more than a hundred half brothers and sisters walking about today, living evidence of man's surplus intelligence, my father's spirit of scientific enquiry, and they won't necessarily feel the way I do. Bang, bang, you're dead! Gotcha! That'll teach you to do nature's work for it – weeding out the unfit with your own peculiar Darwinian mix of random-ness and purpose, which got you labelled back in 1949 at the Nuremberg Trials, even in the days before punchy headlines, the Mad Sadist of Bleritz. You should have tried cosmology, like me, professionally, not taken up genetics as a hobby. Daddy! But then the discipline was hardly invented, back in the twenties, the thirties, when you got given your particular world view.

Now I admit that when I realised my mother's mad tales about my father were in fact true, not mad at all but quite, quite true, which happened when I was fifteen (Frances's age), it was quite a shock. I resolved never to have children, never to get married. In the first I have succeeded by way of three abortions (I am remarkably fertile, or so I have been told – my body managing to foil contraceptive devices in the most remarkable way): in the second I failed, more's the pity. I read Pure Maths at Oxford, worked on a space programme for a time (mathematicians end up everywhere); became a cosmolo-gist, and then developed an interest in simple astronomy, of the sky-gazing kind. Our research team was based at the Greenwich Observatory. I saw this period as a sabbatical, in fact, and it was my good luck, rather than the result of any particular endeavour, which made me the first to postulate, then verify, the existence of Athena. In the meantime, of course, I had had affairs, even fallen in love with, various men: most wanted children: those who did not I did not like. Sad. To prefer a Porsche and a peaceful annual holiday abroad to the creation of children may seem sensible, but it is not likeable. My more complex reasons for remaining childless seemed to me both reasonable and noble, but I seldom wished to discuss these complexities, let alone my family history and shame, with those men I loved, fancied, or felt would do me some good in the world – that is to say, professors, employers, and so on. So they thought me hard and unkind, tough as old boots, which of course I was not. It is not easy to go against blind instinct: it is not easy to do away with babies who have managed to get so far, so very far, towards a viable existence, and now must be blotted out, refused their chance, because I, like my father in his way, have decided to use my surplus intelligence and interfere in evolution's plan. Still, I had my work to get on with.

But after the 'discovery' of Athena, that miserable lump of rock, in its distant, unlikely orbit – and quite when an asteroid stops and a planet begins is merely a matter of scale, but the Royal Astronomical Society was short of funds (whoever isn't?) and could do with a bit of publicity, and nothing like a new planet for making a splash and putting up the member-ship, and I sometimes think Athena was perhaps actually put in my way, one dark night, rather than I seeking it out, but never mind – I have a low self-image, according to a therapist I once visited; which is why these feelings of omnipotence and paranoia keep warring in my rather inadequate bosom (see?) and find it hard to credit myself with any real achievement – anyway, there I was on television rather a lot, and I look better on screen than off it (thank you, Daddy, for your Aryan cheekbones, your thin straight nose, your rather square shoulders, narrow waist: you looked smashing in your SS uniform, especially designed for the likes of you) and I kept getting phone calls and letters from this Matthew Sorenson who really admired me for my mind, my independence, the way I dealt with success. In other words, fame turned him on. He was, he said, a barrister. Now that did impress me, and I agreed to meet him for dinner, and before I knew it he was a frequent visitor to my rather pleasant two-room flat in Bayswater, pacing up and down, talking, talking, about every subject under the sun. Now I rather liked that. Most people knew could talk about one or two matters – few ranged widely over the spectrum of human interest. He had a rather pink face – he drank quite a lot – and a self-important jaw. I did not fancy him in bed at all, which did not stop me getting into one with him from time to time. It wasn't that the talk wasn't interesting, it was just sometimes I longed for silence, and the heave, heave, grunt, grunt of mindless sexual congress was the nearest I could get to it. There was no escaping him, I don't know how it happened. He was always there; when I opened the front door; when I finished at the studio; on the phone at the observatory; picking me up for lunch. He bought me jewels. Jewels! He introduced me to his friends, who were impressed by me, this woman of achievement. How they all talked, and laughed, and shrewdly, wittily commented as if the world was there for their observing, and all the suffering in it meat for their witticisms. I remember after one particularly scintillating evening, after Matthew had brought me home in the Mercedes (a rather perky little vehicle) and I had kissed him goodbye on the step, and he had groaned his passion, 'But *why* won't you let me in? You did last Saturday' (he had such a *memory* for names and places and times which I somehow did not believe in at all), I waited for him to go and then took a ride on the underground just to be with ordinary, incoherent, tired, stumbling human beings again. Why then, you ask, did I marry him? Because he narrowed down the paths of my exits, until they were all blocked except the one signposted 'wedding' and that was the only one I could find, as I ran blind and dizzy here and there, with the Press on the phone and the cameras at the door, and journalists wanting to know who I thought this year's worst-dressed man was, and what was my favourite scent/cause/dessert and what was my star sign, and literary luncheon-organisers wanting me as their speaker. I had a feeling that only lawyers and barristers could keep any of it in calm proportion, mocking at it as they did. 'Sandra, darling, you can't take it seriously. You're a nine-day wonder!' So I just plain and simply married Matthew and moved into his house in Dulwich, the one his last wife had vacated a year or so before, leaving her very tasteful, boring, everlasting pure wool sea green carpets behind her, not to mention a Magimix in which was still wedged a piece of fungoid carrot. The home felt like the Marie Celeste.

'Did she leave in a hurry?' I asked Matthew.

'Not soon enough for me,' was all he said, bleakly, and I wondered how she had offended. Well, it should have been a warning.

'What did she *do*?' I asked.

'What wives do,' he said. 'Nothing.' That should have been more than a warning. 'But you won't be like that, will you? You'll keep an outside interest. Your little programme.'

Now that we were married my programme had become not a major contribution to the world, or to celestial affairs, but a 'little programme'. Well, what did I expect? Why should it be different for me than for the generality of women? I made my contribution to dinner-party conversation, ideas for the coming next month's programme would be postulated over the melon and parma ham and consolidated over raspberry mousse and discarded over rather inferior goat's cheese: I made a pretty enough picture at the end of the dinner table and presently there were fewer solicitors and more judges on my left and right. That, it seemed, was the object of the exercise, of the marriage. Matthew wished to be promoted to the Bench. It was, I supposed, not too bad a bargain. Matthew paid for my bed and board and I was able to save my not inconsiderable earnings. Central paid for at least some of my clothes, and the Tax Inspector kindly agreed that what I spent on the rest was tax deductible, and Matthew all but encouraged me to buy the kind of little black dresses he felt suitable for an accomplished dinner-party hostess. Rather boring design magazines came to photograph the inside of our house: the *Mail* did one of its pieces on 'Who's to Sunday Dinner' and Matthew clocked up four judges and wives over very traditional roast beef.

'Well done, Sandra,' he said, on that occasion. 'I'm very proud of you. Now if only we can persuade the Press to drop the Starlady Sandy absurdity –'

'They would drop it,' I said, 'and very quickly, if you were not so anxious to have them around.'

'Good God,' he said, huffing and puffing – I was sure that he would be a Judge very soon – he had the looks and the mannerisms and the habit of getting things wrong and falling asleep quite suddenly in the middle of a sentence – really, he had no need to worry – 'I don't encourage them! Seedy lot! Media rubbish. Gutter press: your kind, not mine.' I don't think, personally, he could tell the difference between *Interior* and *Woman's Realm*.

'Anyway,' he said, a little feebly, 'it's touch and go. Sandra's bad enough, without Starlady in front of it!' One of the unclassed, that was me. Once we were married, he made me very aware of it. I was without a proper family. Susan's father, my great-grandfather, had been a bishop, but that was a long way back and didn't count any more. The women round the dinner table (I will not call them friends) had names from the English counties – Melissas and Amandas and Fionas – but Sandra? Where did that come from? (Clare, of all the guests, was the one I became fond of. She too had married her solicitor more or less by accident, and her general air of delinquency kept me going through many a scintillating, awful evening.) 'All I'm trying to say,' said Matthew, 'is play it cool.'

And he put the phrase in quotes and laughed with self-satisfaction. How clever he was! The language of the streets. 'Just for the moment.'

'What do you mean?'

'No scandal,' he said. 'No more topless bathing. No more transparent blouses. Nothing for the press to get hold of.'

'I am not in the habit of making public demonstrations of myself,' I said. Nor was I. I rather enjoyed the general modesty of my clothes; and my general air of sobriety and responsibility on screen. I knew I was joking, but few others did – only those who (rarely; I was busy, and tired from cooking) got to raise my skirt and see the red suspenders underneath, in an age when women wore tights and suspenders were definitely not for holding up stockings. With Matthew I put on an old flannel nightie – well, it seemed hardly worth the effort to wear anything else. Grunt, grunt, groan, groan, and the same old position.

'What's good enough for missionaries is good enough for me.'

Had it not been for the sense of time passing – which so afflicts women of spirit and aspiration – I would really quite have enjoyed myself with Matthew. It was not hell. One has to live somewhere.

It was a day or so after his plea that I did not attract attention to myself – what can it be other than a generalised guilt which makes men so convinced that their wives are always on the brink of bringing about their downfall – think of Adam, eating the apple and blaming Eve – when he himself had behaved so

89

badly to his previous wives, Lilith (who argued) and Talith (who was unutterably silly) that he was beyond taking any moral responsibility for himself – that we attended the 'do' at the Astronomical Society in the Observatory Grounds. Some centenary or other: another PR ploy.

It was a beautiful spring evening. Food was served on tables outside the Marquee: the Thames flowed grandly by, and these days even sports a live fish or so, not just those grimly floating belly upwards. The great and famous were there. You know what these occasions are like. (If you don't, you haven't missed much, except, I daresay, the opportunity to dress up.) A girl very seldom meets the man of her dreams on such occasions. The men are far too closely escorted. Fights almost never break out: the food is unexceptional, colleagues meet colleagues and compare notes, contacts are made and information passed on about vacancies arising in the astronomical world. There are always a few cameras, and sound and lighting men from local, not national, TV, some rather bored and yawning newshounds and the mere stringers of gossip columnists, seldom the real thing. Though of course of late there's also often been *me*, Starlady Sandra, always good for a pic or two and what's in the stars for her, not that anyone out there is interested, it's just if not her, who? Whom? With a few mild and kind exceptions, astronomers are on the whole plain and boring people, of interest only to each other – at least until Athena and myself hit the headlines, which did I admit stir everyone up a little. Anyway, there I was, wearing a thin white silk dress with a perfectly respectable button-up-to-the-neck front, but slightly on the tight side – all these dinners, what did Matthew expect? – and my breasts, if small, and hardly worth so much as enclosing in a bra, so I never do, are certainly boldly nippled.

'Sandra, are you sure –?'

'Sure of what? What's the matter with it?'

'Nothing, nothing.' Breasts embarrassed him. Nipples embarrassed him more. I was always rather surprised that he so stuck by the missionary position, which put him in such intimate contact with the fleshy things. I don't think I disliked Matthew at the time as much as I may now seem to; it's just that he did some fairly unforgivable things, the following day.

So there was me, and there was the Band, filling in between the Brady Quintet, who agreeably played extracts from the *Water Music* and (of course) 'Jupiter' from Holst's *The Planets* and a little Mozart, and a Scottish pipe ensemble who played sentimental Scottish ditties. Then the Citronella Jumpers came on loud and strong. I never drink at these functions – I like to go home clear-headed and be able, being hangover free, to have the whole thing well and truly in the past by the next morning. But this time I thought, fuck it, and I did. I drank. I drank glass after glass of champagne and I studied the Band.

Well, Karl was more classically handsome and Pedro more soulful and Sandy leered lecherously at the crowd in general and me in particular, but Mad Jack the trumpeter was the one for me.

Let me say I don't usually look at men in a predatory and salacious manner, but tonight the prospect of being a Judge's Wife had got to me and I was fighting back. I wanted to annoy Matthew. Now you may think this trivial and stupid of me but what's a girl to do? A woman, that is to say, rising forty-two and never had a baby, nor wished to, and not wanting one, and her life being somehow unsatisfied: the past so neatly and tightly packed away, forgotten: depression and elation both denied, scored out with a thick black line. Compromising, as women so often do, with their own happiness, because they must. But there was no 'must' for me – I had chosen to drift with the current into this peculiar role; acting woman, not really being one, unentitled as I always felt I was, by virtue of my birth, to an ordinary existence. Unclassed, de-natured, disallowed. Say I was desperate, if you like, latched on to Mad Jack the trumpeter – jazz musicians are unclassed, unentitled by choice – as if he were a tree trunk and I falling over a cliff. Oh, a tree trunk! How apt! But I think it was nothing to do with that; I think even were I married to someone I actually loved, liked and admired, I would still have gone off with Mad Jack that night. Say rather that like called to like. It takes one to know one.

It was Greenwich where the mean, mean time comes from and the stars are particularly poignant, having offered themselves there first for human study. 'PMT and GMT' I'd sing round the Greenwich house, if I broke a saucer, or burned a sauce, to Matthew's irritation. I'd explain the joke but he did not see it was a joke. Forget Matthew. Oh, forget him! And the green sward shimmered beneath my silver sandals and my dress was far too tight. It clung to me and constricted me, as if the fabric itself had taken on the role of lover. Jack looked me straight in the eye, tapped in the beat, raised his trumpet to that hardly innocent angle and sang to me, about me, for me, of me, by, with and from me, and right, I may say, into me, and what could I do? Except dance, for him. Such things do not come to many of us. Many of us do not come to such things, if you'll forgive the indecency. At the end of the set Jack smiled, and I saw Matthew drifting – not quite drifting but sidling in a both nervous and aggressive way, like a fire-ship into an enemy harbour – through the dancing astronomers and their groupies – takes a lot to get an astronomer to dance – I think the Brady Quintet's *Water Music* had sapped their will quite profoundly – to take me away, or at least dance with me, so my exhibition of arm-stretching, hand-waving, hip-rolling solitary dancing pleasure would not come to any more public attention than absolutely necessary – Starlady Sandra seldom behaved like this, though she got by, I might say, on a kind of hint that she certainly could if she wanted, and that one day if you watched carefully enough you might catch her out – and Mrs Sandra Sorenson – you know, the High Court wife – certainly must not be caught. So I didn't smile back at Jack, nothing so ordinary, I gave him one of those grave intent looks which agrees everything then and there – the same kind, but with a different and more interesting purpose, of course, as when car drivers meet at crossroads, and by telepathic communication, passing through those unsmiling glances, decide who's to go first, and how, and act upon it, unerringly. And Jack nodded towards the bushes and I went after him and Matthew stood gaping behind us.

'Do you know what you're doing?' was the first thing Jack ever said to me.

'Yes,' I replied. My dress was unbuttoned and round my ankles and I stepped out of it.

'You haven't been drinking?' was the second.

'Not so it counts,' I said.

'I wouldn't want to take advantage,' was the third, as he kissed my breasts and nipped the nipples between his teeth. And that's as far as I'll go because here I lie in the shade, trying to come to terms with my past, and I do not want to drift off altogether into an erotic stupor. My task here must be to speak the truth, hide nothing from myself, and peel away the successive onion-skin layers of the past, no matter how it makes me cry. Sex is the great forgetting, the great drug, the great consolation, the great mopper-up of tears: the mover to action, the enhancer of courage, the gauge to the self. It shows full or empty, something or nothing, and steps in between. I shift about on the hard ground. The grass is not soft enough. I want a bed, and Jack in it.

Enough. I am not a person to waste time. This holiday, this run-away, this beginning of a new life, whatever it turns out to be, must afford me the time for self-discovery. Every day a better day: a step further on the road to understanding. If Sandra Starlady lies on her back in the sun, eyes closed, don't think nothing is going on.

'I love you,' was the next thing I said to Jack. Now I know better than to say that mid-sex to any man (other than a fiancé or husband, for whom it is more or less required listening, at least from time to time). It quite puts a strange man off his stroke; the prospect of commitment; the dread of female pain to come. None the less, meaning it, I said it.

'You can't say that,' he said, taken aback.

'Why not?'

'You hardly know me.'

'Well enough.'

'You're a person of instant decision, then.'

'Yes.'

I saw him smile, or did I feel him smile? The moon was behind a cloud shaped like a weasel; nevertheless the light of the Plough over Greenwich is not negligible – I might have seen it.

I daresay it is absurd to seek so patiently and earnestly after truth, when self-delusion is so much more comfortable. Truth in any case is no constant thing; it changes from day to day. Even the two and two we used to trust to make four can no longer be relied upon to do so. By *assuming* two and two make four we can get to the moon and pay the Band; for all practical purposes two and two still make four; but the fact is that they merely approximate four. The fact of adding destabilises the wretched numbers. Try to make two approach four by ever-increasing fractions and you'll never, ever get there. The components of the universe are too infinitesimal, too occupied increasing their infinitesimality, to devote any energy to joining themselves up. We great clumping clumsy creatures, looming through the macro world, grasping at the moon, know little or nothing of that other micro state.

What the hell, Jack smiled. I'll swear he smiled in the light from the emerging moon. He was pleased. He was not frightened off; he knew how rare the feeling was, and that I spoke the truth. 'In that case,' he said, 'we'd better stick together. What's your name?'

'Sandra Harris,' I said. Well, it could be anyone's name. He made no comment beyond 'Hi, Sandra.'

'Hi, Jack,' I said. I knew his name. He introduced himself when he introduced the Band. 'Mad Jack the trumpet-player,' he called himself. What a treat, after my mother, after Robin, to have the word so blithely used. Not the black, black devil's side of us, but the pearly animation of the spirit, heard in that mad music.

'You're here with your husband, I suppose,' he said next.

'No,' I said. 'He's here with me. I'm a research assistant.' Well, it was true, in its way. I answered to the Astronomer Royal. Lies must always be as close to the truth as possible.

'I'll have to go back for the next set,' he said. 'Stay where you are,' and I lay on my back in the twigs and the leaves, under his jacket, and stared at the Plough, and listened to 'Hindustan' and 'If You Knew Susie' and to Jack playing for me, and thought about nothing, not even where Matthew was.

After the last set I joined Jack in the old Ford Transit van in which he lived, and stayed with him all night.

'What are your circumstances?' he asked. 'Are you free to stay with me?'

'Yes.'

'Your husband doesn't mind?'

'We go our separate ways.'

'No children?'

'No.'

'Thank God.'

The van was fitted out like a makeshift caravan. The bed was a foam mattress on the floor: there were shelves for a book or so – he read economics and *Small is Beautiful* and John Fowles' *The Maggot*. His clothes were few but neatly folded. His dishes likewise, neatly stacked. A plastic water container hung from a hook: he was a tidy man. The van smelt of sex, garlic and toothpaste – a good mix, I thought. We parked and struggled on the floor all night, and slept just a little, intertwined.

We had breakfast in a bacon-and-egg café behind King's Cross. One place seemed much like another. I used the loo and washed my face in the wash basin. I wore a shirt of Jack's over my white dress. It came down to an inch or two beyond the hem. I thought it looked rather good. My mouth was swollen and my chin scratched and that was fine by me. My arms and neck were marked with tooth bites.

'You can't go home looking like that,' he said.

'I know,' I said.

He told me a little about Anne: he'd left her a year ago, at her request. He went back once a month or so to fix the washers and see she was all right. They didn't sleep together. His daughter Frances was doing her 'O' levels. They were apart, but free, and stayed friends.

'There must be more to it than that,' I said.

'She gave me an ultimatum,' he said. 'My music or her.'

'So it was the music.'

'I couldn't be her pet poodle,' he said.

'Of course not,' I said.

'Now, I've found you,' he said, 'I wouldn't want to lose you. Come live with me and be my love, in a van parked over a sewer.'

'All right,' I said.

'You can leave work just like that?' he asked, surprised.

'Oh yes,' I said. 'It doesn't mean much to me.' And it didn't.

We went back into the van. It had curtains over the windows, hippie-style. We made love. I use the words advisedly. Such things happen. Buses pinged and taxi meters clicked outside: a police car siren made us both start. The heads of passers-by were at window level. If they looked down or in what did we care? We re-made the universe: they were just the raw stuff of our dreams.

'You do take something?' he said. 'I mean, precautions.'

'Yes.'

'Good.' He hadn't heard of AIDS, or if he had he meant to take no notice. Nor was I going to remind him. It would be a death worth living for. Fuck Jack and die? I thought. Too right, I thought. Any day.

'I'd better go home and collect a few things,' I said. 'You park here and I'll take the tube.'

'I'll drive you,' he said. 'I'd better know a few things. Besides, there might be trouble.'

On the way I asked: 'Do you usually live in the van?'

'Or with friends,' he said. 'My things are still at Anne's. Such as they are. I travel light.'

So much was clear. He'd been to Manchester University, from a South London grammar school. Read Economics, smoked too much dope, half-dropped out, played trumpet, got his degree. Taught for a time; married Anne, bought a house, raised a family, got thrown out. What did anyone do with their lives? What else was there to do but get through it, enjoying yourself on the way?

Well now, I'd always had the feeling people ought to do more with their lives. Become SS officers and do scientific experiments, train as psychiatrists and treat Robin for his illness, grow roses and lament the past like my grandmother Susan, establish stable carpeted households and be ambitious, like Matthew: discover planets and get high-powered media jobs – pass exams and keep on passing them – I had equated not so doing with madness, which was my mother's occupation.

Throwing all control, all sense of future, to the winds, and hearing voices. Listening to Jack, I perceived all of a sudden there might well perhaps be another way. I won't say the awareness came like a flash of lightning, but I certainly blinked once or twice as the van took the road to Greenwich. It was a diesel van and rather old; it had a rocking motion, most unlike that of Matthew's Mercedes.

Which was in the drive when we got there. So he hadn't gone to work, as I had rather hoped, indeed assumed. I needed my passport, my cheque book, a credit card or so: some jeans I had worn properly into, and a favourite sweater. That was all. I was throwing off the past.

'Well!' said Jack, looking at the house, which had a circular gravelled drive leading up to it, two false pillars flanking a boring dark blue door, and a few tedious pots of hydrangeas placed here and there, to suggest the place was somehow in a natural setting, which of course it was not – Mock Georgian, 1920-ish. But the rates alone could have kept many of Matthew's clients in comfort and tranquillity, and unobliged to commit their frauds and murders.
'So this is home,' said Jack. 'Well, well,' he repeated.
'Not very well at all,' I said, and went inside.

Matthew was reading *The Times* in the morning room, or pretending to. He was wearing last night's clothes. He hadn't been to bed, either. His face was red in all the wrong places, his square English chin wobbled as if all the flesh that surrounded it was suddenly spare, and no longer needed as a framework for the conviction of his opinions. I was ashamed to have spent so much time in his bed, even in the missionary position.
'Oh, it's you,' he said.
'Who else?' I said.
'Surprised to see me, I expect,' he said. 'Sneaking home from your night on the tiles. And don't tell me any of your lies about being with friends. I can see through lies. It's my profession. You can't deceive me the way you do everyone else. I know you through and through.'
'I did have a night on the tiles,' I said. 'I don't deny it.'

I think if he'd been nicer, that is to say more upset and less self-righteous, I might even then have sought his forgiveness and stayed. The force that seeks to preserve the status quo is to women the same as gravity is to the apple in relation to the earth. That is to say, very great indeed. It was the 'I know you through and through' which got to me. He didn't, but, knowing so little about anything, he really and truly thought he did. Of course, his forgiveness might not have been forthcoming. I had tended to forget that – again, women do. They forget the man's desire to shake a marriage to breaking point may be almost as strong as theirs. If you ask me, in real life it isn't Eve who tempts Adam with the apple: it's the husband who puts a lover in a wife's way, and then says 'There! See! I can't possibly ever forgive you. It's the end, and all your fault!' Beware the husband who's blind to the lover – he knows: of course he knows: he's plotting his own freedom. And when you, discovered, say to him (with truth) 'But I was only showing you how much I need tenderness, love and affection, how desperate I am, please can we talk about this and save our marriage' he says 'What marriage? You have destroyed the marriage.' And so, by God, you have!

I'm not saying Matthew put Jack in my way: not at all: he hardly had time and how was he to know – as a husband often knows just how much more suitable a spouse his best friend would be for his wife, before pushing them into each other's company: just that it fitted in fairly well with his plans for disposing of me. My ratings were falling again. I'd listened to his bright friends rather too often: forgotten the dreary plodding through fact and idea that produces a programme of any real value – I have great faith in readers, viewers – the consumers of culture. You can con them a little, some of the time: but not much, not all the time: very soon they switch off. They hate 'repeats' with justice. They're being despised. And back home who wants their Sole Bonne Femme served by a failing TV star, Starlady Sandra, has-been, and in the papers as such? Oh, it's a hard life at the top.

And here I was, jumping for the cliff, mouth rounded in a cavernous O, like the mad Munch woman, clutching at stars:

standing in Jack's shirt, searching for words to pacify my husband.

'I've just come back to collect some things,' I said. 'Then I'm off.'

He put down his paper. He was reading the city supplement. He got richer by the minute and thought he deserved to.

'In that case,' he said, 'good riddance. The sooner the better. And clear the wardrobe of your tarty clothes, will you. The little black numbers that shop-girls wear. All you ever were was a trumped-up shop-girl.'

That hurt. What would my father have said? Child of his officer loins, a trumped-up shop-girl?

'Take the smell of you out of my sight,' he said. 'I can't stand your smell. You're dirty.'

I swear I bath as much as anyone, but of course one never knows. Armpits? Where? I had no mother to tell me these things. And my grandmother couldn't tell a rose from a cess-pit, or so, walking through her garden, one could only assume. My friends would hold their noses.

'You smell of sex,' he said, disgusted. That reassured me.

'Good,' I said.

'Disgusting,' he said. 'Who with? How many? Would you care? How much, is really the point. I know your sort. I meet them in the Dock all the time. You withhold sex to lure a man into marriage, to get your meal ticket for life; then you sit back and watch him squirm. But you can't keep away from the streets for long, your sort. Because at heart you're a trollop, a whore, a prostitute. Your pleasure is to sell yourself. And that's your downfall, because in the end, with any luck, some poor devil you've driven to distraction chokes you to death with your own tights.' Stockings. I wore stockings. Nevertheless, it hurt. The nearer things are to the truth, the more they hurt.

'And I'll tell you what,' he said, 'I'd give a man a year's probation for murdering the likes of you. That dress last night. Those – what do you like to call them? Titties?'

Now I'm sure I've never called my breasts 'titties'. Why should I?

'Well,' I said, 'anyway, you'll be hearing from my solicitor.'

'I look forward to it,' he said, and I went upstairs to pack a bag, conscious of Jack waiting outside, my heart beating fast with a mixture of fear, exhilaration and amazement at my own daring. I opened the wardrobe and saw there was precious little there for my future life; but I do not like waste. I extended my requirements to include a cashmere sweater and a rather good black silk skirt with an agreeable swirl around the hem: and face creams; no, really, at forty-two I could hardly ignore their necessity. I am a great believer in creams and unguents for the skin, the more expensive the better. (One has to believe in something and astrology was barred to me.) I began to roll choice jars and bottles carefully in tissue. I found a Raynes shoe bag into which they could be safely packed – taking out for the purpose a particularly pretty pair of high heeled coffee coloured shoes. I'd give Clare a call and she could sneak in and take what she wanted when Matthew was out.

But of course I should have known matters would not proceed so peacefully, nor I think did I want them to, or I would merely have grabbed such things as I needed and run, and not bothered with tissue and packing. There was a bang bang up the stairs and Matthew threw open the door and roared, and threw jars and bottles into the mirrors, and then tried to murder me by stuffing a pillow into my mouth – a year's probation from a friendly judge, I suppose, probably one who'd been to dinner, had he succeeded – and I struggled out and away – he was weeping, and he could hardly see what he was doing, I suppose that's how I managed it – and though I could hardly suppose the circumstances had been quite so drastic, I understood the feeling of Marie Celeste which had struck me when I first came to the house – of a place left in a very great hurry indeed. The lump of mouldy carrot in the Magimix. I'd gathered Sylvia (his first wife's name) was houseproud, so supposed an uncleaned utensil the equivalent of my rumpled clothes, everywhere, as he'd tossed them out of the wardrobe, and ripped and ripped.

Well, what did I need with any of it? Or him? I had my cheque book and cheque card in my pocket, and some fifty thousand saved pounds in the bank. But his voice still rang in my ears. 'Hard, vulgar little tart! No background and no taste. If you knew how people laughed at you behind your back; how I tried to protect you from yourself. Picked you out of the gutter to make something of you! But you can't resist it, can you. You must go whoring!'

Well, how little we know ourselves! Starlady Sandra, she of Athena fame, picked out of the gutter that was Central TV. But I mustn't go on. Matthew really got under my skin. Five years of my life dissolving thus into insult.

'Well,' said Jack, when I returned to the van, 'you don't seem to have come away with much.'
'No,' I said. 'It turned out not to be worth the effort.'
'I expect he was upset,' he said. 'I would have been. Under his nose, and everyone watching as we went off.' I didn't ask whose side he was on, because I know there is a sense in which men are always on each other's side, no matter what.

He looked through his diary and said, 'In a couple of months I'm going to France with the Band; a Festival Folklorique. I'd stay here with you but I can't let the Band down. So perhaps you'd better come with me.'
And that's why I now lay here, on a grassy bank in a sunny clime, and heard Jack say 'Oh there you are; I was looking for you,' and it was music to my ears, and life and event started up again. I stood up, dizzy, and swayed, and he caught me, his long thin arms around me, as the past caught up with the present.

16

Truth Being Stranger Than Fiction

But the next day I was confined again to the haunted Hôtel de Ville, this time not on account of sulks or wilfulness, but because of a few spots of blood and a pain in my stomach, which I suspected might get worse before the day was out. I do sometimes get the most fearful menstrual pains; I think myself it comes from staring so hard at the stars: the body is determined to root one here on earth; makes its horrid point: woman, woman, female! it keeps saying, in tones of disgust. What makes you think the likes of you can ever be all spirit, understand more than a fraction of what there is to know? Take this, take that! Ugh! Ugh! Or perhaps it is the cramping, crumpling revenge of the unborn baby. I'll teach you to keep me out – a pinch here, a snatch there: I'll double you up, I will, since you so decimate me! I have often thought of having my womb removed altogether, but something holds me back. I suppose this something had better now be considered.

Jennifer was most considerate and kind: made me comfortable in the truckle bed: lent me the feather pillow she never travelled without; insisted Frances stay with me to look after me. And oddly, Frances did not protest too much. For some reason or other today she wanted to keep out of the soldiery's way. Her eyes had a hooded, wary look. Well, she would tell me, or not, what had happened. She sat by my bed and scratched her insect bites and told me about school: she had forgiven me. Well, she had to, or there'd be no one to talk to, and she admitted to finding the Hôtel de Ville somehow quivery and spooky.
'No such thing as ghosts,' I said, though when Jack kissed me goodbye – rather quickly and nervously, for my being ill was somehow not included in his vision of our relationship – and went, I had been briefly conscious of the watcher back again.

My ghostly lover. Don't ring me, I'll ring you. And I had not picked up the phone.

I lay flat on my back, for that seemed to help the pains, and felt his hands over my stomach, my breasts, a breath on my cheek. Or perhaps that was merely the shadow of Jack, still lingering? I shut my eyes: I tried to sleep: even ghostly lovers sleep: when one does, the other does: I was in no mood for love. My stomach ached too much. The hands, if such they were, seemed insistent on a response I was not prepared to offer.

But presently they gave up: my body was my own again. I had choked off this unwelcome visitation. I had the sense of being alone: the pains were not too bad: in fact had all but ceased. I was free to think. And obviously it was the matter of my own birth which must now be thought about. Doctors could find no physical reason for the acuteness of my monthly affliction: 'Covert stress,' they said, as if I denied the existence of anything unusual, and to date I had huffed and puffed my scorn at their diagnosis.

Well, a sexually active woman with no children by the age of forty-two, can, when it comes to a gynaecological history, be only a collection of negatives. A story of pains, spasms, blood, fluxing, flowing and failing, which no one wants to hear about, since it's all to no avail. I took the pill for a time, which calmed me down to a brisk, regular, calculable flow, but it made the thoughts in my head somehow confused – I can only describe them as coming two at a time, instead of the swift-stepping neat brisk one-after-another kind I am accustomed to, and can cope with.

However, many's the time I have lain on high hard tables, legs apart, with male medical hands inside me, rubber gloved if one's lucky, feeling a this or feeling a that. What can they *know*? What can they be feeling for? Some ritual here that is beyond rational understanding, but part of the male desire to be in on the female act of creation: and of course my experience has not been a patch on that of my friend Alison; she of the twins and the genetic counselling. And yet male interest in female insides, the determination to be there helping, with scalpel, light, tweezers, dabs of chemicals, squirts of hormones and whatever, gets us nowhere, except increasingly to indicate that we are all without guide, leader, Prime Mover – God, that is – but all hopelessly, helplessly accidental.

This is, I think, what my father set out to prove, when he impregnated my mother in the manner he did, a manner hardly likely to lead to a peaceful and ordinary gynaecological history. Mind you, ordinary people are in pretty short supply, if you ask me. Because something is unlikely, doesn't mean it can't happen. Life on earth is unlikely to the factor of 48 to the trillion, or some such statistic, but here we all are. And here I was, daughter of a man who back in the late forties, before the invention of computers – which have made actual genetic experimentation unnecessary – did his best to discover this and that about inheritance, and was enormously interested, I read in the Press cuttings, or at least according to the officer for his Defence, in not just the whats and hows of the human race, but the whys. A polygene, a polygene – what I inherited was a pretty fine group of characteristics! His murderous nature, his capacity for killing is undisclosed in me (as is his particularly long penis, myself being female) but might well show up in the next generation. All the more reason for me to keep my genes to myself. It was fortunate that I was bleeding, evidence of my non-pregnancy. Not a lot, just a little, but with occasional spasms of pain. Well, heaven knows what goes on within, in the dark and murky recesses, what physical or psychological disturbance Jack has stirred up, if I was thus to be kept at home.

Home, this crumbling haunted place, with its tiered, high, square rooms, each one empty save for the four-cornering of the truckle beds, waiting, no doubt, for some evil emergency! Fire, explosion, flood – or the arrival of an unexpected jazz band into an already overstretched community, with some slight moral right to housing, inasmuch as its members are prepared to stand under the War Memorial and incite the citizens to revelry! Home! What have I come to!

Now my father was no doubt an intelligent man and too bright and civilised for promotion to the very highest ranks of Nazi thuggery. He became medical officer in one of those camps where non-desirable races – those most closely aligned to the monkeys – that is to say gypsies and Jews and others recognisable from the shape of their skulls as being very like chimps, and lagging behind in the evolutionary race – were used as work-horses. It seemed a really bright idea to my father and his lot – you got all the lowest grade humans to work in the factories – a) they wouldn't mind and b) it would free the rest for visionary and artistic activities. Well, fair enough. Our educational system achieves much the same end, though by way of IQ levels and not racial characteristics, though both of course being matters over which the individual has very little control. But the Jews and the gypsies didn't have the stamina it took, and weren't cheerful about it, so the camps became death camps, where the unwanted, and those who were messing up the genetic pool, could be eliminated, for the sake of the future. Well, it happens all the time. Many a generation has to suffer for the general improvement. All those young men in World War One, dying for a World Set Free from War. All those citizens in Hiroshima, dying so GIs could live. Oh yes, it happens all the time. If you ask me, my father's defence counsel made a hash of the job: all he offered was the genuine spirit of scientific enquiry which motivated my father, and it wasn't enough.

Of course it's true my father was offered promotion outside the camp several times – a point made much of by the prosecution – but he *chose* to stay. That is to say, he wasn't commanded to stay, in the ordinary manner of military affairs. He declined – but again the defence made pitifully little of this – on the grounds that he wanted to do the human race a good deed. He was acting in the same spirit as did Alison's surgeons, when they offered her a selective termination: just have the one, mother: not the two! – thus offering Sophie's choice to a later race of mums – remember Sophie, of the Styron novel, who was told to decide by a Nazi officer which of her two children was to live? It was seen (by a man) as a hard and beastly choice, but if you ask me it was better than none. Why didn't she just grit her teeth and get on with it, or kill herself and both children with the materials at hand if she couldn't bear it? Moan, moan, moan, Sophie! I'm my father's daughter and have eliminated a number of my children in my time, and paid the man who held the scalpel very well to do it. That too was to perfect the race, by keeping my father's seed out of it.

My father's trial took up only two columns in *The Times*, which in those days, I grant you, was more closely printed than now. Fewer people read it but paid it more attention.

My father's name was Oscar von Stirpit. My mother's was Tamara Wells. She was half-gypsy. My grandmother Susan, the bishop's daughter, had this Lawrencian encounter with a gypsy behind the bushes. Off with the raggle-taggle gypsies oh! But she didn't go off with them. No. She stayed home and gave birth to Tamara, and everyone was enormously kind and forgiving.

And haven't I succeeded where my grandmother did not? At least I ran off, with the leader of the Band, the King of the Gypsies: I didn't just cower at home! And, dear God, even as this thought occurred to me, I heard the telephone ringing, English style, somewhere, nowhere. And how could I answer, stop it: don't ring me, I'll ring you. Coming out tonight, sweetheart? Oh, dear Lord, Thou who dost not exist, Deliver Me!

I put my head under Jennifer's pillow but it didn't blot out the sound. I counted. After thirty non-existent rings the non-existent bell stopped. Thirty. Why thirty? Thirty pieces of silver? The image of betrayal? Or something to do with that imaginary line that separates the woman under thirty from the one over? The rise in the figures for abnormal births? Take your pick, according to your therapeutic discipline. Fried, addled or hung, as my grandmama would say. Freud, Adler or Jung.

My abnormal birth. Okay. A pun. Not exactly an abnormal baby – I had all my parts, thanks to my father's skill – just abnormally conceived. Though now I came to think of it, fairly matter of fact these days, just done with anaesthetics and willing patients. Whipping out eggs by the dozen and fertilising a few and replanting them, and selectively terminating, or freezing the rest for later surrogate mothers, and test tube babies, and other blessings. Thank you, Father, first in the field! It's just in those days those young women didn't understand: would rather have done it in the normal way, in bed with the central light turned out, but the little light on the bedside table softly burning, not my father's way, in the hard bright cruel light of meaning. That's what it was: they didn't understand. I'm proud of you, Father, in spite of your War Crimes Record! I'll be proud of you if the effort kills me: doubles me up with pain once a month.

Footsteps outside, now. What prowls around? Gather your courage, look out the window. No one. Silence. Something sticky and red on the window sill, where your ring finger rests; the one that wears no ring, and wouldn't, couldn't. (Matthew's gave you a detergent rash beneath it.) Your own blood? No. Brownish and aged; a stain, a splash. No, not even blood, a trick of the light. Oh Lord, Frances, anyone, where are you? What happened here once at the Hôtel de Ville? Those little dents in the building's façade — bullet holes? Could blood have splashed up as far as this? And rain and wind and time simply failed to remove it, wash it away? Surely not. An atrocity is no more than the sum of its parts, hardly an excuse for haunting. We all die. Some die young. Many die unfairly. What's so special? The trouble with studying the macro-universe, dealing in infinitesimal distances and sizes to the trillion, and the micro-universe, dealing in fractions likewise, is that, as I keep complaining, all this middle ground of lumbering shapes and unwieldy minds and primitive sensibilit-ies lacks impact, lacks horror. Especially if you are determined to be proud of your father. Forget your mum. I look again: the stains are gone.

No, mum must not be forgot, though she always wanted to forget me. Tamara's raggle-tag dad, the dark-eyed gypsy, kept in touch with the girl he'd wronged. That never happens in song and fable, where girls lean their backs up to thorns and weep their days away for lack of a good man, the one that's so hard to find once they wear their apron high. In 1939, when she was ten, Tamara was taken off by the batty bishop, my maternal grandfather, to visit her gypsy dad, whose home base was in Bohemia: a place even then a tourist trap. My grandmother's father the bishop Edward took the child across Europe, and then went on down to Italy; to take a look at the Religious Art of Venice, planning to come back up when the month was up. Traumatic enough for my mother, I would have thought, as an event; but very few in those days paid much attention to the emotional sensitivities and whims of children. Nor indeed had Edward seemed to notice the news-papers were suggesting that war was about to break out and everyone had better stay home. So while my maternal great-grandfather Edward was inspecting the Grand Canal, my maternal grandfather was swept up with all his tribe and incarcerated for the sake of future generations, who could well be spared the nomadic subhuman messiness of the gypsy. And little Tamara, with her dark eyes and hair and olive skin, ended up in my father's laboratory.

It is odd, isn't it, this notion of the genes not blending. I think my father, unacquainted as he was with the notion of particles of inheritance, but assuming there would be one gene for dark colouring, and another for fair, was trying to work out, while more or less accepting Mendel's laws, which suggested other-wise, the truth of the old limerick:

> There once was a white man called Starkie,
> Who happened to marry a darkie.
> The result of their sins,
> Was quadruplets, not twins,
> One white, one black, and two khaki.

Now of course scientists and doctors often do come up with truths convenient to politicians and employers. Think of wicked old Lysenko, proving the inheritance of acquired characteristics, so convenient to Marxists! Listen, you! You just behave like a good revolutionary, be brave, strong and true, and your children will be likewise! And how about all those doctors employed by Imperial Tobacco, insisting for decades that cigarettes weren't bad for you at all, if anything mildly beneficial: a gentle disinfectant. The Nazi party *wanted* genes to blend. Father just helped prove they did.

Obviously the younger the women who bore the babies the better: and the fairer the donor, and the darker the receptor, the easier to trace various traits through the generations. So very dark girl children – especially the gypsies, who tended to be pretty – were fed oestrogen from fresh placentas removed from other mothers at various stages of foetal development and brought to maturity early. Then impregnated – the techniques of fancy fertilisation not yet having been developed – in the natural way, by the blondest and best. Look, the same kind of thing happens to animals, all the time, in laboratories all over the world, and the animal liberation theologists would argue that this is not better than using human beings to find things out, but worse. Humans have voices. They can protest. 'No, no, no!' I daresay they got used to it, though pulped fresh placenta must be pretty disgusting, sometimes drunk as it was from tubes attached to still living women. That's the worst of it. And it worked: that at least was something. Girls as young as nine had babies: it was also interesting to find out what effect the immaturity of the mother had on the foetus, so many were removed for study. My mother was really lucky, and was all of fifteen when I was born, at the very end of the war; difficult to fertilise (a sign of natural superiority) and one of those chosen to live in comfort and tranquillity listening to Mozart during the course of her pregnancy. I like to think perhaps my father was fond of her, though I don't know why he should have been. She was never very likeable, as I have already detailed, by virtue of her illness. Last time I visited her she asked me who I was, and when I replied 'your daughter', she fetched one of the nuns and told her I'd said I was the gasman, but there was something odd, because she only had electricity, so she wasn't to open the door to me, was she? In other words, she gibbered. And, as I say, though her early experiences were certainly traumatic, and my brother Robin's were not, he ended up as peculiar as she. Unless of course Lysenko was right, and acquired characteristics can be inherited? Or perhaps it was just a simple, if unlikely, coincidence (but that's all coincidences are – unlikely events) in which case at least 50 per cent of my reason for not having babies is out of the window.

And the other 50 per cent, the world's condemnation of my father, is beginning to look a little weaker. If I could only establish him in my own mind, as a reasonable and well-motivated man.

There were, of course, other charges against him at Nuremberg, other than those of the untoward vivisection of women and children (no one bothered about the exploding women and children of Berlin, at the time, since they weren't innocent victims, being German) but I try to dismiss this as hearsay. Those SS officers all looked pretty alike. One blond God (or Devil, depending) is pretty much like another. My father (or someone) had a whimsical way of turning up every now and then and shooting sometimes every tenth, or sixth, or fifth, or third or whatever, inmate as they queued up for their soup. There was no discernible system at work – no simple number added or subtracted, nothing to do with odd or even numbers, the days of the week, the number of guards, that anyone could work out, and so no knowing where in the queue one could safely place oneself. So most simply queued, trusting chance and being hungry, and on bad days would even rejoin the end of the queue, there being, as the result of my father's activities, extra soup to go round. I see no point in denying the slayer was my father; it seems probable enough that he was at it again, mimicking in the camp the random deaths of evolution. Those things which happen by simple accident to a species – the wiping out of a continent by an ice age, say – random, putting a stop to such evolutionary forces as are at work there. Yes, perfectly possible. Oscar would, I suppose, had he lived, now be in his eighties. I am glad I do not have to visit him. He would be an old man in an armchair, with a scarf round his neck, mulling over the adventures of the past, thrilled with all the new statistical evidence and computer models and cunning proofs the Darwinists can these days mount in their denial of the Prime Mover, the Creator, the Intending Mind of the universe. I bet he'd be glad to find he was right, that God didn't exist. But then again, I daresay he would still see himself as virtuous, as does Edward Teller, Father of the Bomb. Innovator. Saviour.

I wonder why I see him with the scarf round his neck? Unless there's some connection between a noose and a scarf, and I have a vision of seizing the old wool rag and pulling it tight, in a cloud of dust and frayed fabric, with just enough strength left in it to do its work. Most of us are ambivalent about our fathers. They didn't hang mine, mind you, they shot him. All that and in the end to prove nothing: but of course the adventure's in the race, isn't it, not the winning. An attempt to re-create the universe must always be worth while.

So that's the horror story at the nub of it all. We are all misbegotten, by one form of monster or another (listen to our mothers). Mine is just an extreme case of an everyday event.

My mother was liberated by the Americans, and taken to a hostel where the diet was less satisfactory than in her little oasis of plenty, and the music was not Mozart but from the American Services Network abroad. Nevertheless, one month later I was born, safely, to all accounts a perfect little replica of my father. How had he managed that? Did he have some inkling of the cloning processes, or were my looks a mere matter of chance, it so happening that all, or nearly all of those that pertained to his looks were disclosed in me, and those from my mother undisclosed, just waiting to pop up in future generations? If Daddy had only realised the unblendability of male and female, he could have desisted from his tinkering and enjoyed my mother in peace.

So really, I suppose, I shouldn't be surprised that my mother, forty years on, accuses me of being a gasman in disguise, a robber knocking on her door to gain entrance under false pretences, the better to hit her over the head and take all she has. Her neat little blonde baby, her enemy, bursting out from inside her like the creature in *Alien*. Not much fun, you must agree, for her, or for me, of course, who always wanted her to look at me softly, kindly, and she never did – or only once, when she mistook me for a kitten, but then got cross because I didn't purr. I remember it well. I was five at the time, and took her censure to heart. She threw me across the room.

'Forty years on, growing older and older . . .' – I can't remember the rest of the song.

My great-grandfather the kindly bishop who got home safely enough from Venice in November 1939, feeling guilty, I expect – but I daresay also a little relieved – to have so easily mislaid his gypsy granddaughter, presently had no option but to claim her and her little SS baby back. It was happening all over after the war – relatives thankfully lost were turning up everywhere, while (as is so often the way of the Great Creator, who has this passion for irony; a sign no doubt of His great intelligence) those genuinely missed just never came back.

Tamara grew up to ride to hounds (she loved animals), and tear foxes to pieces (an inferior race, I always think: nasty smelly bony things with odd shaped muzzles, though it must be admitted splendid brushes) and met Simon, a pleasant person though of rather shifty financial habits, while he was trying to sell a dodgy horse to the Master of Hounds. He took her and her misbegotten little baby – that is to say, me, little Sandra, on. Robin was born. Tamara got carried off by the men in white. So presently did Robin. I mean not to be.

English telephones ringing in France, ghostly footsteps, splashes of blood! Not insanity, merely myself, wanting to speak to myself; Sandra Harris has an urgent message for Mrs Sandra Sorensen. Dear God, let me not be mad.

Oh Holy Father, Cruel God, All Powerful Simulator of an unkind universe; He in whose image I am made. Male and female created He them, the bastard! That's the point. They shot you, nailed Him: couldn't stand it. Quite right too. All this misery, inadvertent human woe, random cruelty – from avalanche to divorce to child neglect to typhoon, the rages that create war, the greed that creates hunger – made He all them. Disgusting, if you ask me, from the slurp of copulation to the strawing up of pulped placenta. What the hell, Daddy-oh! Perhaps it's you on the telephone.

17

Chew You Up and Spit You Out

I felt better. The pains had gone. I got out of bed, feeling the floor dusty and splintery beneath my feet. I put on T-shirt and jeans. I washed. I did not look behind me. It wasn't that I was frightened. I just did not want to see what still might be there to see.

I remembered Eugenie, our pretty neighbour when I was a child; when our peculiar family lived in what once had been a vicarage, and she lived in the church; allegedly deconsecrated: but personally I always felt a vengeful God still dwelt therein. She was a wide-eyed, very thin, nervy creature, a weaver of tapestries depicting country scenes. She had her bed in what had once been the minstrels' gallery, and her weaving frame where once the altar had stood. Plaques remembering dead babies and brass dedications to village benefactors were embedded in the walls. On the anniversaries of their deaths, Eugenie (I expect she was born Joan or some such name) would place little pots of flowers beneath their memorials; more in hope of keeping their spirits quiet and not making a nuisance of themselves, than from any real sentiment, or so it seemed to me, even as a child. Eugenie suffered a series of disasters emotional and financial while living in the church – and of course laid the fault at the building's door. Even as a child I could see the folly of this – if you live in a damp cold building difficult to heat, you will contract rheumatism: if you engage in a non-profitable profession (and the crafts are simply not well paid) you will run into debt: if you believe all you need is a man to make your life complete, that man will not turn up – or if he does, will stay for a night or so, and briskly depart, before you can lay claim to his soul. And a night or so, what's more, does not constitute an affair, does not entitle you to talk publicly about your broken heart, as did Eugenie. But she was a good neighbour, and kind to myself and Robin, and would sometimes let us use the bath, installed in what had been the vestry and the only warm place in the church. The window of our Rectory bathroom was broken, and remained so for year after year. Through the hole icy winds blew, in winter, and in the summer wasps would drift in from their nest in the apple tree, a branch of which had thrust itself right into the room, through the open pane. We took very few baths. When I was fifteen I sawed off the branch, went to the glazier, bought some putty and fitted a new pane, thus upsetting my grandmother very much. She ranted and screamed and said I was no flesh of hers. She apologised next day – it was just, I think, that sometimes the sum of the male side of my being was too much for her, its accumulated foreignness. I learned from my grandmother how little people like change, how much they value the problems caused by their own inefficiency. This, of course, was brought home to me, vividly, as the Citronella Jumpers journeyed through France.

Eugenie finally ran out of the church – literally, one Sunday morning – refusing to go back. She left it in a truly terrible state for the next purchaser, an architect, who complained to the Estate Agent and argued that a couple of hundred pounds should come off the asking price. The place was riddled with dry rot, wet rot, deathwatch beetle. Eugenie had neglected it. He wanted her back to prove his point, to thrust his competent knife into rotten beams, crumbling plaster, so she would not have the face to argue.

'I can't go back,' she said. 'It's haunted.'

'Don't *say* that,' said the Estate Agent, 'or you'll lose the sale altogether.'

So Eugenie lost the couple of hundred pounds that would have bought her a nice little car: which if she'd had she wouldn't have been knocked down as a pedestrian on one of the new zebra crossings, would she, and been killed, six months later. The Curse of the Haunted Church! The architect, a shrewd man, as you can tell, made no complaint at all about the ghosts of dead babies, or misfortune dogging his footsteps: his business prospered and clients loved to dine beneath the vaulted beams. Mind you, he'd had proper central heating put in, and spotlights shone against the stonework, and he objected to the Parish Council about the way every now and then villagers would come into his garden to put flowers on the gravestones he kept as conversation pieces and he had the practice stopped. That's the way to deal with the past! Keep it in its place, or it'll get you, even if it has to trail you across fields and cities, and make you stumble beneath a bus: your own past or someone else's. And above all keep the house in order: keep it placated.

Eugenie failed to keep the place in order: so it got her. Reached out and got her. Perhaps it was not my past, but the Hôtel de Ville itself, which so oppressed and haunted me.

So I took Jennifer's brush and swept down a wall or two, and pinned up some falling wallpaper. I went out into the fields and picked some wild flowers. I put them on the table in the jam jar which had contained the excellent French apricot conserve. But it was not enough. The sense of desolation merely increased. What was it I'd picked up; what was it had fallen in behind me, on my way back from the square to the Hôtel de Ville, down the back road, past the shuttered bungalows with their neat pots of mauve hydrangeas and red geraniums and yellow dahlias, standing smart and orderly like Napoleon's Grand Army in 1814 before it went off to the slaughter: a summer dream defeated by a Russian winter. The lifelessness of France in summer! The ghosts of dead men under every hedge; bodies swing in memory from every lamp-post. The people have forgotten: the land itself has not. It still mourns. My ghostly lover, some young man who can't forgive death for the denial of his pleasures. Just as my unborn babies will not forgive me. Oh, I could have picked up anything, anyone, along the road.

18

Tell Me About Your Wife

'Jack,' I said that night. 'Jack, tell me about your wife.' When I was in bed with Jack I forgot all about ghosts.

'My ex-wife.' He nibbled my ear as if to muffle the words.

'Ex in law or in your heart?' I asked.

'In the one that's most important,' he said. So I knew he was still married.

'Did you really ask her to come on tour with you?'

'Yes.'

'Why?'

'Ask me no whys and I'll give you no becauses.'

My ears were blocked by his fingers, my mouth by his mouth: all my orifices were agreeably blocked up, so for a time the sensations inside me were all-important. But it could not last for ever. These things can't.

'What are we going to do when we get back?'

I felt a wary stillness in him. I should not ask. But how could I not ask? Join your life to another's, and you must know what goes on inside their head, if only in order to dovetail your actions to theirs. Herein lies the penalty of company. To live alone is to be free, but who wants to live alone? I even joined my life to Matthew, rather than be on my own. The cosmos is a kind of company, a never-ending puzzle, but gives the impression of being dreadfully *still*; judgmental, even – though one knows just what a whirling, buzzing, roaring, dancing maelstrom it is. If all the bits were just moved closer together, stripped of the illusion of immensity, we'd see that clear enough. Listen, folks, it's just *tiny*, compared to – compared to what? Alas, we don't know. All we know is that it's there, beyond our comprehension, still further, greater patterns made not by divine intent, but by the cumulative chance events of endless aeons.

And of course, since the small echoes the great, and the differences between the world of simple rocks, stones and isotopes and that of living matter are not so dissimilar, save in the latter's complexity and its capacity to reproduce itself in more or less identical form (the more or less being the crux, of course, ending up in the difference between the amoeba and the giraffe) it should not surprise me that illusion is inherent in what goes on between me and Jack. More (or less) than meets the eye, the nose, the ears, the mouth, the fingertips, or that other sense we traditionally ignore – the sexual responses somewhere inside us; that seventh sense. Because, if you ask me, I'll tell you that's what it is, which combines the other six with its own peculiar awareness of *meant, meant, meant*.

Nature's way, you may piously say, of stopping my monthly bleeding, my horrid pains, the unseemly tricks me and my Dutch cap get up to, my version of the Thames Tidal Barrier, wilfully barring the onflow of history into the future, crying fuck you all – what about *me, me, me*? diverting it elsewhere, until the tide ebbs, gives up. Not nature's way, I say. Illusion.

We don't talk much, Jack and I: not in the way of exchanging ideas, comparing our particular visions of the world. Rather less than before, I think: before he found me out as Starlady Sandra, she who has the heavens at her fingertips. But I don't mind. Though I love to have friends, intimates, confidantes, I have never felt the need for what is called 'intellectual companionship'. Mathematics is a solitary activity: I became accustomed early to keeping my thoughts a private matter between myself and some sheet of paper, or some blackboard, or later some computer. Others were welcome to look in, of course, but could scarcely expect to contribute. Space scientists and astronomers are not on the whole the liveliest people in the world: they tend to see only detail, not the wonder of it all. (I hasten, politely, to say but of course, of course there are exceptions.) Perhaps they are right; stare into the heart of things too long, and be blinded! More prudent to tiptoe round the edges, taking sneaky sideways glances in, pretending not to. Only when I came to preside over Matthew's dinner table did I meet people who dealt easily and eagerly with ideas, but with a kind of condescension, such a swift, ironic sense of their own superiority as quite gave me indigestion. They made their bread and butter the incoherent of the world, and I didn't like that. I prefer the Citronella Jumpers, who squabble and rankle all the time with one another, on the simplest level, but have some kind of intuition, a non-verbal wisdom, which they in all generosity love to communicate. What harm can they do? The singers and dancers of this world?

I said to Matthew once:
'As well sentence a rock to three months' imprisonment for standing on a footpath and tripping you up, as a man for getting drunk and breaking a window.'
'Nonsense!' he said. 'A man has free will, a rock doesn't. Where is my dinner jacket?'
'Arguably,' I said, 'no man has free will.'
'Argue away,' he said. 'But where is my masonic apron? Put your drunk in prison and he won't do it again.'
'Computer studies prove a period of imprisonment makes no difference one way or another,' said I. 'If you put rocks in prison you could still earn your living and the warders do without all that nasty smelly slopping out.'
'You are impossible,' he said. 'Save this kind of thing for your programme. Hand me my tie. No, not that one, you fool. The dress tie, not the bow.'

And so on. In other words, he wasn't properly concentrating. Alison, my good friend, suggested he didn't concentrate because I was a woman, but I don't think we have to look as far as that. Most people would rather just go on doing whatever it is they're doing, bother the sense of it, let alone the morality.

Jack and me; separate, trying to be one. 'Ask me no whys,' he says, 'I'll give you no becauses.' 'Jack,' I say, 'what will we do when we get back?' Jack the wild trumpeter, leader of the Band, husband of Anne, father of Frances, lover of Starlady Sandra, astronomer and media hack! 'Jack, Jack, what will we do when we get back? Where will we go? What's to become of us?'
'Do about what?' says he, a man of few words, but offering a warning. Think too much about the future and you'll have no present at all. You'll live your life tomorrow, never today; be

dead before you know it. Song of the wanderer, the nomad, the traveller, dweller on this stretch of the road, self-righteous as all such songs are. I'm right to live as I do: you're stupid: and here are the words to prove it. Listen to them! How they sing!

'We have to live somewhere,' I say, persisting, and he sighs.

'Women are all the same,' I feel him say, though do not hear.

'Must have their pots and pans, their washing machines.'

'I'd love this to go on for ever,' he says. 'But it can't. I have things to do back home.'

'What?'

'Gigs,' he said. 'A wedding, a funeral, a fête. The usual things. Except the funeral. That's not usual. Not much jazz at funerals. Piano player. Dropped dead over the keys, playing "Body and Soul". In the wrong key. Mind you, it's tricky. Three chord changes. But he was never much of a musician. And there's every Monday at the Bell. That's in Cardiff.'

'A lot of travelling.'

'Yes. Now I know who you are, do you still want to tag along?' There's a trace of anxiety in his voice, just a trace.

'Do you mean because I am who I am, or because you know who I am?'

He laughs and holds me closer. He's not slow, this Jack the mad trumpeter. Agile enough in the head. But he doesn't reply.

'Of course I want to tag along.'

'That's settled then,' he says, relief in his voice. But how he hates to be held to plans, confined by the patterns of other people's expectations. Of course, nothing is settled at all. I am used to rotas, work schedules, menus, lists of guests, Christmas cards received and returned (Matthew's era), production dates, and the certainty of knowing where I am going to lay my head each night and, what is more, having a clean nightie. Look, I would like to know where I am going to live.

Even Godfrey the Goatherd, he of the vibes and the rural crafts, with whom I spent five wretched years, understood the necessity of having a roof, albeit one that was thatched, and with an ancient thatch, in which insects of every kind sported and worked out evolution's particular plan for them. Wooden-top Cottage (I ask you!) was eighteen miles from Manchester

University, which meant a tedious daily drive for me, but Godfrey couldn't stand living in cities, and his general view was that if I insisted on pursuing my career that was okay by him, but since he was happy enough to support me, there was no real necessity for me so to do. (Happy to support me he might have been; but he earned barely enough to keep himself in vegan foods, let alone me. One of his theories was that if pushed we could live on grass, like King Nebuchadnezzar.) Work, he said, was a replacement activity: better for me to give up and live next to nature, in tune with the seasons.

Godfrey the Goatherd 'worked with' young male schizophrenics and somehow managed to contain my confusion and distress before and after Robin died. That's why I moved in with him. I came to be sceptical about the 'working with', which seemed to add up to sitting around in the company of what even he called 'weirdos', drinking wine, smoking marihuana, reading R. D. Laing's *The Politics of Experience*, and occasionally offering the kind of advice one drunk, high man will offer another – for which he was paid a small salary by the Social Services. But he seemed to do no better or worse with the young men than did the more orthodox psychiatrists; the clients lapsed in and out of babel in just the same exhausting way, earnestly buttonholing both the sane and the insane, just as loosely connected to reality as ever, but at least, and for the most part, in the same kind of amiable, hazy daze as Godfrey himself. Sometimes violence and horror erupted, but not often. There was a lot of leading in and out of the goats which lived in the fields at the back, and which often got out to munch the forbidden plants which grew under my kitchen windowsill, and sometimes I would come back from the University and find goats as well as men sitting on the broken sofas of the living room.

'Mad,' I wept, once, as I made them all borage tea to sip, goats included.
'You mustn't say that,' Godfrey said, gently taking me by the hand – he had a beard and soulful eyes: Pedro the guitarist and he are much alike, now I come to think of it – 'these people must not be called mad. Theirs is the true experience. You do yourself no good, or them, by using these labels.'
'Nor them, you,' I said, and wept some more. I very seldom

cry but I was weak; I had recently had another abortion, through which Godfrey held my hand, deploring the while my rejection of the life force – but not sighing too loud, in case I changed my mind, for even he could see the inconvenience of my being pregnant. He did not understand my determination not to propagate, which I rashly attempted to explain to him, for he saw insanity as a blessing, not a tragedy. But we needed my small salary as junior lecturer to help support the dope-smoking, borage-sipping, goat-keeping habits of himself and his coven of patients. I was a year into my doctoral thesis, too – a mathematic model of sexual selection: how height and weight in humans is affected by polygenes, leaving out diet and other environmental variables. (Large groupings of genes, each one of which will have an infinitesimal effect on the growing organism, but which together add up to something significant, are known as 'polygenes'.) Those were the days in which I was having to work late into the night on my thesis, and, what was more, by candlelight. Godfrey felt that electricity had something to do with the increasing amount of mental disturbance (or whatever it was that was so described): one had to be careful in our contemporary society. Since he also felt that the colourings and preservatives put in food could affect the mental processes, and was heartily laughed at, loudly, at the time, by nutritionists, it is perhaps too early in the world's history to declare him wrong about electricity.

Where was I? Oh yes, my concluding conversation with Godfrey. I wept, as usual. He was benign and fatherly.

'Mad!' I wept.
'Don't say that,' he rebuked, 'these people are as sane as you, probably more so.' (Or words to that effect.)
'I wasn't talking about them. I was talking about you!' I remember saying, through my tears.
He breathed in, hard, rolled his big brown eyes upwards in the attempt to forestall wrath and said:
'Poor Sandra, you're tired! Why don't you give up this silly work of yours, and help me with something really worthwhile!'

It was shortly after this that I left. But I continue to hold Godfrey in some esteem. He and his kind pulled up the blinds, as it were, on those long dark lonely corridors of madness: made it almost a sign of grace, a gift from God, to have madness in the family. The blinds have been lowered a little since, of course: the mad are grouped with the socially inadequate, and certainly not admired any more, as they were in the sixties and seventies; their asylums are closed and they are left to stand about on street corners, occasionally gibbering and erratically jerking, and from time to time raping, strangling or mutilating a passer-by; but they are not hidden, strait-jacketed, to be a source of secret shame and disgrace.

My stepfather Simon died of cancer of the stomach when I was twenty. Cancer was then a word still scarcely spoken: a hushed whisper: a misfortune: yet another source of family disgrace. But little by little, as madness came out of the closet, so did cancer. The dying crawled out of their back rooms to sit at the family table, and guests even came to tea: and Nancy Reagan told the world she had cancer of the breast. Some things change for the better.

So good for Godfrey the Goatherd, say I, and may his herds flourish, and his dope grow strong and green, but not with me. No. After Godfrey I lived with my Professor for a little; and then, when that broke up, on my own, until in a moment of weakness, after all the business of the hard-rock little Planet Athena, I married Matthew.

19

Where Will We Live?

'Jack,' I say, 'Jack, where will we live?' How hard it is to be a free spirit!

'Why,' he says, 'in the van.' So I am to live like a gypsy, am I, without a postal address?

'You take your washing round to your wife,' I say. 'I can hardly do that.'

'No,' he says. 'She'd put your delicate things through the heavy soiled white wash. She does that to me when she's angry. I have no socks left unshrunk.'

'I'll take them to the launderette,' I say, 'along with mine. Your future will be soft socks, delicately laundered.' Anything I will do for him, anything: or that part of him which so wonderfully, nightly, becomes me. I will bath in the public wash-house, if I must.

'You'll miss your work,' he says, 'your friends.'

'I'll sit in the van and write a book,' I say. 'I'll follow you to every gig. I will never be bored. We could,' I add cautiously, 'get a radio telephone.'

'I suppose so,' he says, 'but it might be the beginning of the end.'

'Then we won't have one,' I say. 'There will be only you and only me.'

'Anne keeps my diary,' he says. 'The bookings come through to her. I call her once a week, from a pay phone. Or go round.'

'I'd rather you called her,' I say.

'I think I'll have to,' he said, 'at least for a time. She'd got herself into a real state. Perhaps I'd better call her tomorrow, calm her down.'

'I'd rather you didn't,' I say.

'I have to have someone to keep the diary,' he says.

'I'll do it,' I say.

'How can you, from the van?' he asks. And he starts to sing in a husky voice, like some old, old black folk singer, 'Smoke

Gets In Your Eyes'. I realise he's a little drunk. He gets through two bottles of wine a day at least, and quite a lot of beer. Playing the trumpet is thirsty work. Matthew drank no more than half a bottle of wine a day, and unlimited Perrier water.

A kind of cold creeps into my heart: and worse, I have the sensation that the hot hard fleshy tool around which my own soft flesh is wrapped, is not flesh at all, but cold metal: like some kind of makeshift rod – wire coat hanger not hazel dowsing twig. The effect is the same: the wire twists and turns as does the twig, but the process is different.
'What's the matter?' he asks. 'Don't you like my voice?'
'I love your voice,' I say. 'I love you,' and the magic works, and he is warm again, and the ghostly lover, the grave dweller, who was there for a moment, is gone.

Jennifer Says . . .

'But where will you and Jack live?' asks Jennifer.
'In the back of the van,' I say.
'It won't last,' she says.
'It will,' I say.
'He'll go back to his wife.'
'He won't,' I say.
'She keeps his diary,' says Jennifer. 'He'll have to. And there's Frances to think of and one thing leads to another. What he usually does is live in the van all summer and with Anne all winter.'

We're whispering. We're in the kitchen. It's four in the morning. I couldn't sleep, and got up and came downstairs, braving ghosts. I found Jennifer wrapped in a blanket, head on the table, dozing. Sandy felt too hot and sweaty to have her in his bed, she said. So she got out of it.

Hearing this, I feel an expression on my face that quite shocks me. I remind myself of my grandmother. I borrow Jennifer's mirror – she has one in her bag, of course, and study my face, and yes, there it is, in my pursed and disapproving lips! My father's narrow, perfect Gestapo lips – he must have been the handsomest SS officer in the whole German army – but on them my grandmother's expression whenever she said 'I don't approve of that!' or 'Oh no, it wouldn't be safe'. Is this the result of environmental variables, or of the dreaded polygenes? What the hell; I pull myself together. If Jennifer wants to play masochist it's nothing to do with me. I rearrange my face so it displays less disapproving lineaments.

'She won't have him back,' I say.

'She will,' says Jennifer. 'She's the kind who thinks half a man is better than no man at all. And he has no right to ask you to live in the back of a van. What will people think of you? You'll amount to nothing.'

'The back of the van's just fine by me,' I say. I, Sandra Harris, Stargazer Supreme, Lady Astronomer, aged forty-two, non-procreator of the race, herself an end in itself, not a mere hander-on of life, will live in a van to the end of her days, if that's what Jack the mad trumpeter decrees.

This woman I hardly know, who appears to be me, goes back to bed and settles her body in beside the man she hardly knows. His hairy arm moves round her smooth back. Forty-two she may be but her skin's as smooth and pale and freshly ironed as ever, and she's off with the raggle-taggle gypsies oh. Oh, and oh, and oh again.

'Hush,' he says. 'Remember Frances.' In some matters, let it be said, he is more delicate than she.

20

The Unclassed

The 'unclassed' is a word seldom used these days, but much in vogue at the turn of this century. It refers to people who by virtue of personal choice, happenstance (a very recent word, this one) have lost their position in the world. Or who chose to throw it all away and live in vans. They may be defiant about it, or wretched, or try to hide it, but those who remain firmly fixed and secure in their position in the world, who make lasting and sensible marriages, who look after their money properly, who have clean tablecloths at properly laid tables, recognise them for what they are at once, and look to their pockets, and to their daughters. It is often, but not always, a matter of money.

The classed sleep with the unclassed but do not marry them, because then they become unclassed themselves.

These are the ranks of the unclassed:

Any man or woman who married too far above or below them on the social scale.
Any woman divorced and not speedily re-marrying, preferably her lover.
Any man made redundant and not quickly re-employed at a higher salary.
Anyone on Social Security.
Anyone dying of an incurable disease.
Anyone 'in the media'. That is to say, anyone questioning or commenting on a society in a way disruptive to that society.
Actors, artists, writers, musicians and so on, who seem to prefer the company of the unclassed to that of the classed, and who form a demi-monde, of some slight interest to the classed, who will sometimes have one or two to dinner at a time.

(Painters, in particular, oddly, often make great efforts to appear classed. In England they appointed each other RAs, that is to say, Royal Academicians, and put on dinner jackets and smoke cigars and comment on the wine, but it doesn't really work.)

Anyone whose parents do not have a fixed abode, or are not married.

Anyone who was born as the result of a genetic experiment, or conceived in a test-tube, by in-vitro fertilisation.

Do you understand? It is not a matter of snobbery (a bus driver can be as classed as a stockbroker) but of belonging, or not belonging, either intentionally (which is at least something) or unintentionally by virtue of birth, which is – as the French say – bas de gamme. The unclassed are rubbish and that's the fact of it. Yet there are so many of us, and more every day, test-tubes popping all over the land.

Astronomers are not normally unclassed. But Sandra Harris, astronomer, forty-two, struggling to be classed all her life, by way of passing exams, gaining degrees, changing partners, moving house, making and saving money, pretending her past did not exist, was de-classed yet again when she discovered the mouldy Planet Athena (mouldy! would that it were. Mould implies moisture, warmth, fungus, life) and became the object of media attention, and not even marrying Matthew Sorensen made it any better. Stargazer Sandra!

To be unclassed is one of the most painful experiences of being alive, if you ask Sandra Sorensen, S.S., or anyone in a Social Security queue for the first time.

Yet Jack the mad trumpeter seeks unclassification willingly, embraces it for all our sakes. That's why I love him.

21

How's Your Pains?

'How's your pains?' asked Frances the next day. She must have fallen asleep while sunbathing; her system had broken down and her long left leg was bright red, and her long right leg was pale.

'Much better,' I say. She doesn't seem too pleased.

'Would you like to borrow a Tampax?' she asks, and I realise she wants to be sure I'm actually bleeding, which will prevent my sexual congress with her father. Little does she know.

In actual fact I was now hardly bleeding at all any more: perhaps my body, knowing where its maximum pleasure lay, was taking steps to make itself properly available to Jack the mad trumpeter. Buggery is okay, but not okay: not quite true love. What is the best that can be done in certain circumstances is always in danger of being the thing that needs to be done: like valium or heroin: an addiction, self-defeating: pleasure turning into necessity.

'The curse!' laments Frances. 'Why do you think God invented it? Punishment, I suppose. Serving women right.' We are sitting next to each other on the bus. Jack is up front with Sandy arguing over the day's programme.

'But why should we be punished?' I had a feeling she might somehow know, that she possessed her father's intuition, would put her finger right on it.

'For being such messy things,' she said. 'God didn't get us right, if you ask me, something went wrong, so He's taking it out on us. Do you think I'm mad? I'm always saying things like that. People at school say I'm mad.' She spoke with the complacency of her age: glad to be mad.

I wonder what it would be like to have her as my daughter. She's sixteen; I'm forty-two. She was born in the year of a termination, the one I had by Godfrey the Coatherd. I am revising my opinion of Frances. I rather like having her about. I might even teach her to read, write and think, as her mother has so singularly failed to do. Her father, of course, cares nothing for the education of a daughter. On the whole he thinks the better informed someone is the more boring they are.

'Discover a planet!' I found myself apologising the previous night. 'Anyone can discover a planet! All you have to do is have the right backing and look in the right place.'

I know it is not given to many of us women to make precisely that statement, but its like is made up and down the country by successful women in various professions, as male members wilt and quail.

'But, darling, it's only a *little* promotion.'

'I won't really be making more than you, darling, not if you take the babyminder into account.'

'Darling, I'm only the token woman on the Board.'

'Darling, they're so short of women to be Dames they'll choose just anyone. Now to be an OBE, like you, is *really* something.'

'I only make all this money because the public has no taste. The more you make, the worse you are. Everyone knows that!'

And buggery is all the rage, in certain circles. If you think there's a connection, that's up to you. Male frustration constructively contained. I'm not complaining; Sandra the Stargazer is not complaining, only mentioning. The way round it is to lie there and enjoy it. That way family life continues. I might have got on better with Matthew if he had only heard of it.

22

A Certain Rhythm

What, live without a fixed address? Me? I'm not sure about all this. Receive no letters? I am accustomed to certain rhythms in my life. I like the morning paper to come through the letterbox. I like my day to start with very cold orange juice. I like the sense of my mind starting from cold, like the engine of my car, to its agreeable morning purr. I like my fingers on the computer keyboard; the pen in my hand. I like a full-length mirror on the wall, unsmudged, unsmeared. In fact, I feel pretty much as my grandmother must have done, when she declined to abscond with her gypsy lover.

I, on the other hand, like Mad Jack's stubbly chin: I like his wide mouth, his even teeth, his bright eyes and long fingers. I like the music he makes. I like his past, meeting up with mine to form this powerful present. If I have to, I will do without my certain rhythm, and think the privilege of a fixed address well lost for love.

I sit at the window where lately the splashes of blood appeared and disappeared – there is no sign of them now – clearly, the way to deal with these little demonstrations of a traumatic past, seeping through the barriers so sensibly erected by our conscious minds, is to ignore them, as one might the tantrum of a naughty child. I watch the Band getting out of the van, instruments glinting in the pale light. For once their voices are lowered – in deference to what? Me? Frances? I hardly imagine so. More likely the moon. Jack, long, lean-thighed, quick moving, somehow elongated, fit for a Goya portrait. My breath catches in my throat. My heart lurches. I speak advisedly. Love it may be, but the symptoms of love and death are not so dissimilar. I have an ECG trace of my own heart to prove it. (Where? Where are my belongings? Where are the traces of my history?) I have always travelled light, but this is going too far. I should have taken more from Matthew's house. I should not have provoked him. Now he has control of my past, as a witch has control of the person whose fingernail clippings she possesses. I thought I was happy enough with the contents of the nylon bag I brought with me in the bus – I thought that some money in the bank, a cheque book, a credit card or so, an address book with the numbers of friends and colleagues, and a change of pants and a change of jeans was all I needed – my past, after all, being carried in my memory if I needed to refer to it, my present being an ongoing situation – but here I am, wanting sight and feel, the physical actual sight and feel of a strip of blue, waxed, lined paper containing a portion of my cardiac history. Oh, how much weaker am I than I thought: where is my home? where are my slippers? – and I remember how I once did possess, in my late twenties, a pair of mauve high-heeled fur-lined slippers of wonderful vulgarity, which I can only have bought to annoy Godfrey the Goatherd – whatever became of them? – of the copper-bottomed saucepans I like? my manuscripts? My familiar desk is still at Central, it's true, and in it the kind of pleasant, familiar things one keeps in office desks – nail varnish, love letters, unanswered fan letters, a few floppy discs which contain my attempts at writing, as recorded by a kindly secretary attached to the Wild Life programme, the producers of which spend so much time hovering over burrows or lying in wait for foxes – the miracles of nature taking for ever to film – that she is only too glad of something to do, if only my typing. Perhaps the ECG trace is in my desk at Central?

On this strip of pale blue waxed paper that I now so irrationally miss, is the record of the pattern made by my heart in one of its occasional attacks of tachycardia, when it reverts to its foetal speed, some 200 beats the minute. The pattern is aesthetically pleasing: a steady, satisfying, regular beat driving across the paper, as a pen drives along the page; it is just that the upstrokes and downstrokes are far too close together for comfort – as they can be, to continue the analogy, in various groups of words.
'Pipetting up palpitating placenta' for example, and all those s's – Starlady Sandra, Sandra Sorenson – but that I daresay is fanciful. These attacks of tachycardia (see what I mean? the

upstrokes again? the overheated rhythm?) are brought about, depending on what doctor you care to listen to, by black coffee, alcohol, a shortage of potassium, stress, undisclosed emotion, the attempt to deny the past, or by the possession of an extra bundle of nemones in the heart, through which the electric cardiac charge can short-circuit. (Oh Daddy-oh, was this your doing? A defect, running through your genes, or those of my mad mother? Or just a copying mistake in the DNA?) The ailment is professionally linked – doctors, writers, journalists and media folk tend to suffer from it – nature's way, perhaps, of eventually phasing out those people too sharp for their own good or that of the species – the sick should really die off before they can reproduce, and the weak remain unprotected – a point I put to a casualty doctor while he prepared to return my heart to normal by injecting intravenous Verapamil, but he remained grim faced and merely wrote something in my notes. (I took the opportunity of reading them, later – 'patient agitated and rambling'.) These medical men are not great ones for laughing on duty. I daresay my father was not a bundle of laughs as he worked. Tamara, of course, laughed a lot, rather as poor Mrs Rochester did, up and down dark corridors. As a child, I frequently woke to its sound. My version of the primal scene. Well now, my heart, as recorded on this particular strip of blue paper, was in the throes of one of its pets, its little demonstration of its traumatic past – I do try to take my own advice and ignore its childish tantrums, and sometimes it works, gives up and reverts to normal, but more often nowadays it requires the paternal intervention of the medical profession, and injections of this and that. The 'that' on the blue strip I so particularly miss is the record of the time they injected stryamine intravenously, instead of verapamil, and first I had a catch in my throat, of the kind I have now, waiting for Jack in the moonlight, my love, and then my heart lurched, and lurched again and I cried out first in love and then in terror, as I died, I swear I died, and came alive again, and there is the record on the page – the heart just stopping, stopping, the straight line running across the page, unmarked, running across, not even upstroked, down-stroked by palpitating placentas or Sandra Sorenson, or Nazi SS; then, thank God, thank God, starting up again all over the place, the beats leaping out of control, off the paper, like seismological needles shaken right off the page, then by some miracle the steady habitual beat reasserting itself, starting up again: regular, even, conventional. Thank you, Daddy: you engineered me well, whatever else you did.

'Thank you, Doctor,' I say, when I am able. 'I see I am alive again.'

But they don't care for jokes, as I say. When he's gone Sister says, 'We'd run out of Verapamil. But you're all right now, that's the main thing.'

'That's the main thing,' I agree.

But now, as my heart lurches, I think of death as well as love. I wonder where my home is, and why I have never had one. 'Home is where the heart is,' Frances said today. She speaks so seriously, her great eyes so solemn, uttering the myths of our society with such reverence I don't like to dent her faith and start arguing. Oh, pitter-pat, pitter-pat, returning to the pre-natal state!

Starlady Sandra Sorenson, S.S.S. An extra S, an extra bundle of nemones. What terrifies me is the way it all ties up.

23

Highs and Lows

Jack said, between numbers, between swigs of red rough wine, as if casually, but I know by now it was not, 'Someone in town was looking for you.'
'Who?' I asked, alarmed.

I wanted us to go to bed but the party was still going on. It was past three. We had to be up by seven. Nobody seemed to care. Jennifer stifled her yawns and smiled brightly. She knew it was no use protesting. The Band was winding down from its night's performance. Nothing a musician despises more than a party pooper, someone who can't stand the pace, puts earplugs in their ears, hides the drink, departs, or stands between him and the girl of a passing, drunken dream. Frances had gone to sleep over the table: well, that was allowed. Her red hair spread over a surface dark with spilt wine, dirty plates, sodden labels, bread crusts and broken glass. (Jennifer had had beans soaking all day. She'd cooked them up when the Band returned. She put salt in the boiling water. Salt should never go near beans. It toughens the skins: makes them more indigestible, more fast-food. Never mind. Who was I to say? I am a lady astronomer. They will forgive me if I keep my knowledge specific to my trade, and profess ignorance of nearly everything else, from how to keep a man to how to find my way to how not to cook beans.) Frances's delicate white hand curled in her sleep, around the encrusted cup used as a serving ladle. She had not lost her virginity to Douglas, only her heart. He was married, and had foolishly told her so. I was proud of her: not because she was virtuous, but because her will had triumphed over her inclination. I felt somehow it was my doing. I had shown her it was possible to get by without being too agreeable.

The instruments were out. Pedro was playing folk, Jack New Orleans, and Karl something that sounded like the Birdie

Song. Glasses were filled from mammoth plastic containers that looked like petrol cans, and whose interiors were corroded, I was convinced, by the crude red wine they contained, of the vinegary kind Jesus was no doubt offered on the cross. Thirst quenching, pain deadening. Much of it got spilt: flung away with cries of disgust, and then more, optimistically, poured. Jennifer did not clear up, though I knew she longed to. The sight of a dishcloth would have offended. The talk was mostly of why all were playing in different keys and how this could be remedied. It was not. Sandy was convinced Pedro's guitar was a banjo. Pedro became angry. When he was angry he moved his crowned tooth with the tip of his tongue, and glared, gat-toothed, but it did not stop him playing. Strands of his long greasy hair fell into his wine: he tossed his head back in his rage and splattered the room. I was glad I was wearing my black T-shirt and not my white. There was some familiar talk about how the Band was being billed by the Festival Organisers: fists and feet were banged: murders and rapes planned. Bente sat patiently smiling as if nothing untoward were happening. Suddenly she began to cry, and left the room. Hughie followed her. Deprived of one of their number, they contented themselves with agreeing amongst themselves that he was a rotten player anyway, and no loss to anyone.

It would have been difficult in such circumstances for any ghost to materialise. I wouldn't if I were it, not if my ears were in any way responsive. I wondered if I was in the right company, and thought perhaps I was. I preferred this to gliding amongst Matthew's friends, in my little black dress, answering questions about the Planet Athena or discussing the property boom, and drinking Muscadet, or in Godfrey's world, in my Laura Ashley smock, discussing ley lines and listening to nonsense about birth signs, or with my academic friends, in skirt and sweater, agitating about university appointments, the achievements of children, the vintages of wine. Different worlds, different parties.

Though frankly I would rather be in bed with Jack, and was hurt that he was somehow pushing at the borders of our unspoken spheres of influence – like Russia invading

Afghanistan, the US establishing its bases in Turkey – and claiming these late hours for the Band, not allocating them to me.

Jack's idea to get out the wine: Jack's idea to start playing. Jack's idea to keep everyone out of bed as well as himself. Jack was angry. Someone was looking for me. Well, what made me think I could just disappear, that I was of so little interest to the world they'd just let it happen? Was I not a kind of fulcrum, that present point where the past and future balanced, where the dead met the living, not to mention heaven and earth: they wouldn't let me go so easily.

'Who was looking for me?' I asked again, after Jack had finished playing 'The Red Flag' (or 'Maryland', depending on who was paying for the gig) while Pedro played 'Strawberry Fair' and Karl a fandango. Oddly, it sounded rather good.
'Man or woman?'
'Don't know,' he said. 'It was just a note with your name on it, on the Festival noticeboard.'
'Written or typed?'
'Handwritten, in green ink. Some lover, I expect.'
'Why would I have a lover who used green ink?'
'I don't know,' he said. 'I don't know anything about you.'
'If it seemed urgent,' I remark, 'why didn't you bring it back for me?'
'Because it's nothing to do with me. If that's how you want to live, lovers leaving you urgent messages all over France, that's your business.'

Karl has taken up 'Hindustan'. Jack can't resist playing too. And Pedro. They manage a fair rendition. I give up and go to bed, on my own. No ghosts appear.

24

A Hot Time in the Old Town Tonight

Yes indeed! They're all here. Jack's wife, Matthew and Jude from Central TV with her frizzy hair, her powerful personality, her muddy complexion and her straight nose. They all turned up today.

Jude and Matthew have the last two rooms in town, Jude in the Hôtel de Cheval Blanc and Matthew (naturally) in the Hôtel de France, where they take American Express Cards.

There is nowhere for Anne, so she is sleeping next door to Jack and me, in Frances's room.

I write this by moonlight: sitting at the haunted window, writing pad on my knee. Jack lies asleep in the bed. He had a great deal to drink tonight, and besides, the day's events have shaken him. Out like a light, lucky him.

What made me think I could just disappear? I am the point where the mad, the bad and the infamous meet. I am an ordinary person, but carried to extremes.

'Come back to bed,' says Jack.
'No,' say I.

This is what happened.

The minibus left the Hôtel de Ville at nine forty-five. The first gig was to be at ten thirty, au-dessous du Monument aux Morts. The Band had actually held a *meeting*, after breakfast, to decide what to wear, what to play, and various technical matters about breaks and keys. A week into the tour, and they were actually getting it together. As for me, I was practising inefficiency. It had occurred to me – forget the personal

satisfactions my failings aroused in other people – that ef-
ficiency is neither wanted nor needed in the modern world.
There is not enough to do and far too many people to do it.
Better just for all of us to bumble along. I wore a white T-shirt
– Frances had kindly washed it for me – and jeans. She had
lent me a pair of her bikini briefs, too.

'Fit enough to travel today?' asked Jennifer.

'I'm feeling much better,' I said, politely.

'That's good,' she said. 'Because we can't have poor Frances
stuck away on nursing duty, can we? After all, this is her
annual holiday.' Meaning, the likes of you can holiday any
time, with other people's husbands, forget about the likes of
us. I was feeling pretty good, I must say (except for this pain
which would suddenly dart in from the left to somewhere
beneath the navel, hover for half a second, and then depart:
enough to startle, not quite to hurt. I rather liked it.) And I
was looking rather good. Too much sex may weaken you, but
it gives you a pleasant swollen-mouthed glow as well. I looked
better than Jennifer did. She had a bad mosquito bite just
beneath her left eye. Perhaps that was the matter with her. I
offered her some Boots' Sting Relief, without which I never
step abroad.

'I expect one of the good things about getting older,' says
Jennifer, 'is that the curse gets shorter.'

Some women just sit there, working out how old you are from
things you let slip – old films you say you've seen: what age
you were when you had a beehive hairdo – and Jennifer was
one of them. But I blamed her husband Sandy – he was one
of those men who talk about their wives as 'old bags' and talk
about their sexual conquests in their presence. So I forgave
her.

'It certainly does,' I said brightly. But I thought, for all I felt
so good, I would call in and see a doctor when I got to
Blasimon-les-Ponts. The French have this agreeable system
which actually allows you to go to one and *pay* for a diagnosis
and treatment, which they will actually discuss with you. In
England doctors like to keep their conclusions to themselves,
or written up in very secret notes. You are not even allowed
to know your own blood pressure, as registered by them. A
strange, barbaric country. (This can only be my father talking:
sometimes, when my mouth is not moved by my polygenes

into its disapproving moue, I feel it stretched into a kind of Dr Strangelove grimace – tee hee hee! the mouth goes in a kind of sadistic mirthlessness and I am then quick to reform my thoughts and feelings, making them, as far as I am able, more mine than my forebears. What more can a girl do?)

Besides, visiting the doctor would occupy the time between eleven thirty and twelve thirty, while we waited to go up to the school canteen for our free lunch. Salades de saison would be served to some 200 musicians and hangers on, along with pork chops and white beans which Frances hated and Jack loved and I put up with, and musicians from other nations, who had strong religious feelings and cultural preferences, would noisily refuse.

Jennifer and Sandy sat in the front of the bus. He drove. She offered advice, consolation and sips of Perrier water through straws, while he reproached her for various matters over which she had no control (the weather, her bosom) and those she had ('look! there, there! a parking space!' 'It's a double yellow line, you fool!'). There was room for a third up front, but the double bass sat between them. Well, it would, wouldn't it. She had to lean across it, the instrument which spoiled her life, keeping him out all hours, splitting his loyalty, which she gladly did. I will say this for Sandy, that he exuded an air of great genial sexual confidence – he blinked and winked into the morning sun and preened himself in his wife's esteem.

Pedro sat behind Sandy: his eyes closed. He was asleep or meditating. His reddish beard glittered in the sun. His body was littered with talismans of one kind or another. He was barely talking to either Jack or me: Jack, on account of being brought in the night before on the wrong chord, or some such matter I did not fully understand: but Jack, according to Pedro, had done it once too often. Jack for his part merely said Pedro was impossible, and didn't understand jazz. He should stick to folk, where he was so much at home. (The Jumpers despised folk almost as much as Dixie.) These quarrels would flare up amongst the Band, rage for a time, and then subside over a glass of beer on a good break. Jennifer and Frances were used to it. I was not. Pedro was not speaking to me because I had refused to sign his copy of *Athena, planet of the Aquarian Age, bringer of peace* published by the Astrological Society. ('But why won't you?' Jack asked. 'Because it's an outrage to common sense,' I had replied, and Jack said, 'For God's sake sign, or he'll break another string tonight. The man's a menace. He's bringing the whole band down.' But I wouldn't.) Now, as I say, Pedro's soft, kind eyes, with their cold deeper level of hate and resentment (I had seen the same in Godfrey's) were closed. Sandy speeded up to go over the railway crossing for the sake of the extra bump; he likes to do that.

'Hold tight, everyone!' cried out Jennifer, and everyone held tight and the instruments twanged and wine bottles clattered and Frances shrieked, and a strong smell of body odour came from Stevie the trombone player, and Jack and I held hands.

I went to the doctor's surgery, just up the road from the Crédit Lyonnais, and sat only briefly in a small white room amongst posters of poisonous snakes and mushrooms, before being allowed into his consulting room. The French seem a healthy lot – or else begrudge paying doctors money. Doctor Tarval was, or so I thought at first, a not very bright young man in his middle twenties, with an owl face, cropped hair and perfect French manners. Language was a slight problem, since he spoke no English, but the vocabulary of pain can be mimed. He seemed to understand: required me to go behind a curtain and pee into a container, and come back at four o'clock. I asked why, but he was almost as unforthcoming as an English doctor, and said there would be time enough to discuss it then. Jennifer and Frances had come with me. Sandy had locked the keys inside the van, somehow circumventing all Renault's ingenuity to prevent just such a thing happening (the Band blamed Pedro, clearly today's whipping boy, for leaning on a lock at just the wrong time) and fortunately after the shirts and instruments had been taken out – but not the Band's cassettes, which it was Jennifer's job to display – for which Sandy roundly and publicly blamed Jennifer. Jennifer had for once had enough: her eyes glinted not with tears but with rage, and she shouted (to the amazement of the passers-by – the French are a controlled lot), 'You mad disgusting insane bully, sell your own fucking cassettes. They stink, anyway. Call yourself a bass player? You couldn't strum a mandolin.' Well, she wasn't going to live that down for quite a while, was she, especially since even I know that a mandolin is a very difficult instrument to play.

So I took her off to a café and bought her a brandy, and Frances came too, and Jennifer cried and shrieked for a little, and I said Sandy must be feeling a fool for having so stupidly locked the keys in – she hadn't thought of that. Her loyalty was so ingrained, she believed he must have somehow done it on purpose – and she would do better to laugh than cry. And presently she felt better, and told us a little about her past – an only child brought up by an elderly father, without the gift for friendship, envying other children their large families, their busy lives: Sandy's secretary originally, then deposing his wife, moving on, taking over their three children, having two of her own; but they were now almost grown and the loneliness was closing in again. People know so much about themselves, I thought, yet remain so powerless to control their lives. It explained Jennifer's 'come on, everybody' syndrome; the need to be necessary, the short cut to being loved. I thought then that it would make a good short story.
'I'm sorry for his first wife,' I said. 'With you coming flashing along like a dreadnought.'
'You can talk!' said Jennifer, and Frances shrieked, 'Hark at her!' and pointed at me, and downed a brandy, fifteen going on forty, and we all laughed some more. It was a good half hour. We were all, I suppose, under what might be called tension. But I thought perhaps I was undergoing some kind of sea change, due to the sun's heat, and the music, and Jack, and all this writing down of the past; and that perhaps there was such a thing as 'discovering yourself' and that indeed you might end up being nicer than you thought, at least on the top layer. Then I went to the doctor.

When I came out I saw Matthew's car outside the Hôtel de France. Shiny Mercedes are rare in this part of the country. They tend to keep to motorways and major cities, where they don't get dusty and scratched. It took up too much of the road: other vehicles queued to get past. There was no doubt it was my husband's car. I leaned against a wall.

'What's the matter?'

I looked round, I can only suppose wildly, for I am a contained kind of person, usually, and found myself staring straight into Jude from Central's eyes. I fainted.

I have never fainted before. Very occasionally I have wept, but never fainted. It is not pleasant, and pleasant. Not pleasant because of the black whirling nauseous tunnel which swirls through your head and sucks you in and takes you over; pleasant because of the sheer sensuousness of it all, as body takes over from mind, simply takes it upon itself to wipe it out. I wonder if animals spend a lot of their time in this agreeable, sexy state? I hope so, for their sakes.

I need time to collate everything that's happened inside my head and out of it, although for the most part I'd just been sitting and writing while I waited for my lover to turn up and the erotic stupor to take over. Like being on drugs. But things had been going on, more than even I quite understood. The past was catching up with me – well, that was okay; I'd just stood still and let it – but here it was in practical reality, in the stolid shape of Matthew and the lean and hungry one of Jude – and I hadn't reckoned on that. No wonder I fainted. I was playing for time. Still am.

Where was I? Back in the café, feeling fine, my wits collected, my eyes wary, Jude saying Central had sent her down to make sure I was okay.

'Going to come up with next month's programme, you mean,' I say.

'To make sure you're okay,' she repeats, patiently. 'You can have a year's sabbatical, they say. They understand what pressure you've been under.'

'What does that mean? I haven't been under any pressure at all.'

That stops her. I just fell in love, lust, with Jack and ran off. I wasn't under pressure; I was bored.

'That's not what Alison and Bobby told me. They would have come themselves if only they'd had the time. Anyway, it's a face-saving thing, isn't it,' she says vaguely. 'If Central are going to give you a year's sabbatical they have to justify it to

142

the accountants. So it doesn't look so much like a bribe, more like a medical matter.'

'You mean they want to get rid of me for a year?'

'Oh God, Sandra,' she complains, 'you're difficult.'

'I'm not difficult,' I say. 'I just like to know what's going on.'

And so on. There'd been a small piece in the *Mail* about my going off with a jazz band to the South of France. Central's spies had followed it up. I wonder who'd put the piece in?

'Anyway,' said Jude, 'either way, they want to know what's happening. Production dates are looming and there's been nothing from you.'

'I just can't be bothered,' say I. 'Have another drink.'

The sounds of Dr Jazz echoed up the street from the War Memorial.

'You look very odd,' she says. 'Exhausted and not very clean. Are you living rough? Do you want to come home with me? We can fly back together from Bordeaux, at five o'clock.'

'The thing is,' I say, 'I have nowhere to go, once I'm back. My husband threw me out.'

She looks surprised.

'That's not what he says. He says you had some kind of breakdown. You know he didn't get his Judgeship, or whatever it's called?' She sounds severe.

'Actually I didn't know that,' say I. 'Still, try, try, try again! He'll do it one day.'

'You know he's here in Blasimon-les-Ponts,' she says.

What's she playing at?

I rise.

'I'd better go and help the Band get back into the van,' I say. 'They're kind of locked out. It's the sort of thing that happens. See you around, I expect. Don't you just love this kind of Festival? There's two whole hours of Bulgarian State Folkdance at two this afternoon. That's in the stadium. They do a splendid knee-slapping turn. The thighs are a real turn-on.'

Even as I spoke, I wondered who and what I was betraying, for I heard myself fall back into the old media side-speak; the making of jokes where none should be. Jack was right: I had

143

become infected with the dreadful virus of urban worldliness, and there was no health in me. Some vital sensibility had been deadened by long exposure to studio lights. I could not maintain my interest in Bulgarian wedding dances for more than an hour at a time. They entranced Jack. They wearied me. We were not altogether at one. It had to be faced. I was at home with Jude. I did not trust her, but I was at home with her. We talked, as they say ('they' being those I most despised), the same language. I could laugh with the Band, and listen to the Band, and spend my nights with the leader of the Band, and involve and concern myself with the women of the Band, but who could I speak to in the Band who would have the slightest notion what I was going on about? While Jude would get at least 80 per cent of what I had to say, and put a researcher on to the other 20 per cent, checking on the detail. Why, one day a team of us might even come to some conclusion about the Nature of Experience, given a little help from the Religious Affairs department.

'Look,' I said to Jude, using the language I deplored, but knew she would understand, 'I'm sorry, but I need some space. I'm trying to make some kind of choice here; you understand?'
She'd lately produced a Drama Series called *Life Choice*: she ought to understand. Women wondering whether to change jobs, leave husbands, have babies, tell lovers they had AIDS, that kind of thing. A real bore, straight off the pages of *New Society* – unless the choice happens to be yours, when of course it can only be of considerable interest.

'Okay,' Jude said, 'you can have till tomorrow.' (In radio they move slowly: they're all on thirty-seven-year contracts and it feels like it. In telly it's here today and gone tomorrow, so stamp on a foot, make a mark, stab a back, while you can. I love it!) 'But at least go and talk to Matthew. He's come all this way to see you.'
'You talk to him,' I said. 'What's more, you marry him.'
'He has asked me to,' she said.

I remember the moment when I discovered Athena – poor Athena! I had been so angry with her! All she did was whirl about in her own rather unexpected orbit; a simple thing, a lump of stone, incapable of reproduction, helpless in the grip of her own qualities, which kept her suspended there between heaven and hell, and not so different, when I come to think of it, from myself. And what a shock it was, understanding how all the figures worked out, wondering why it hadn't been obvious before: the same kind of shock, come to think of it, as fainting. Not an altogether pleasant shock, because one's been such a fool not to have realised it all before; but pleasant because it all works out so well, fits together so admirably. Oh, what a flash of light. Matthew and Jude.

'Wait a moment,' I said. 'But you love that other fellow, that director.' (See Appendix III!)

'It's never done me any good,' she said. 'And I'm very fond of Matthew; not in the neurotic way I love Andreas.'

All this talk of love! It is absurd.

'But I don't want to hurt you in any way,' she added. Well she wouldn't, would she?

'Matthew needs building up,' said Jude. 'You really sapped his confidence.'

'Poor Matthew,' said I.

And there I will leave that scene. I went up in the bushes behind the castle and there Jack the mad trumpeter and I embraced, and the sun shone, and the butterflies crossed bluely past my hazy eyes, and green grasses tickled my arms, and oh, oh, oh again, but I don't know, I was scarcely concentrating. Of course one doesn't have to: in fact it often seems the less one does the better it goes, only afterwards you can hardly remember, and I like the memory to be there, the seventh sense still feeling its input, only barely tamped down, waiting to go again; while at Greenwich I turn and open the dome to the skies, or at Central I wait for the studio lights to shine, or the computer at Imperial College to come on line, or the graphite rods to rise (I'm talking about the old Magnox, I know; now all but obsolete) and the pile to start up, and the mind, which the body feeds – I swear to you, for all this love and lust, the body is just something that feeds the mind, through the seven senses – to get going –

Look, what am I doing on this hillside with this itinerant musician, while everything collapses around me? Jude means to move into my horrible house, and it instantly seems not so horrible, merely mine. She means to have my dreadful husband – and likewise the 'dreadful' fades and the 'my' looms.

'Is something the matter?' asks Jack.

'No,' I say.

'Frances said you went to the doctor.'

'I have a little hay fever,' I say, not the sort to claim pity for female problems. The pain seemed to have gone. Fainting had quite shaken it out of me. Afterwards Jack went off to lead the Band in a parade round the streets and I went to the Hôtel de France to face Matthew. Jude wasn't there. My husband was very formal and correct, in open-necked shirt, blue trousers, white socks and black city shoes.

'Did Jude pack for you?' I asked, ever curious.

'Jude's been very busy,' he said, 'but yes.'

'She certainly has,' I said. 'I've only been gone three weeks.'

'You haven't been idle,' he said. 'You look like the slut you are.' There was no suggestion of reconciliation, then.

'How long has it been going on between you and Jude?' One has to ask.

'Nothing's been "going on". After your leaving in the manner you did, I had no option but to look round for someone else.' His jaw is beginning to tauten, his lip to tremble; his nose is inflamed and his cheeks getting pinker by the minute. I understand now why he has come so far to speak to me. He wants not to speak, but to hit. We're in the bar of the Hôtel de France, however, not in our bedroom. He may have to restrain himself.

'You bitch,' he begins. 'You witch. Do you understand what you did to me? First you humiliate me in public, then you lose me the only thing I've ever wanted. You cold, cold bitch. Do you understand? Is there no way of getting through to you?'

'I hear what you say.' It is bound to madden him. It does. I don't like myself.

'I could kill you,' he says. I feel very depressed. I can see he is justified in his desire. I married him to suit myself. Well, he did the same to me but the strong (me) should look after the weak (him) and not let self interest win. I am sorry to see Jude falling into the same trap.

'How long was there between my predecessor going,' I asked

'and my arriving?' I had never thought to ask. That calmed him. It was clearly a matter of pride.

'Seven weeks and two days,' he said. 'She was another one!' Another one like me, by inference. Greedy, self-interested, loving him for his big house and his nose for a good bottle of wine, not *him*, the boy his mother had loved. Or perhaps she hadn't loved him. Some people are just born unlovable.

'Well, I'm sorry,' I said, with some sincerity. To my horror he began to cry. Seven weeks and two days. He'd be breaking his own record with Jude, I expected. At least I'd left more for Jude to clear up than a mouldy carrot in the Magimix.

'Don't do that,' I said, 'it's embarrassing.' So it was. The bar was filling up with African dancers; wild, lean men with feather headdresses and painted bodies. They made Matthew look very strange. I offered to go out and buy him a pair of canvas shoes from one of the market stalls, and that started him off again.

'You never even liked me,' he said. I shan't go on with this account. Neither of us came out of the episode well. He'd come because of the new divorce laws – which he himself, of course, had helped construct. He wanted a divorce as quickly as possible, and he wanted me to sign an affidavit as to my generally impossible behaviour, which I duly signed. He said he'd thought he'd better catch me while he could, before I disappeared – as he put it, smiling, his temper much improved now he had my signature, my mark, as if that somehow contained and controlled me, and now he could work magic spells on me in my absence – into the wild blue yonder. And I suppose he was right.

Jude came in on the dot of three, no doubt as planned. She'd had lunch at the Café des Routiers. I'd had none. My jeans were beginning to feel very loose upon me, and no longer agreeably tight. She'd had snails, faux-filet, a nice goat's cheese and café noir. I asked her. She seemed surprised, but Matthew explained my love of such detail.

'You might be able to get into my dresses,' I said. 'You'll have to go to all these functions and give dinner parties. It's part of the job. No such thing as a free lunch.'

'We're going to live very quietly,' said Matthew, 'and raise a family.'

147

Well! His jaw and her nose: her liveliness, his determination. 'I hope it's a boy,' I said, and left. What had seemed very trivial, being the sexual relationships of the childless, now attracted to itself, in my eyes, a certain gravity. If people, even the most unlikely, come together to raise children, there seems a certain inevitability about it all. And it is interesting how often it *is* the most unlikely, the least apparently suited, who want to have children, as if nature for ever scoops up those who stray too far from her net, and flings them back in there, willy-nilly. There! You of six foot four and you of four foot eight! Deviate from the norm, would you? Oh no. You Jewish Princess and you lumberjack – thought you'd keep it going your way? Not on your nelly – it's twins for you! Even the participants in these evolutionary dramas seem to feel surprised. They certainly look it in wedding photographs. No wonder the guests get drunk.

Matthew took me to the door. He handed the signed affidavit to Jude before he left the bar, surreptitiously, but I noticed all the same. He thought I'd snatch the paper back. He couldn't believe his luck. No doubt I'd signed away home, maintenance, everything. I didn't care. Jack would be pleased with me. Can't go one way, have to go the other.
'See you back at Central then?' asked Jude.
'I'll think about it,' I said.
'Don't think too long,' she said.
'Why – do you want my job as well?' I asked. But you can go on like that for ever. I said goodbye as nicely as I could, disappointed in her. I'd thought she was a romantic figure, and here she was, consenting to the missionary position for the sake of a gravelled drive and a nice letter box and my bath salts. I went down the road, drawn by the sound of the Band, squeezing back against shop fronts, as trails of enormous lorries did their after-lunch (fuck you) dash for wherever, feeling as affronted as Elizabeth Bennet when she turned down boring Mr Collins only to have her best friend Charlotte take him.

I wondered how much to tell Jack of all this and decided it would be very little. One of the benefits of being with someone so unacquainted with one's way of life and thought is that there can really be no point in the exchange of confidences

148

and the asking for advice. I have always been very bad at the latter. Jack, not being interested in my marriage, could hardly be interested in my divorce. And I could scarcely expect him to be sympathetic with the internal tumult, the nervousness, that tends to ensue when the one you think you're leaving turns out to be leaving you.

It was to my surprise that I discovered a plump, agitated figure weeping upon Frances's shoulder, as she sat on a stone bench beneath the trees of Blasimon-les-Ponts' central square, where the cars neatly parked in the shade, at that agreeable and tidy angle so admired by the French, but which leaves a useless triangle at either end of the row. The English, with their blunt four-square approach, at least find room for one more car. However, I daresay I digress. The weeping woman was of course Anne. The Band played on; 'Hindustan', followed by Jack singing in a hoarse croak 'The girls go crazy about the way I walk –' (walk, of course, being a euphemism for you-know-what) – rather bravely, I thought, in the circumstances. I sat down beside Anne. She moved abruptly away so that my flesh did not touch hers. I understood the feeling. I had not wanted to touch Jude after hearing her intention of marrying Matthew. He'd assured me nothing had been 'going on', but then he'd said to me all kinds of things that had not proved true – most importantly, that he'd do everything in his power to make me happy. Now I do not believe it is any man's obligation to make any woman happy, and I would not hold him to that – she should learn to make herself happy – but he should have refrained from making me actually unhappy.

Anne. I asked how she'd got there. She said by train. She glared at me. She had blue swollen eyes, and bits of her, not all, had been in the sun. The left side of her nose was particularly pink.
'Facing the engine,' I said. And Frances, said, interested, how do you know that, and I said well, she'd have been travelling south-west and getting the sun from the east, and Anne slapped Frances for general treachery, and Jack sang louder and louder and the crowd caught on and clapped and cheered and stamped. Anne didn't slap me. I would have, in her place. How did you know where Jack was?' I asked.

'He sent me a postcard,' she said. And I didn't believe her at first, but she took it out of her well-worn, very English, crocodile bag with its stiff metal clasp (people are extraordinary, really) and showed me a postcard of Blasimon-les-Ponts. She allowed me only a glimpse of the other side but I registered Jack's writing, a letter-post stamp, and a brief message. I am not slow. Anne put her trophy back in her horrid bag.

'I'm staying,' she said to me, defiantly.

'You can't come all this way and not stay,' I said, reasonably. I saw no reason now to be kind. 'Would you like me to ask at the Hôtel de France if there's a vacant room. I'm afraid the town is very crowded. I expect Frances has told you. The Band and us lot are billeted up at an Hôtel de Ville – that's a town hall, you know, not a proper hotel, with no proper facilities – simply miles and miles away.'

'You lot!' she said, 'you lot! You cold shameless woman. I think you're insane. What are you doing with my husband!'

'Fucking him,' I'm afraid I said, and somehow that defeated her. She looked horrified, and wept some more, and turned her head from side to side, hopelessly, as if there was nowhere now she could crawl to and hide, so as not to show her shame and defeat. Well, I recognised that feeling too, though I hadn't had it for a long time. Not since I'd been a student and went to call on my boyfriend one night, to surprise and please him, and found him in bed with a friend of mine. Such friends women have! Think of Jude, and her so keen on God!

'I'm sorry,' I said, 'but there it is. He's a musician, and you can't tie them down.'

'You tell me!' She was getting angry again. 'You tell me that. Do you think I don't know that? My Francie, my Colin?' Had Jack even mentioned Colin? He hadn't! I looked at Frances.

'Colin's my little brother,' remarked Frances. 'He's five. He's over-active. Little pain he is too –'

Anne was mouthing; the words had trouble coming out of her mouth, as if she'd had a stroke. The words were willed, but somehow just not there properly.

But I could understand more than enough of what she said. A tale of martyrdom and misery, of masochism and monstrou male manners. (Ms were the consonant she had most troubl with, oddly enough.) Jack off with his trumpet, no prope family life: practising all day and the neighbours complaining; him not there at the children's births because he was off at a gig; his drinking, his wretched leaving capacity, the friends who could pull him away, the nights out with other women – 'But of course,' I said. 'Of course. Didn't you know all this when you married him?'

It didn't stop her. On she mouthed and mumbled. A dreadful absentee father: she left them with him for a week – they lived on chips and he brought his girlfriend home.

'But why *have* children, if it's all so terrible? Why carry it on?' On she went. On Jack played.

'Oh don't, don't,' begged Frances. People stopped listening to the Band and started listening to Anne instead. That wouldn't do. Jack wrapped up the gig. His lip was going, that was all; or he'd have carried on, I had no doubt of that.

Jack stood over her and sighed. She seemed old and he seemed young.

'What are you doing here?' he asked. 'It will only upset you.'

'I came last year in the middle,' she said, perfectly clearly when she spoke to him, her victim, 'and you sent her away.'

Her? My predecessor?

'This time it's different, Anne.'

'I've heard you say that a hundred times.'

'Hardly a hundred.' How amused he seemed. But how else was he to deal with her? Such a dreary old woman! One longs for a decent rival.

Frances said personally she was going off to the café, but I didn't move. So she lingered, looking depressed.

'You knew when you asked me I couldn't leave Colin,' moaned Anne. 'He's right in the middle of his allergy tests.'

'He doesn't have to have allergy tests. All he needs is for you to cheer up and he'd be fine. You shouldn't have come. It was very naughty.'

'But you sent me a postcard.'

'I sent you a postcard asking you to start the car every few days, or the battery runs down. I didn't say come.'

'But it's what you meant.'

How dare she look at him like that, speak to him like that, as if she were in his head! How dare she have his car in her garage, as she presumably did. And what car? He hadn't spoken to me about any car.

'Frances and I will go down to the café,' I said, 'and leave you two together. Let me know what you work out.'

It was time for me to go to the doctor. I thought he might well have something of importance to impart, it being that kind of day.

'Madame,' he said, 'puis-je vous offrir mes félicitations. Vous êtes enceinte.' Or words to that effect.

'Pardon?'

'Seulement deux ou trois semaines, mais vous êtes certainement enceinte.'

Pregnant. Ah yes. They have the most sensitive tests for extra oestrogen these days. But the pain? An ectopic pregnancy, perhaps? I had to draw a diagram before he understood what I meant. Then he shook his head vigorously.

'Mais non.' Just one of those things: one of the Fallopian tubes a little swollen. It sometimes happens. A week or two and all would be well.

Oh yes, I thought, it certainly would.

'Everything okay?' asked Frances, as I came out.

'Fine, fine.'

'Mum shouldn't have come down. It's embarrassing for everyone. But she's like that. Dad's always had women. I'm used to it, why can't she be? She could just wait quietly at home and look after Colin and wait for him to come back.'

'But, Frances, this time he isn't going to come back. This time it's for keeps.'

'Oh what a mess,' she carolled, with a sudden burst of good cheer. 'What a mess! What a mess!' She was like her father, like the whole Band.

'Do you play an instrument?' I asked, suspiciously.

'I play the accordion,' she said, 'and I sing quite a bit. Not with this band, though. I'm folk.'

Well, there it was. I was feeling very tired. Rather a lot had happened. I left her in the café being chatted up by the waiter and found Sandy and the bus, just as a mechanic finally levered the back door open; I piled coats in the long back seat and lay down and fell asleep. Enough was enough.

I woke up to find the van was on the way home to the Hôtel de Ville. Anne was sitting next to Frances. Jack was sitting by himself. In the front, Sandy and Jennifer sat stiffly, not talking. Presumably Sandy had not yet forgiven his wife for her outburst of ingratitude. Pedro was asleep. Stevie sat upright and disapproving, staring out into the bouncy night. I looked at my watch. It was ten thirty. Jack came and sat next to me.

'I didn't want to wake you up,' he said. 'You know I love you. I wouldn't have had this happen for the world.'

'Um,' I said, and went back to sleep. Starlady Sandra, Jack's fancy woman, impregnated yet again! Oestrogen makes you sleepy, even so early on in a pregnancy.

We got out of the van in front of the Hôtel de Ville. Anne was still crying, but silently. I bounced around, organising her bed for the night: blankets, a spare bolster; one of the horrid hard French kind.

'You'd better share Frances's room!' I said brightly. The Band was silent, disliking Anne for her misery, me for my cheerfulness, my capacity to organise. No one blamed Jack. It was just the women again, making trouble for men.

'Night, everyone,' I said, firmly and loudly, and got into my half of Jack's bed, and presently heard Anne get into hers next door, and then Frances, and a few murmuring words between them. The Band was having their goodnight drink in the kitchen, winding down after a day's playing. You know what performers are. It was two o'clock before Jack came to bed.

'Hi,' I said.

'I thought you'd be asleep,' he whispered. 'Anne's going back on the train tomorrow.'

'Thanks for telling me!'

'Don't be sarky!' He'd drunk too much. What was too much? I no longer knew.

'No. I meant thanks for telling me.'

'You're too tough to worry,' he said. That shook me. 'What I like about you,' he said, 'is your toughness. I've never met anyone like you. I'd be safe with you.'

Well, I could see it. He would. Never feel sorry for anyone in his life again, never feel obligated. 'You won't ever leave me, will you?' he says. 'I need you.'

He falls asleep. Well, I don't know. What does it matter? The whole human race is doomed. How can a species survive if a disease turns up which is sexually transmitted and invariably fatal in mothers and babies? The species will struggle along an aeon or two, but that's it. Fight it back with the tools of civilisation, drugs and vaccines, but the first major earthquake, ice age, war and that's it. Some such disease carried off the dinosaurs, if you ask me. Humans, cats, monkeys, all now get AIDS: heaven knows what else; they haven't started testing. I don't give any of them long. Not that it makes much difference: presently too the earth must fall into the sun: and it's all words, all word games, all these notions of immensity, because our own individual deaths come first.

That dreadful woman lies awake and snivelly in the room next door, and her boring daughter who plays the accordion likewise. And here I lie, whatever it is in there splitting and twisting and copying and growing; my father's blue eyes, or my mother's brown: Jack's sinewy neck, my pretty straight toes. We will never know. What's the point: the species will never be perfected, were perfection in mind, which of course it isn't, just endless workable forms. Of course Jack's and my set of variables would *work*; would breathe, eat, sleep, fuck; but what would it *mean*? Why bother? And what of this child Colin, with his hyperactivity and his asthma? Does his fool of a mother know about additives? Colorants? Tartrazine? Probably not. Why has she left him behind; why isn't she at home looking after him? A mother's first duty is to her child, not her husband. I feel my grandmother's pursing of the lips. I don't even bother to rearrange my face in denial of my ancestry. Look, who wants a child? I am the only child I properly know. I got my father shot, I drove my mother mad. My brother Robin killed his father with grief, nearly did the same for me, his half-sister. There's children for you. I think of my grandmother in her garden. Susan. The quick sudden smile. A kind of glitter of life, glimpsed behind hedges, between roses. No wonder the gypsy vaulted the lych gate, for all her pious ways.

Does Bloody Anne weep because I'm here with her husband, who no longer loves her, or because if he'd gone to a different

154

gig, the night the moon shone over Greenwich Observatory, she'd be in his bed instead of me? Is it me she hates, or the permutations of fate? What can I do about it?

I know very well what I can do about it. I am the fulcrum where the past and future balance, in which I am like anyone else. But I am also the point where the mad, the bad and the infamous meet: the possessed and obsessed. I had better get it right – this infinitesimal spark of moral decision which is apparently required of me. Let us pray! Great Father, Cruel God, simulator of the Universe, in whose image I am made, etc? No, better not: no help there, God the Bastard! What the hell, Daddy-oh! I shall have this baby, even though it looks at me with your cold blue eyes. And Bloody Anne can have her Jack back, Jack the mad trumpeter, though it breaks my heart. Frances can learn her accordion in peace. Central can have me back, and I will go on patiently instructing the millions. Matthew and Jude can copulate in peace and tranquillity, pursuing both the future and their own ambition. I shan't mock it. No. I shall listen one more time to the Citronella Jumpers and then go home – I can stay with my friend Clare while I sort things out – to nurture this baby and allow it its passage into daylight, since it's so determined to get there. He, she or it. The 'it' is what I worry about, of course. Who doesn't, these days?

Appendices

I

Alison's Story

A Libation of Blood

'Mum,' said Alison, 'give me some advice.' Mum was sixty-five and Alison was thirty-nine. Mum was widowed, which is never a nice thing to be, but what can you expect? Women outlive men.

'You?' asked Mum in some astonishment. 'Me give you advice?' Mum had left school at sixteen and gone into the WRACS and packed parachutes. That was as far as her education and training had gone. Alison had gone to college and taken a degree and then a diploma in the Social Sciences. Mum had one child: Alison had three. 'What can I know that you don't know?'

Alison wept. Mum, astonished, made her a cup of tea. Mum had a touch of arthritis in her fingers. She lived, as she had always done, in a bungalow on the outskirts of Exeter. Dad had run a TV repair business, and had left his wife well provided for. His daughter, of course, could look after herself. She lived in London and did well enough; very well, in fact. She worked for a charity, raising funds for mentally handicapped children, and ran a small specialist agency besides, which provided research material on handicap for similar organisations. She was tall, energetic, good-looking, usually laughing; and now suddenly here she was in Mum's small kitchen, laughing and crying at the same time.

'Tea's no answer,' said Alison. 'Oh, Mum, you never change.'

'Tea never was an answer,' said Mum, 'but it was always something to do with your hands, while you got your act together.' Do not suppose that because Mum was sixty-five, and had had little education, and no other lover (or so Alison supposed) than her husband, she was stupid or ill-informed. The television and the library make one knowledgeable nation of us all.

'As for never changing,' added Mum, 'that may be so, but

I don't weep as much as you do. Now what's happened?'

'I don't know what's going on inside my head, that's what's happened. And when I press my breast it hurts. Do you think I've got cancer?'

'You're probably pregnant,' said Mum, 'and it's affecting what's going on in your head.'

'I can't possibly be pregnant,' said Alison. 'Bobby and I take precautions.' On the telephone a week ago Alison had been all set to move in with Bobby: fortyish, good-looking, a crusader for the handicapped, famous up and down the country for his goodwill and good works. Marriage was spoken of. What a wonder! True love at last – and for a woman of thirty-nine with three children and two marriages behind her.

'Precautions, schmecautions,' said Mum. 'Condoms, schmondoms. When did they ever not break? How do you think you began?'

'You're so frivolous,' complained Alison (whoever liked to believe they sat thus accidentally in the world?) and asked Mum to come up for a week and babysit Caroline, aged nine, and Wendy and Wyndham the five-year-old twins; the twins' father William being unexpectedly in hospital for his varicose veins and William's new wife Annabel declining to look after them if William wasn't in the house, and Alison having a conference and what with one thing and another –

'Just cool it, Alison,' said Mum, 'will you? You'll give yourself a heart attack. Okay, okay, I'll come up for the week and childmind but you didn't come all this way to ask me that. You could have done it on the phone.'

'I wanted some peace on the train,' said Alison. 'I wanted my own space. Just a couple of hours.'

'I suppose you travelled first class, or you wouldn't be talking about space.'

'Why not? I can afford it.'

'And thousands starving in Africa!' said Mum. 'Sometimes I think you earn too much for your own good.'

'You'd never say that to a man,' said Alison, and wept again. It was true. Her head was all to pieces. She'd been all set to move in with Bobby, give up her own house, her independence, everything: all for love. But now she wasn't sure she wanted to: supposing it all went wrong? She couldn't bear it. Better

162

not to try, than try and fail. This way and that, things went in her head. Yet wasn't little Caroline happy with the idea: Bobby for a father! Wasn't that reassuring? Of course William wasn't happy about it one bit but nothing made William, the twins' father, happy; Alison could never do anything right: it was the self-righteous Annabel whispering in his ear, no doubt. What difference could it make if the twins visited their mother alone every second weekend, or their-mother-with-Bobby: she, Alison, put up with Annabel not to mention Annabel's hordes of mimsy little children when she visited the twins; why should William begrudge her Bobby? Or was it that she was begrudging him to herself? Alison wanted a whiff of home, in fact, where nothing ever happened, except in her mother's head, and all was always the same, even the brand of tea. PG Tips.

'Multiple marriages,' said Mum. 'All change, but all the same! Why didn't you stay with Andrew?' She'd liked Andrew, in the way mothers do seem to like their daughters' first husbands. Or perhaps it was just the pattern of names from the beginning. Alison and Andrew, Andrew and Alison – they'd got used to it, that was all.

'He was a mass murderer,' said Alison, 'that's why.' Andrew had worked as a designer for a firm which produced, amongst other things, leaflets for a cigarette company.

'Now who's being frivolous?' said Mum. Andrew had pronounced himself bisexual and Alison had left, running shrieking into the night, Caroline under her arm, straight into William's waiting maternal arms. Had she been right, had she been wrong? What is intolerable, what is not? Andrew hadn't kept in touch with Caroline, or Alison for that matter, though he rang Mum from time to time, feeling the need of a mother. Well, these days, who doesn't?

'How can you even speak to him?' Alison would shriek, in the early days of their parting, when she was still flayed red and raw.

'But you didn't *want* him to keep in touch with Caroline,' Mum would remind her. 'He's only doing what you wanted. And you're right, he is a very sexually confused young man. But I am not going to condemn him for that. Surely you wouldn't want me to? And it's all turning out for the best, with William. Surely?'

Well, it didn't quite. Alison's next baby, by William, was Down's Syndrome, and the hospital saved its life, and Alison rejected it, and said since the hospital had saved it, the hospital should look after it, a reaction which shocked the noble right thinking very much, and William was nothing if not a noble-thinker. But he bit back his thoughts, rather noticeably, for love of Alison, and supported her, and the baby died at three months, anyway, never well enough to come home. After that there was a lot of genetic testing and detailing of hereditary factors and the odds of William and Alison's next baby being born similarly affected was declared at one in fifteen. But the couple could take advantage of a newish procedure called amniocentesis by which babies could be tested in the womb at four months and aborted if necessary. So you only had the worry for four months. Then if anything was wrong – terminate! Of course by that time it was like going into a proper labour – 'At four months?' Mum had asked, in horror. 'Aborted at four months? It's practically smiling by then.'

'Especially if it's Down's Syndrome,' said Alison. 'You know what gutsy little smilers they are!' (William raised his eyebrows when Alison said things like this; but she was still in shock, he let everyone know, and himself wonderfully patient.) But four months was the best the medical profession could do at the time. And not even the pro-lifers made much of a fuss at aborting imperfect babies, though Alison couldn't quite understand their rationale. Life in itself being so important, according to them, not the quality of life. William wished she'd just shut up about it. And there Alison was, pregnant, somehow or other, in spite of her Dutch cap (the pill bloated her: the coil made her bleed and hurt) while they were still trying to make up their minds. William and Alison rejoiced – well, almost. You know what these things are. They'd rather have trusted their judgement than their luck. Who, well and properly informed, would not?

At seven weeks the doctors diagnosed a twin pregnancy, which meant that the odds of at least one baby being Down's Syndrome went up to one in eight: and if the twins were identical, one in six. And Alison was being sick not just in the mornings but lunchtime, teatime, dinnertime and all night too, and

Caroline, aged five, was coming out in sympathy and kept banging her mother's tummy with her head and saying she hated the baby and no one had the heart to say 'babies, actually' and the temptation just to terminate now, and not later – whoosh, the good baby going out with the bad, should such there be – though the likelihood of them *both* being Down's was now up to one in five, because Mum reminded her of a Down's great-uncle, never before discussed, plus identical twin great-aunts on William's side – good Lord, those sessions at genetic counselling, William staring at Alison, Alison at William, each wondering whose the bad seed was, and the whole weight of society (not to mention William) blaming the mother, though it's often enough old fathers, not old mothers, who produce Down's Syndrome babies – as the specialist was at pains to point out. Not that maternal or paternal age affected their particular case. Though Mum wouldn't have it.

'The thing about William,' Mum said later, 'is that he was just plain *born* old' – she'd just plain liked Andrew, sexual ambiguity and all, and that was the fact of it. Andrew had needed a mother and William was all the mother to himself he'd needed – just watch him bandage his own cut finger, cosseting and comforting! Anyway, William and Alison kept their courage going and Alison took time off work – 'Caroline *needs* you at home,' said William, 'at a time like this' – and got through to the amniocentesis at four months – only first Alison had flu and then the clinic had been closed because of some virus – and the twins had actually got to nineteen weeks before the test, and Alison pretty much bonded in spite of her efforts not to be: and in went the needle once, into the amniotic sac – ping! – one baby done – and in went the needle twice – second baby –

'I say,' said Alison, 'when you got the first one it moved, you know. Didn't like it one bit. You got the baby as well as the sac. I hope it wasn't an eye!'

'Nonsense!' they said. What a mother! Pity the poor father, with a woman who could joke at such times.

Joke?' said Alison. 'I wasn't *joking*.' They put her on tranquilisers until the results came through. She was very thin, what with the vomiting and the flu, and Caroline's little arms curling round her legs whenever she tried to leave the room. But the test results came through in ten days or so – two boys, both okay – no Down's, no spina bifida. ('Any tests for blindness in one eye?' asked Alison.)

'Isn't that wonderful!' said the doctors. 'Aren't you relieved? We certainly are! You were taking quite a chance.' Ah, the wonder of modern science.

'Wonderful,' said Alison, but one or other of the babies was pressing on the sciatic nerve, or they were taking it in turns, those two healthy, crowded boys, and the pain was terrible.

Well, Alison was worrying. That never helps, does it? The trauma of the previous baby's birth was still with her, of course, but more than that: she was troubled by the nature of the universe. In hospitals other than the one she'd attended, she'd been told, efforts to save severely handicapped babies were not nearly so strenuous. Luck of the draw, all luck of the draw. This hospital, that. Her birth, Andrew's dual sexuality (genetically determined, he maintained, no matter how she shrieked 'you're doing it on purpose!'), Caroline's wilting nature, her imperfect baby's survival, the twin pregnancy, William just being there waiting with reassuring arms: luck, luck! Work wasn't luck. Cause and effect operated in offices. Effort was rewarded by money. She pulled herself together and dragged herself to work every morning.

Her father died. A stroke – luck again. The blood clot was incapacitating or not, fatal or not, depending on where in the brain it happened to stick. It stuck in a bad place. That was that. She watched her mother carefully. Mum wept, mourned, recovered properly. It had been a good marriage. Death was, they said, more easily survived in such circumstances. Consciences were clear. Luck again. When you married, who you married, staying married: luck, all luck. The genetic counselling clinic denied luck and claimed probability, but Alison thought she'd rather just hang a lucky charm around her neck.

Mum came up to be with her before the twins were born. A long and painful affair, but at least relieving the pain in the sciatic nerve. The first twin was a boy, the second a girl. 'Ooops!' said the hospital.

'You tested the same baby twice,' said Alison. 'Told you so. See, two puncture marks. One on his chin, one on his ear. Lucky you missed the eye. Just test the girl for Down's, will you.' She went back to sleep. Ungrateful and difficult, they decided. The girl had the right number of chromosomes, so all was well. (Better luck than she deserved, one or two muttered.) Of course, amniocentesis was in its infancy. It is more sophisticated today. Don't worry.

Well, twins! Something in Alison's attitude upset William. It wasn't that she hadn't bonded. ('Have you bonded yet, mother?' Sister actually asked Alison. '*Both* twins, you're sure?' 'Quite sure, thank you, Sister,' said Alison, primly.) She longed to be up and active now the sheer physical weight of the pregnancy, not to mention the pain and the anxiety, was gone, and William had his two perfect children, the pigeon pair, and even Caroline seemed to find the reality of the twins quite tolerable, and her little white face had become pink again, and she'd been to stay with Mum down in Exeter for a whole week without howling for home – in fact Alison's spirits had been so high, back in the world of cause and effect, not just luck, that the twins had been three before the marriage broke up. Alison wouldn't stay home, that was the trouble: she would go out to work. William took her absence as an insult. He'd lost his job (he worked as an accountant with a small firm which unexpectedly merged with a large firm. 'Luck!' cried William. 'No,' said Alison, 'cause and effect. You could have seen it coming. If you'd looked, which you didn't.') and wouldn't even try to get another, having gone off figures anyway and wanting to be a writer, and Alison argued that someone had to bring the money in, but he'd argued that it was better for them all to live off Social Security, and how could he look after twins *and* write, and so on and so forth, and it had all ended up as musical chairs, with him in one household, sometimes with the twins, sometimes not, and Alison and Caroline and an au pair in another and Alison going out to work – unsatisfactory, said William, but I suppose it's what Alison wants and what Alison wants she gets (a lot of aggro and acrimony there) and somehow or other within a month or so William was living with this Annabel, about whom Alison had never known – but perhaps she should have seen it coming

– who had a little money of her own and could stay home with William so he could find the time to write – and Alison, who was earning good money, found herself legally obliged to support both households (and morally obliged, of course. Hadn't her unreasonable attitudes been the cause of the marital break-up?).

Alison grieved for the twins in their absence, of course she did, but she had her sanity to think about (well, didn't she?) not to mention Caroline, who wasn't even William's child (as he kept saying both in public and private, once the arguments started) and both households to support and fortunately Annabel turned out to be both kind and competent (though financially more than canny) and the twins liked her and she had the knack of somehow turning William's motherliness into fatherliness, but anyway all that was in the past. Alison had met Bobby, and she was happy, and her future was in her own hands, whatever she did with it, and seeing her mother had cleared her head, and she thought she'd just move in with Bobby but put off marrying him for a few months until she was absolutely sure it was all going to work – then she would be acting responsibly and not trusting to luck – and she and her mother travelled back to London first class.

'I'm perfectly happy going second,' said Mum. 'Why don't you save your money for more important things?' Well, she was like that. It made Alison feel safe. Except on the journey up she was sick, twice.

'Pregnant,' said Mum.

'Travel sick,' said Alison, but she felt her breasts and they were sore.

She went to her conference, and it was wonderful coming home to Caroline and the twins and Mum and Bobby visiting, and Mum liked Bobby, and he liked her and it all felt like home and she wondered why she was still hesitating, and forgot to wonder why she'd suddenly gone right off wine and coffee. And when William came out of hospital – his varicose veins stripped – ('Isn't he rather *young* for varicose veins?' asked Mum. 'But I suppose as he was just born old, it's got to his legs first') the twins went regretfully but happily enough to their other home, and she felt that even though they liked and appreciated Annabel, who kept their socks so clean and organised, it was she, their real mother they loved, and what's more now they were older, less babies, more people, she was beginning to come to terms with them and the trauma and anxiety they had caused, not to mention the months on her sciatic nerve. She blamed the hospital for making what was blind and instinctive somehow rational and required, so the mind cut in and observed the body, just when it shouldn't. Really, she thought, the way things were going in the gynaecological world, new human beings should just be grown in petri dishes, sperm joined to egg, forget love between man and woman, let alone parent and child, the once dark, once secret act of procreation now so brilliantly, clinically lit.

'Love you, Mummy,' said first Wendy, then Wyndham.

'I love you too,' said Alison.

'So do I,' said Caroline. 'And William a little bit. But Bobby more.'

'Isn't that all nice,' said Mum, who had quite come round to the modern habit of expressing love through words, she who had never in her youth or middle age been demonstrative could now see the pleasure of so doing.

'Come along, little ones,' said Annabel, briskly. 'Daddy's waiting in the car with Saul and Rachel and Dodie. Daddy's got to walk two miles every single day for a whole month. Think of that!' They thought of that.

'Oooh!' they said. And William, pale and brave, framed in the car window, spoke kindly to Caroline, who beamed and blossomed, and indeed to Alison too. So everything was just fine except there was no denying now that Alison, somehow or other, was pregnant. She did a home test and sat and through a slanting mirror watched the little orange ring forming out of yellow dust and wondered whether the new baby would increase the sum of the world's good, or do the opposite, and shatter what had been so precariously achieved? No twins in Bobby's family, let alone Down's Syndrome (or as far as she knew) which helped: but once you had one set of twins the likelihood of another multiple pregnancy leapt up and with it the dramatic halving of the odds against a perfect baby, and of course every year that passed, even with a single baby, put up the odds of it being Down's, having already had one, and how old was she now – thirty-nine – there was a kind of compound interest going on here: some cosmic penalty for happiness.

'What shall I do?' she asked her mother.

'Trust to luck,' said Mum. Luck! Good God! What good had luck ever done her?

'You must do what you want,' said Bobby. 'Though, of course I want us to have a baby. Very much.' And of course now the baby could be tested at ten weeks, through the cervix, so that took at least some of the anxiety out of it, not to mention risk to the baby, should the pregnancy proceed and they decide to go ahead. No termination, not yet. They postponed rejoicing until after the test. It could be done. Just. You went on pretending morning sickness was food poisoning and not referring to it. The baby was not a baby, just a growth, until declared valid by medical decree. But it was okay. They loved each other. That much was now certain. Only at eight weeks a scan showed twins. Two sacs. 'What will I do?' pleaded Alison. 'I can't go through with it. Not twins!'

'I might as well tell you,' said Mum, 'since you're already in such a state, you were twins, Alison. You had a sister. She died at birth. Of course these days they'd have saved her, but goodness knows how I'd have coped. Your father was better with a TV set than with a baby.'

'But why didn't you tell me?' Alison was astounded. 'You knew it would alter the odds. You must have known it would.'

'But knowing the odds made no difference,' observed Mum, 'since you got pregnant by accident, anyway. All knowing ever did was worry you more. Now you know you're terminating two, if that's what you're going to do, all that's happened is the decision's twice as hard. No one likes doing away with a perfect baby. Better to wait till they're born, if you ask me, then do away with the one that isn't right, if it isn't, and keep the one that is.'

'You go to prison, and I couldn't possibly do any such thing. Kill a baby, once it's born! Allow it to die – that's different. That's natural.'

'Might as well tell you,' said Mum, 'your twin wasn't right, mongol as we called them then, and the midwife did away with her. That's what midwives were for. That's why we had our babies at home. More danger but less interference '

'She couldn't have been identical,' said Alison, too obsessed by these genetic matters to worry about Mum's deceit, let alone the real function of midwives, 'or I'd have been Down's too.'

'Would you?' asked Mum. 'Down's schmown's, a baby's a baby.'

'Bet you were glad yours didn't live, all the same.' My sister, she felt. The sister I never had, always thought I ought to have, killed by my own mother.

'I was,' said Mum. 'Your father would never have stood for it.'

'You may be right there,' said Alison. Statistics certainly showed babies that weren't right broke up families quicker than anything. The handicapped end up with mothers, seldom fathers, hardly ever both. And she thought sadly of William, whose good opinion she still somehow couldn't quite seem to do without, and grieved for her poor baby, with his extra chromosome and dicey lungs, who had clung so studiously to life, and for so long – long after others would have given up and allowed themselves to be sluiced away in a flood of pre-natal blood. But the conversation, though it shortened, or was it lengthened, the odds, strengthened her mind. Termination. To go ahead with twins was absurd. She didn't have the physical strength, either before or after the birth. She just didn't.

'Oh!' said the specialist, 'if it's twins that worry you, these days we can terminate one and let the other go to term.'

'Which one?' Alison asked.

'The first one we come to,' said the specialist, a little stiffly.

'You mean you can't test both and remove the one with Down's?'

'Not yet. Though no doubt soon we'll be able to. And of course we must look on the bright side. Neither might be Down's.'

'I don't think that's the bright side,' said Alison. 'I don't think terminating a perfect baby can ever be called the bright side.' Difficult, wasn't she. Well, wouldn't you be?

'We would recommend a selective termination in any case:

you might have trouble carrying two babies to term. We do it often, nowadays. The procedure's been developed to cope with the number of multiple pregnancies we get nowadays – the result of fertility drugs.'

'That's different,' said Alison. 'This baby of mine – these babies – were created naturally. Conceived in love and passion, if by accident. How can I possibly terminate one? It might be the wrong one. And if it was okay, how could I tell the one that lived, when it came to their turn for genetic counselling, that I'd got rid of the other? What would it think of me?'

'It would at least be alive to do the thinking. I could terminate one now,' said the specialist kindly, 'and test the other at sixteen weeks, though there would still be an increased risk of miscarriage, and dispose of it for you if it were Down's.'

Sixteen weeks! 'No, no,' said Alison. 'Never. No counselling, no testing, I'll have them both and trust to luck.' She could already feel the pain of the sciatic nerve but she didn't care. She'd never said or felt such a thing before. It quite shocked her to hear herself speaking so loud and clear. And as it happened, the gods of chance must have heard, and looked down on her, or somebody or something; at any rate as she left the clinic she felt the first sticky flow of blood, and presently more and more, so much blood there seemed no end to it, so many regrets, so much relief, and within twenty-four messy, painful hours the putative twins were gone, male or female, good or bad, identical or fraternal, no one was ever to know, in such a flow of welter and crimson even the hospital was surprised.

'So much blood!' exclaimed the au pair, in the ambulance.
'Don't look,' cried Alison, 'it might put you off.'

Later on, when she was feeling steadier, she'd try again, and trust to luck it wasn't twins. Caroline, Wendy and Wyndham were all just fine – weren't they?

'Just as well,' said Mum, 'though I don't suppose you want to hear that. You have quite enough to think about as it is. How is the inside of your head?'

'Clearer,' said Alison. 'It's the sudden drop of oestrogen.'

'Reminds me of the time I miscarried the first lot of twins,' said Mum, who was, as ever, full of surprises.

172

'Just as well. They weren't your father's. Now drink a lot of water, and replace the lost blood, and here's to better luck next time. It'll happen. Blood's the libation the God of Chance requires. Lots and lots of blood. Always has, always will. Afterwards things go better. Didn't I have you?'

II

Jennifer's Story

Come On, Everyone!

All kinds of things puzzled Maureen Timson when she was eighteen, and nothing puzzled her more than her friend Audrey Thomas. If she was a friend. They were both at college, doing languages. They shared a room, being next to one another in the alphabet; a kind of fated closeness. Maureen had all the advantages, Audrey (in Maureen's eyes) very few. Yet Audrey led and Maureen followed, and Maureen could not understand it, and chafed, and was riled. Maureen liked to get to the bottom of things: to work away at them like a knotted shoe-lace, yet here there was something bottomless, ununknottable. And it was not fair.

She, Maureen, was pretty: she only had to look in the shared bedroom mirror to know. (Maureen's mother had discouraged mirrors, being the kind who said it was your character that counted, not your looks, but mirrors are everywhere, aren't they? Puddles or shop windows will do, or the interested eyes of others reflect back at least some kind of image.)

Audrey was not at all pretty. She had a face like – as Maureen's Great-Aunt Edith would say – the back of a bus. (Maureen's mother had eight aunts and Edith was the one she most disliked – but then Maureen's mother disliked almost everyone, scorning the weak, the frivolous, the idle, the soft, which meant almost all the human race, excepting only sometimes Family.) Maureen was an only child, Maureen's mother having scorned her father right out of the house, shortly after Maureen's birth. (Maureen had a vision of him, stumbling with thick boots and beery breath, up the damp path between the sad rhododendron leaves and away for ever, her own infant crying echoing from the right hand upstairs window.) Maureen had a tidy little waist, and Audrey had rolls of flesh above and below hers: that is the kind of thing you get to know if you share a room. Maureen had never shared a room before. It puzzled her that for all her bodily imperfections Audrey could wander around it naked and easy. And she didn't like it. Maureen was clever: from the age of thirteen she'd never let a past participle not agree with a verb, not once. Audrey could hardly tell a grave from an acute. Heaven knew how she'd wangled her way into college. Maureen read Machiavelli and Audrey read women's magazines. But still there was something Audrey had, that Maureen didn't. Audrey led, Maureen followed, half grateful, half resentful. Maureen was solitary, Audrey was not. Maureen hated to be solitary.

'You make friends so easily,' said Maureen to Audrey, making it sound like a reproach, some inbuilt lack of discrimination. 'How do you do it?'

And that seemed to puzzle Audrey, who was so seldom puzzled.

'You just talk to people,' she said.

'Anybody?' asked Maureen, with distaste.

'Well, yes,' said Audrey. Sometimes it was more than talk, it was into bed with just anyone, and then into someone else's, so the first anyone would go off in a huff, and Audrey would weep and weep but as Maureen said, keeping her virginity to the last possible moment, and then surrendering it to the Secretary of the Debating Society, a steady and reliable boy with a car, what did Audrey *think* would happen?

Audrey was popular with boys but Maureen could take her pick of them, so that wasn't the matter. But she felt when she looked in the mirror of their eyes she saw less than Audrey did. Now why should she think that? She tried to talk about it to Audrey.

'What *do* you see?' asked Audrey. 'I mean, apart from general lust?'

'Self-interest,' said Maureen, before she had time to think. They were sitting together in a Chinese restaurant after a film. Audrey was eating crispy banana in batter, which Maureen of course had declined.

'Oh,' said Audrey. 'I see them liking me.'

Maureen felt such a spasm of rage she swallowed too great a mouthful of too-hot calorie-free China tea and burned her mouth, and it was dry for days. But she didn't say anything. What was there to say? She forgot it.

What she didn't forget was Audrey standing on top of a sandhill one day in spring, in a one-piece swimsuit, hair flying in the wind, turning back to the group that followed her, that would follow her anywhere, calling out 'Come on, everyone!' and everyone followed. Friends. Company. Party times, good times, crowded times, peopled times; the whole human race whizzing round the benign fulcrum that was Audrey. 'Come on, everyone!' and everyone came, and so did Maureen, against her will yet by her will. She thought of the quiet, damp regularity of her childhood home, the single cat shut out at night, breakfast for two, mother and daughter, laid before they went to bed, and part longed to escape and part didn't want to: some blight had entered her soul too deeply. Up the sandhill she ran with the others, and Audrey was in the sea first. 'Come on in, everyone! The water's lovely!' But of course it wasn't, she was joking, it was icy, everyone screamed and Audrey splashed. How dare she! Maureen was furious. But everyone had a good time, and so did she. Orchestrating Audrey, weaving everyone into patterns of pleasure! How was it done?

Then of course their paths parted. Audrey with her II2 went off to muddle through some Social Science course; Maureen, with her II1, went off to Brussels to work for the EEC, always her ambition. There was something so clear and wholesome and ordered, not to mention well-paid, about the notion of a job in such a city; a little car, a little flat. And so there was. She had to chuck the Secretary of the Debating Society, because he went to work for Marks & Spencer in Newcastle, but these things often happen to student relationships. Maureen was put out when she found he'd married within the year, a colleague ten years older than himself, and that summer she went home to her mother in Paignton for her annual holiday, but it was miserable and boring, and she resolved never to do it again. Twelve years in Brussels, and now creeping up in the Agricultural Division, and lonely, and getting herself involved with a married man (but they were all married: what was she to do?) which kept her lonelier because of all the waiting about for the telephone and the secrecy and the unkept promises and the no social life, all of which she could see, but it took her forever to break it off (what had *happened* to her?) and finally she did and then she got a letter from Audrey. What had become of her? Could they meet? Just like Audrey, Maureen thought, why should anyone want to keep in touch with anyone just because they'd been to the same college, been close together in the alphabet. But she wrote back, Audrey invited her to stay for Christmas. Yes, she was married (of course, the unchoosy bitch) with three children: in the country, with lots of animals. Just like Audrey, thought Maureen, come-on-everyoneing into something no doubt damp, muddy, messy, noisy, with cat crap in corners. But Maureen went; she had come to dislike Christmas, after seven seasons with a married man.

The house was a mess. Of course it was. Maureen put on rubber gloves and helped clear up; helped get the over-decorated Christmas tree steady on its pins, the stockings done, endeared herself to the children by handing out Mars Bars in a sugar-free household, and keeping Audrey's husband Alan entertained while Audrey muddled through the children's bedtimes and prepared four kinds of stuffing for two small turkeys because that was more fun than one stuffing and an apple in a large turkey.

'But it's more work, Audrey.'

'I know it is, Maureen, but we've all got used to it. Family life is all ritual.'

Maureen doubted that ritual was enough. Alan was a political journalist with modern left-leanings; he had to reinspect his own political stance at least three times a year and it didn't seem to Maureen that Audrey was taking much notice of what was going on in her husband's head: rather she favoured a kind of ongoing warm emotional demonstration to keep him happy.

'Darling, what's the matter, what's the matter?' she would cry, flinging her arms round him and embracing him as he stared at the electricity bill (two turkeys cost a third more to cook than one, as Maureen pointed out) until he unwillingly smiled. Maureen understood the unwillingness very well. In fact she thought she understood Alan very well. She looked round the ingredients of the household: the children, the warmth, the animals, the mud tramped in and out, the friends coming and going – they came for miles – and thought, with a little reorganisation this would do me very well. She thought she would have it for herself.

She had to wait four years. In that time she was a frequent visitor to the household. Then Audrey had, as Maureen knew she would, her affair with a married man, and Maureen knew the anatomy of that very well.

'I feel so bad about it,' mourned Audrey, chopping nuts for one of the turkey's stuffings. 'I love Alan, but I just can't stop myself.'

'I expect you just want attention and flattery and to feel loved,' said Maureen, carefully. She'd read enough women's magazines in her time, oh yes, since her college days. 'The things Alan isn't good at. Such a pity he isn't more demonstrative. Then you wouldn't have to look for love outside your marriage.'

Audrey's tears fell into the cous-cous and lemon peel, and made it a fraction soggier than it should have been.

'If only I could tell Alan, if only I could talk to him about it, I'd feel so much better in my mind.'

'Perhaps you should,' said Maureen, not believing her luck. 'You have such a strong marriage. If Alan knew the lengths you'd been driven to he'd be horrified. He'd really work at saving the marriage. So this kind of thing never happened again.'

'Confess?' asked Audrey, her swift hands pausing, some glimmer of common sense illuminating the dark recesses of her lovesick mind, but only for a moment. Her lover was married too, of course, glooming over his Christmas Eve whisky in some other household, lost to her for the season.

'It's hardly confessing,' said Maureen. 'It's just being honest. How can a marriage as close as yours and Alan's work if you're not honest with one another? I think you owe it to your marriage, and to Alan, to tell him.' Then Maureen went out for a walk with the children, in the woods, where the leaves were wet with mist, and tried out 'come on, everyone' as she produced Mars Bars from her bag. How they rushed!

As the two of them filled Christmas stockings, Audrey told Alan about the affair, about her secret love, about trystings in the backs of cars and offices, and behind hedges – it had been going on since the summer – and how she really loved Alan, if only he was a bit kinder and nicer to her it need never have happened, but he'd let things get stale and how much she valued her marriage.

'Don't talk like the back of a woman's magazine,' was all Alan said, before hitting her from one side of the room to another, and by Boxing Day she had packed her bags and gone; she'd had to, screaming and hysterical, leaving the children, matrimonial home and all, which didn't help her a bit in the divorce. (Her lover decided to stay loyal to his wife.) Just as well there was Maureen to help the family through the rituals of that dreadful Christmas Day – she knew the domestic ropes so well, as Alan's mother said. And by the next Christmas Maureen was not just installed in the house but pregnant as well, with her first child, and calling out 'Come on, everyone!' at mealtimes, along with the best, though she didn't often cook herself, having help in the house, and a very good job (considering the local wage structure) running the local branch of the Farmers' Union.

'Don't say that!' Alan would beg. 'Don't say "come on, every-one".'

'Why not?'

'It irritates me. I don't know why.'

'Then you're just being irrational,' said Maureen firmly, and went on doing it. For a time her 'come on, everyone' was rather less peopled than Audrey's had been – but the friends soon drifted back and everything was just fine, and the damp and droopy rhododendron leaves which rustled in her past, in her dreams, stood up fine and straight and glossy in some kind of imagined sun.

III

Jude's Story

GUP – or Falling in Love in Helsinki

You'll never guess what happened to me in Helsinki. How my life changed, when I was there last October. Let me tell you! The trees in that much-islanded, much-forested Northern country – you've never seen so many islands, so much forest, so low and misty and large an autumn sun – were just on the turn, the rather boring universal green giving up and suddenly glowing into reds and yellows and browns. 'Ruska' is what the Finns call this annual triumph of variety over uniformity; something so dramatic they even have this special name for it. It is, I suppose, the last flaring surge of summer: like a woman of fifty who throws out the black shoes she's worn all her life and shods herself in greens and pinks, feeling she'd better make the best of things while she can. Not that I'm fifty, in case you're wondering, I'm twenty-nine; but twenty-nine can feel pretty old. Older, I imagine, than fifty, because around thirty the tick-tick-tick of the biological clock can sound pretty loud in a woman's ear.

My mother wanted me to stay home, get married, have children.
'Settle down, Jude,' she'd plead. 'It's what I want for you.'
'I can't think why,' I'd say. 'You never did.'
'That's different,' she'd say, and pour another whisky and light up her cigar. My mother is a professional golf coach, and has been ever since my father walked out twenty-five years ago. Well, she had to earn a living. She's a healthy and athletic woman, though she must be over sixty, and men are still for ever knocking at her door, though she doesn't often let them in. The whisky and cigar syndrome is no problem (or only to my sister Chris), it's just my mother's rather old-fashioned way of saying to a man 'I'm as good as you. What do I want you for?'
'Christ,' I say to my sister, 'the whisky's well watered. The

185

cigar goes out after ten seconds. What are you worrying about?'
But she's a nurse. Worse, she's the kind of nurse who always
sees disaster round every corner. It can't be much fun for the
patients. She was seven when my father left.

So anyway here is my mother, who never has, hell-bent on
me settling down; just another example of GUP, or Great
Universal Paradox, which rules all our lives. You see GUP
most clearly at work in any Obstetric Ward, at the very
beginning of things, as is only fitting. There you'll find a
woman who wants a baby but it was stillborn, and another
who's just had a living baby she doesn't want, and someone
in for a sterilisation and another for a termination, and another
with a threatened miscarriage, and another resting up before
sextuplets, having taken too much fertility drug – and all will
be weeping. All want different things so passionately; and
nature takes no notice at all of what they want. Just rumbles
on insanely, refining the race.

What you want you can't have: what you do have, you don't
want. That's GUP.

When I went to Helsinki I was in love with Andreas Anders,
who didn't love me. And I was loved by Tony Schuster, whom
I didn't love. My loving Andreas Anders loomed large in my
life, and had for seven years. Tony Schuster loving me, which
he had for all of seven days, meant to me next to nothing;
that's the way GUP goes. Besides, Andreas Anders not loving
me made me feel fat and stupid: so if Tony Schuster was
capable of loving someone as fat and stupid as me, what did
that make Tony Schuster? Some sort of wimp? In other words,
as famously spoken by Marx (not Karl, but the Brother kind)
tearing up the long-sought invitation to join – 'Who wants to
belong to a club of which I'm a member?' GUP!

Talking about Marx, Finland is just across a strip of sea from
the Soviet Union, though the government is of a rather different
kind and in Finland women seem to run everything, and in
Russia it's the men. It makes a kind of difference. Little
Finnish children always look so healthy and bright-eyed and
well-mittened and properly fed to keep out the cold. Yes, yes,

I know. I'm broody, GUP! Bright, bright clothes they wear, in Helsinki. Terrifically fashionable. Lots of suede, so soft it looks and acts like linen.

Picture me there, last September. Nipping down into the town to buy this or that, the envy of my sister Chris. I earn ten times as much as she does, I daresay. She's two inches shorter than me and I'm five foot six, but she's two stone heavier. She'd look pretty strange in a mauve sort of fluted leather skirt, the kind I bought for me. No GUP factor here. Facts are facts. Chris says it's the hospital canteen. I say 'It's your way of not getting involved with men.'

'You're so right,' she says, munching another Mars Bar, 'look what happens when you are: look at you! Look at Janice!'

'That sugar's worse for you than tobacco and alcohol,' say I, thinking of Janice's (that's our mum) cigars and whisky.

'No it's not,' she says. 'Nowhere near, and I should know, I'm a nurse.'

I love my sister Chris, and I wish she'd go on a diet and meet some man and settle down. GUP!

Anyway, here we were, in Helsinki, making a six-part thriller called *Lenin in Love* for BBC TV, on film. Helsinki's Great Square is the same period, same proportions, same size as Moscow's Red Square, so it gets used by film companies a lot. Filming in Red Square itself is always a hassle: there's a lot of worried security men about and they like to read the script and object if it says anything detrimental about their country – and it so often does, doesn't it: I mean, that's the whole *point* of thrillers – and the queue for Lenin's tomb is always getting into shot, and you can hardly ask them to move on, when they've railed all the way in from Tashkent or wherever to be there. So off everyone goes to Helsinki to film the Moscow bits. They made *Doctor Zhivago* there.

Andreas Anders is the Director of *Lenin in Love*. Tony Schuster is the cameraman. I'm the PA. You'd think a bright girl like me (I have a degree in Politics and Economics: I moved over from Research to Production five years ago; thinking, rightly, I had more chance of being close to Andreas Anders that way) could think about something other than love but at twenty-nine it gets you, oh it gets you! Twenty-nine and no children or live-in-lover, let alone a husband. Not that I wanted all those things. GUP! In the film and TV world there's not all that much permanent in-living. You just have to pack up and go, when the call comes, even when you're in the middle of scrambling his breakfast eggs. Or he, yours. Men tend to do the cooking, these days, in the circles in which I live. Let's not say 'live'. Let's say 'move'.

I was the researcher on Andreas Anders' first film. I was twenty-three then, straight out of college. It was a teledrama called *Mary's Son* and about this woman's fertility problems. It was during the first week of filming – he took me along with him: he said he needed a researcher on set though actually he wanted me in his bed – that I both developed my theory on GUP and fell in love with him. And at the end of the second week he fell in love with his star, Caroline Christopherson, the girl who was playing Mary. And I was kind of courteously dismissed from his bed. Nightmare time. I'd got all through college repelling all boarders, if you understand what I mean. But Andreas Anders! Look, he's got a kind of pale haunted face, and wide, kind, set-apart grey eyes, and he's tall, and broad-shouldered, and has long, fine hands, and what could I do? I loved him. That he should look at me, little me! Pick me out, ask for me! Even for a minute, let alone a week, let alone a fortnight; until he fell for Caroline Christopherson. And he married her. And now she's world-famous and plays lead in big budget movies, and is a box-office draw, and Andreas doesn't like it one bit – he's the one with the talent, the creativity, the brains, after all: she just has star quality – and when it gets bad for him, why there I am in bed with him again and he's telling me all about it. They have a child, Phoebe, who gets left behind with nannies. Andreas doesn't like that. I don't say 'But you're the one doing the leaving too,' because I never say to him what I really think. That's what this one-sided love does to you. Turns you into an idiot. I hate myself but I'm tongue-tied.

How can I compete with C.C., as he calls her? That kind of film starry quality is real enough: a kind of glowing magnetism: a way of moving – just a gesture of a hand, the flick of an eye – which draws other eyes to itself. I don't look too bad, I tell myself. Though I suppose where C.C. looks slim I just look plain thin. Both our hair frizzes out all over the place, but hers shines at the same time as frizzing. I do not know how that effect is achieved. If I did, friend, I would let you know. I look more intelligent than she does, but that's not the point. On the contrary. 'Judgmental,' Andreas Anders once said I looked. That was when we were doing a studio play up at Pebble Mill. *Light from the Bedroom*. My first PA job. C.C. was giving birth to little Phoebe in Paris while we were taping in Birmingham. Andreas couldn't leave the show: well, could he? We stayed at the Holiday Inn. He is the most amazing lover.

I don't let on how much I care. I pretend it means nothing to me. If he thought it hurt, he'd stay clear of me. He doesn't mean to be unkind. I just act kind of light and worldly. I don't want to put him off. Would you? GUP again! If you love them, don't let them know it. 'I love you' is the great turn-off to the uncommitted man.

And now here's Tony Schuster saying 'I love you' to me, leaning down from his dolly as he glides about in the misty air of Helsinki's Great Square. The mist's driving the lighting man crazy. The scenes are meant to be dreamlike and misty, but all prefer the man-made kind to God's kind. Easier to control.
'Let's leave this life,' Tony says. 'Let's run off together to a Desert Island.'
'You mean like *Castaway*?' I ask. I know film people. Everything relates back to celluloid.
'How did you know?' He looks surprised. He's not all that bright. Or perhaps I'm just too bright for everyone's comfort. Anyway, for all his gliding to and fro on his great new black macho electronic camera with its built-in Citroën-type suspension – 'This camera cost £250,000,' he snaps, if anyone so much as touches the great shiny thing – I just can't take Tony seriously. He has quite an ordinary, pleasant, everyday face. He's thirty-nine, and has a lot of wiry black hair. Andreas's hair is fair and fine. 'I love you!' Tony Schuster yells, for all the world to hear. 'Run off with me, do!'

I think his loving me so publicly annoys Andreas, but he doesn't show it. Tony's one of the top cameramen around:

they can be temperamental: it's as well for a Director to hold his fire, unless it's something that really matters – a smooth 50-second track in, for example – not like love, or desire, which everyone knows is just some kind of by-product of all the creative energy floating around a set.

'I love you' is a great turn-off for the female committed elsewhere. GUP!

Sometimes I agree to have a drink with Tony though, when it's a wrap for the day, and we'd all stagger back to the bar of the Hesperia. Except for Andreas, who's staying at the Helsinki Inter-Continental. When I heard C.C. was coming to join her husband and hold his hand through the whole month of Helsinki shooting, I put them in a different hotel (I do location accommodation, inter alia) from the rest of us. I thought I couldn't bear it. We'd be going off to Rome presently, anyway, and she wouldn't be following us there. Going, not back to Phoebe, oh no: but back to Hollywood for some rubbishy block-busting new series.

'It's so clichéd I can't bear it,' Tony would moan. 'The PA in love with the Director! You're worth more than that.'

More than being in love with Andreas? How was such a thing possible?

Tony was thirty-nine. His wife had just left him, taking the children. He'd been away from home just once too often. When she wanted him where was he? Up the Himalayas filming *Snowy Waste* or under the Atlantic with *Sonar Soundings* or in the Philippines with *Lolly a go-go* (he needed the money). When he didn't turn down *Lenin in Love* because he couldn't miss an opportunity of working with Andreas Anders, the Great Director (time, he thought, to move out of commercial film into Art, and get a bit of video experience too), Sara waited for him to say 'yes' to the call from his agent, and he did, of course, having said he'd say no, and then she packed.

'You love films more than me,' she said. And so he did. Now he thought he was in love with me. I knew what was going on. She'd left, he was sad and worried; love on the set's a great diversion. On the whole, you last as long as the project does; not a moment longer. Sometimes it sticks – look at Andreas and C.C.; me and Andreas – but mostly it's all, as I say, just this surplus energy taking sexual/romantic form. I know so much, and so little too. GUP!

'You have no pattern for a happy married life,' laments my mother. 'All my fault.'
'I don't want to be married,' I say. If I was married how could I follow Andreas round the world? But I don't tell her that. His favourite PA! I'm good at my job: by God, I'm good at it. He won't find fault with me.
'Without you!' he once said (that was *Love in a Hot Climate*: we were in a really ritzy room at the Meriden in Lisbon: C.C. was off in Sydney and Andreas thought she was having an affair with the male lead – whose name escapes me though everyone gasps when you mention it – and he was finding solace in work, and me), 'Without you, Jude, I wouldn't be half the director I am!' A real working partnership we have, oh yes! His fingers running through my hair when there's nothing else to do and hotel rooms in strange cities are lonely, aren't they.

Before I left for Helsinki my mother said something strange. 'Your father ran off with a girl from Finland,' she said. 'Our au pair. Just make sure you come back.'
Now my mother never said anything at all about my father if she could help it. And Chris and I didn't ask. Questions about our dad upset her. And it doesn't do to upset a woman who is a golf coach by profession. She gets put off her stroke, and if she loses her job, how will you live? Our house went with the job. On the edge of the golf-course. Thwack, thwee, muted shouts – to me the sound of childhood.

I expect if your husband ran off with the Finnish au pair you wouldn't want to dwell on it much. So this was the first I'd heard of it. Chris and I tried to trace him, when she was twenty and I was eighteen, but we never got very far. And I can't say we tried hard. Who wants to be in touch with a father who doesn't want to be in touch with you? Apart from the fun of the thing, I suppose. And Chris had been oddly worried about Helsinki, too.
'You and your lifestyle!' she said, when I rang the Nurses' Home to say I was off to work on *Lenin in Love*. She'd just been made Night Sister of Men's Orthopaedic. Quite a cheerful

ward, she said. At least they mostly got better. 'Can't you ever stay in one place? You'll get AIDS if you don't watch out. You film people!' (Reader, she had my lifestyle all wrong! There'd only ever been Andreas Anders, apart from a few forgettables, and that just a week or so here and there over a whole seven years. It was pathetic really. Somehow men seem to know if your emotions are occupied elsewhere. You send out 'I belong to someone bigger than you' signals, just as much if you're wretchedly involved as if you're happily married.)

Anyway, Janice and Chris were right to worry, as it happened. Because this strange thing did happen to me in Helsinki. I was with Tony, who was too obtuse, I suppose, to notice the signals, and was persisting, and I was explaining why I wouldn't go to bed with him, and what was wrong with his psyche, and he was looking quite wretched and pale, as men will in such circumstances. We were walking in the open-air Rural Life Museum – a whole park devoted to the artefacts of Finland's past. It was Sunday. There were elegant wooden church boats to hold a hundred people, in which an entire village could row itself to church if it so chose; ancient farm-steads, moved plank by plank from distant places, and so forth, but my attention was caught by one of those familiar groups of people, complete with cameras and sound equipment. This lot were clustered round and filming one of the enormous orange toadstools with yellow spots they have in these parts. Proper traditional pixie toad stools.

And the sound man put down his gear – he was taking white sound, I presumed: a toadstool hardly makes much noise, even in its growing, which can be pretty rapid – and walked over to me. He wasn't young. Sixty or so, I suppose. Quite heavy round his middle: pleasant looking: intelligent: glasses.
'Hello,' he said, in English.
'Hello,' I said, and I thought where have I seen that face before? And then I realised, why! whenever I look in the mirror, or when I look at Chris: that's where I've seen it. More the latter, because both Chris and he were overweight. It looked worse on her. He was really quite attractive.
'You're with the English film crew, aren't you?' he said. 'I saw you in the Square yesterday. It had to be you. Jude Iscarry.'

'Or Judas Iscariot or Jude the Obscure,' I said, playing for time, because my heart was pounding. 'Take your pick!'

'Your mother said you'd gone into films,' he said. 'Chip off the old block.'

'You're my father,' I said.

'Fraid so,' he said.

'I didn't know she was in touch with you,' I said. It was all I could say. Tony just stood and looked on. Moments in a person's life!

'I passed through five years back,' my father said, 'but she advised me strongly to keep away, so I did. Though I'd have liked to have stayed. Quite a powerful stroke, your mother.'

'She's had to develop it,' I said.

'Um,' he said. 'But she always was independent, wanted to be father and mother too.'

'That's no excuse,' I said.

Tony left us and he, my father, whose name was Saul Iscarry, took me out to lunch. We had pancakes, caviar and sour cream, washed down by tots of vodka. The best food in the world. The Finns have the highest heart disease rate in the world. So Chris had assured me, before I left.

My father had eventually married his Vieno, my mother's au pair, and actually gone to the Moscow Film School, and now he was one of the best sound men in the world (he said) and had Finnish nationality, but lived in Leningrad and Vieno was a doctor, and they had three children, and what with visa problems and general business and so forth there hadn't been much point in keeping in touch, let alone the time. (Roubles are just one of those currencies that make it difficult for a father to support his abandoned children.) But he'd thought of Chris and me a lot.

'Big deal,' I thought, but said nothing. What was the point?

Now we were in touch, he said, we must keep in touch. He was glad I was in films. The best life in the world, he said, if you had the temperament. But why was I only a PA? Why wasn't I a producer, at the very least? Ah. Well. He said he'd like to see Chris. How was she? Just fine, I said. She'd have to come over and see him some time, since visas for him were so complicated. If you ask me visas are as complicated as you care to make them, but I didn't say that either.

I said Chris would be over to see him next Easter. That gave her six months to lose three stone. She should be able to do that. A girl likes to be at her best when she meets up with her old dad.

'You've grown up a fine handsome girl, Jude,' he said. 'I'm proud of you,' and you know, that meant a great deal to me. More than it should have. If anyone was to take the credit for the way I was it should have been my mother. Oh, Great Universal Paradox which runs our lives – that what should please us doesn't, and what does please us, shouldn't!

He had to go back to work, he said. The pixie toadstool called. The crew could not be kept waiting. When could it ever, in any country, in any language in the world? We exchanged addresses. He went.

And I took myself off to the little Greek Orthodox church that's tucked away behind the Great Square, and there I sat down. I had to be quiet: absorb what had happened. I didn't kneel. I'm not very religious. I just sat, and thought, and rested. The unexpected is tiring.

It's a small, ancient building: a chapel rather than a church. But it blazes with intricate icons and gold leaf and crimson velvet; everything shimmers: there's no way it can't: there must be a thousand candles at least stuck all around, lit by the faithful at their own expense. It's a sensuous, somehow Mediterranean place, stuck here as if by accident in this cold northern land. The air was heavy with incense: that and candle smoke smarted the eyes: or was I crying? And in the ears was the gentle murmur of the faithful, the click click of the telling of beads. Yes, I was crying. But I don't think from wretchedness. Relief, happiness almost, at something completed. My father: no longer fantasy, just a man.

And there in front of me, a couple of rows nearer the great glittery altar, was sitting Andreas Anders. He looked round and saw me. I wished he hadn't. I wanted to just go on sitting there, alone, thinking. But he got up and came to sit next to me. How good-looking he was. His bright eyes glittered in the candlelight.

'Well,' he said, 'she's not coming to Helsinki after all. Had you heard?'

By 'she' he always meant Caroline Christopherson. 'I think,' he said, 'I'd better give her up altogether, don't you? Divorce, or something drastic. I can't stand the strain.'

'Let's go outside,' I said. 'This isn't the place for such conversations.' Nor was it. As I say, I'm not one for religion, but some sort of God was here in this place, albeit in heavy disguise, and didn't want to hear all this soggy, emotional mish-mash.

So we went out, Andreas and me. And he tucked his arm into mine and said, 'Shall we go back to the Inter-Continental, just you and me?' and I pulled my arm away and said, 'No, I won't. What a monster you are!' and heard myself saying it, and knew I meant it, and there I was, out of love with him. Just like that.

'A monster?' he asked, hurt and confused. But I didn't even want to discuss it. It wasn't worth it. I'd see the *Lenin in Love* through of course, because I was a professional, but that was all. The man was an egocentric maniac.

I left him staring after me, his turned worm, and I went back to the Hesperia Hotel and found Tony in my bedroom and told him to stop messing about and for heaven's sake somehow get his wife and children back. If he wanted to get out of the business, let him do it with the proper person.

'Is this what finding a long lost father can do?' he asked, as he left. 'And I had such high hopes . . .'

And all I could do was suppose it was: that, and simply Finland itself.

In the past Finland has always been conquered or annexed or governed by someone else – this vast flat stretch, on top of the world, of islands and forests – but now it has its own identity, its own pride: it looks not to its previous masters, Sweden and Russia, but to itself. How odd, to identify so with a nation! Perhaps it's hereditary, in the genes: like ending up in the film business. My dad ran off with a Finn: one mustn't forget that.

Perhaps he somehow felt the same connection, and can be forgiven.

And that's the strange thing that happened to me in Helsinki, last October, and how my life changed. And I called this story 'Falling in Love in Helsinki', not 'out of love' because although it's true I fell out of love with Andreas, out of love with love (which is a real blight) somehow I fell into love with life. Or with God, call it what you will, there in that chapel. Anyway, sufficiently enamoured of just the sheer dignity of creation to realise I shouldn't offend it the way I had been doing. I think everything's going to be all right now. I'll make out. I might even leave the film business altogether. No⁺ go into a convent, or anything so extreme. But I might try politics. It's what I'm trained for.

As for GUP, the Great Universal Paradox, that's real enough. What I marvel at now is how so happy so many of us manage to be, so much of the time, in spite of it.

FAY WELDON

THE PRESIDENT'S CHILD

Babies have fathers too, and when that father is soon to be President Elect of the U.S., mothers had better beware. When the interests of powerful men conflict with those of intelligent women, who wins?

A stunning parable of our life and times.

'One of the most readable, articulate, and fascinating of contemporary writers'

The Scotsman

A Royal Mail service in association with the Book Marketing Council & The Booksellers Association.
Post-A-Book is a Post Office trademark.

FAY WELDON

LITTLE SISTERS

Elsa's not really very good at typing, though she tries. Would she do better as a good-time girl? A weekend in the country with her suave new lover and his millionaire friends proves that life and love are both more magical, and more murderous, than Elsa, or any of us, had ever supposed.

'Delicious, effervescent . . .'

Daily Telegraph

HODDER AND STOUGHTON PAPERBACKS

FAY WELDON

THE FAT WOMAN'S JOKE

She is monumental and she is magnificent and her name is Esther and she's one side of every woman who ever lived, breathed, loved, lost and ate!

'Delightfully witty and wicked'
New York Times Book Review

HODDER AND STOUGHTON PAPERBACKS

MORE TITLES AVAILABLE FROM
HODDER AND STOUGHTON PAPERBACKS

FAY WELDON

☐	33965 9	The President's Child	£2.50
☐	23827 5	Little Sisters	£2.50
☐	27914 1	The Fat Woman's Joke	£1.95
☐	36379 7	The Life and Loves of a She-Devil	£2.95
☐	26662 7	Puffball	£2.95
☐	39875 2	The Shrapnel Academy	£2.50

All these books are available at your local bookshop or newsagent, or can be ordered direct from the publisher. Just tick the titles you want and fill in the form below.

Prices and availability subject to change without notice.

Hodder & Stoughton Paperbacks, P.O. Box 11, Falmouth, Cornwall.

Please send cheque or postal order, and allow the following for postage and packing:

U.K. – 55p for one book, plus 22p for the second book, and 14p for each additional book ordered up to a £1.75 maximum.

B.F.P.O. and EIRE – 55p for the first book, plus 22p for the second book, and 14p per copy for the next 7 books, 8p per book thereafter.

OTHER OVERSEAS CUSTOMERS – £1.00 for the first book, plus 25p per copy for each additional book.

Name ....

Address ....

....